FEELS LIKE HOME

JENNIFER VAN WYK

To the boys who gave me inspiration.
You each deserve your own book.
Who knows. Maybe one day it'll happen.

ONE

ANDY

I stand in the doorway to my bedroom, leaning against the doorjamb with my arms crossed, watching while my wife knocks down the last remaining brick holding our marriage up.

Not that it was sturdy anyway.

It had been crumbling for years.

"Well, I wish I could say I'm surprised, but damn, I'm honestly not."

At the sound of my voice, Heather shrieks, her head jerking up from her reverse position on top of some douche with his Hummer parked in *my* driveway. Ironic, since he has something else parked in what's mine, also.

"Andy?" Heather squeals, using the sheet on the bed to cover her chest. Not that it matters. We're married, so it's not like she's hiding anything I've never seen before.

I sneer and turn my head to the side, narrowing my eyes as the guy under her grunts and grips her hips. I'm not sure if he's stupid or in denial. Is this asshole seriously going to try to continue having sex with my wife while I stand in the doorway?

Did he not hear her say *my* name? Or realize that she's stopped moving?

"Yo!" I say loudly.

"Andy..." Heather starts, her voice wobbly and unsure.

His head pops out from behind the back of my naked wife and his eyes widen. Idiot.

"Not now, Heather. You." I point to him then gesture with a thumb over my shoulder. "Get the fuck out of my bed, tuck your dick back into your pants, and get out of my house. You can meet back up with Heather later — she won't be staying here tonight anyway."

"Dude. I had no—"

"Bullshit. You had no idea? There's a picture of us on our anniversary a few years back sitting on the nightstand right next to your fucking head, you asshole," I growl, gesturing toward the picture.

The asshole pushes Heather off him, stands up, and I cringe when I hear him snap the condom off his dick that he was thankfully wearing. Makes the moment even more awkward than it already was. Then he reaches down to the floor and grabs his boxers. Of course, he wears tight as hell short boxer briefs that practically ride up his ass. Like I didn't already know he was a douche, he just added to it with his underwear selection. One day I'll look back on that particular thought and probably seriously question what was going through my head when I had just caught my wife mounted up on another man, riding him backwards.

But the truth is? I knew this was coming. This guy? He's not her first. I know it happened at least once before, maybe twice. Or hell, I don't know how many times. I'm not an idiot. We've argued. Fought. Put our marriage on the back burner. She claims it's my fault that we've grown distant. That she feels like she's living someone else's life. But the truth of it is, she had an affair. Heather can have excuse after excuse, but that's all they are. Excuses. I don't know when she decided that our marriage wasn't worth the effort, but it's obvious she no longer cared — and damn the consequences and whoever she hurt in the process. My heart? It's fine. I can recover. Our sons? Fuck her.

Douche looks me in the eye once he's dressed then bends down and kisses Heather on the cheek while sliding a hand around her waist; she's wrapped only in a sheet. He smirks at me, clearly thinking he's winning here. She has the decency to try to shy away from him, not that it matters much. I already saw everything I needed to see.

I raise my eyebrows at him. "You think you have something special? You think you won? Have her."

His steps falter, and he eyes me; I'm even confused by my flippant response. He thought seeing him kiss her would bother me? Not a chance.

"Andy!" Heather cries out, as if she's hurt. Offended.

I turn and stare at her head on and take a long look at what I'm walking away from.

The mother of my children.

The woman I pledged my life to in front of God and family and friends.

The woman I, at one time, thought I would be spending my entire life with.

It's a strange epiphany.

To discover that your life is no longer mapped out the way you thought it was.

"You think you're anything to me now? You step out on our marriage any chance you get. You may not have slept with all of them, but don't think I didn't know." I know what I'm saying is truth but I'm more saying it to see her reaction.

She squeaks, and her lower lip starts to tremble, but I don't let up.

"What? You thought you were sneaky about it? That you could hide your flirtations? Your text messages or Facebook messages? You think I was blind to it? Don't you wonder why I haven't touched you in months?"

"Heather..." the guy murmurs, reaching for her hand. To what? Comfort her?

"Preston. Just go," she says dismissively, yanking her hand away from him.

I bark out a laugh. Even his name is douchey. Is this really what she wants? He couldn't be more my opposite. Where my hair is short, cropped close to my head, his hair looks like it's been done for an article in GQ, complete with an abundance of greasy product and highlights. While my skin is an entirely normal shade of color, his tacky spray tan makes his skin orange and resemble an oompa loompa. His lack of neck makes him look like he had one too many steroid injections, and the cherry on the top of this shit sundae? I'm pretty sure he's about ten years younger than my thirty-five. If that.

Excellent.

"But..." the wimp says, but his voice is weak. Too high pitched. Whiny.

Fuck this day.

"She'll catch up to you, soon, Preston boy. No worries. I'm not going to take your little play thing away from you."

He blanches, and Heather makes a choking sound, but I couldn't care any less. They deserve each other.

A minute later, I hear his car door slam shut and the engine start up. Heather hasn't moved from her spot, still standing naked underneath the sheet that covered the bed we once shared.

I pick up her yoga pants and shirt off the floor and throw them at her.

"Put your clothes on. Meet me in the kitchen," I tell her,

giving her no room for argument. I turn on my heel and storm out of our bedroom.

In the kitchen, I open the fridge door and grab a beer, thinking that if ever there was a time that called for day drinking, today is it. I twist the top off the bottle and toss the cap onto the counter. After taking a long pull, letting the liquid cool my throat and dampen my ever-rising anger, I place the bottle on the counter. I'm not sure who I'm angrier with at the moment. Her for being such a supreme bitch or me for letting it continue. Amazing what a guy will put up with for the sake of his young boys.

I hear Heather approach but don't turn around. I rest my hands on the counter and take a deep breath, not wanting my mouth to get away from me.

"Andy..." she starts, but I hold up a hand and stop her.

She squeaks but doesn't say anything more.

"I don't want to hear it."

"But..."

"I said. I don't want to hear it — got me?" My voice is strong, firm, and unyielding. The exact opposite of her bedmate from a few moments ago.

She remains silent as I lift the bottle and take another drink, giving myself another moment to grasp hold of the words that I need to get out to her.

I spin around and lean back against the counter. I cross my ankles and arms and stare at her. The mother of my sons. The person I once devoted my life to. She doesn't look anything like the woman I exchanged vows with.

Sure, physically she's basically the same. But she's not the same Heather. She's standing before me in an old pair of black yoga pants, a baggy T-shirt that she stole from me right after we got married, and her dark blonde hair pulled into a ponytail. Typically, this is my favorite look of hers. Casual. Comfy.

Relaxed. Right now, I couldn't be more unattracted to her if I tried.

"How many?" I ask, my voice laced with disgust.

She fiddles with the hem of her shirt and looks away, her eyes glistening with tears. Are they real? I can't be sure.

I slam my hand on the counter, and she jumps at the noise.

"Answer me, dammit!" I shout, my patience long gone.

"I don't know," she whispers.

I raise my eyebrows, sadly not shocked enough by her admission.

"You disgust me," I tell her.

A sob escapes her, and her hand goes to her mouth. "I'm sor—"

"Sorry?"

"Yes," she whimpers, nodding her head frantically.

"For what, exactly? For screwing every man you came in contact with? For risking everything for a quick fuck? For being a sucky role model for our sons? For letting them think that this is type of marriage is okay?" My voice is increasing in both intensity and volume, but I don't have it in me to try to calm down.

She starts sobbing, buckling over at the waist, but I don't give a shit.

"I thought..." I laugh humorlessly. "Man, Heather. I thought maybe it was just a few guys. I had a sinking feeling and kept trying to convince myself I was wrong. And, damn, I wish I were. Do I need to be tested? If you—"

"No. You don't need to be tested. I've been tested, and always use condoms."

I nod my head and scrub a hand over my face, hardly believing that this is my life. I suck in a deep breath through my nose and let it out. I'll get tested anyway. She's not exactly the picture of trust.

"We're done."

Her head shoots up, and she wipes under her eyes then along the side of her pants.

"What?"

"Did I stutter? We're done. Gather your shit. Get out of this house."

"But... don't you want to work this out?"

I let out a breathy laugh. "Work what out?"

"Our marriage, Andy!"

"We haven't had a *marriage* in years! Since the first time you let some other man have a relationship with you, touch you... stick. His. Dick. In. You. How long has that been, Heather?" I'm shouting, the veins in my forehead rising to the point where I feel my head could explode.

"I..." she croaks out.

"Out." I say, my voice now low and with finality I continue, squaring my shoulders and looking her dead in the eye. "I want a divorce. You're going to be honest with the boys. I want them to hear it from you rather than the rumor mill. We're going to sell this house because damn if I can ever sleep in this place again knowing you've been screwing other men in the home we built together."

"You can't be serious?"

"Oh, I'm serious."

"But... Aidan and Reece?"

"Will be with me. I don't want your influence on them."

"Andy! They're my—"

"Shoulda thought of that before you started screwing around on me, Heather. I'll give them the option, but given the fact that you've made it clear even in front of them that you don't exactly love being a mom, I wouldn't count on them wanting to stay with you. Fuck, Heather. What were you thinking?"

"I guess..."

"Wasn't looking for an answer. I was good to you. Even when I knew — and trust me, I *knew* — you were having an affair, or affairs, it seems, I was still good to you. Yes, we may have drifted apart."

She opens her mouth like she's going to start using it as an excuse for her actions.

"Life happened, Heather. Life. It's nothing other married couples don't go through. You made this choice. You did this."

And with that final word, I push off the counter and walk toward her. I lean close, the last time I ever plan to be this close to her, and say right into her ear, "This is on you. You. Did. This. You wanted freedom? You didn't want to be tied down? You got it."

I walk away, storm through the front door, and take a deep breath of fresh air. The first breath I feel like I've taken in years. The first breath of the rest of my life.

TWO
ANDY

As soon as she walks out of our house with a small bag packed, after begging me to change my mind, of course, I climb into my pickup and don't turn back, but I had to make sure she was really gone before I left.

Not having a clue where to go, I just drive.

Eventually, I walk into Dreamin' Beans, the best coffee shop in town, with no doubt a look of pure fury on my face. It's one of my favorite places to be. Christine's pastries are out of this world, and her coffee is the best. I don't know what she does different from others, but it's like magic in a cup. And Heather hated it. Said she would never step foot in the place because she could make coffee at home for cheaper — which makes no sense because she loves to spend money — and she didn't need to think about fattening herself up with all the bakery items. Her loss.

"Um, hey, Andy. You okay there?" Christine asks, looking at me warily. She and I have known each other for a few years now, teetering on that line between mere acquaintances and friends. We kind of run in the same circle, though her daughter, Bri, is a few years older than my boys. But she's friends with one of my bosses, Barrett. In fact, Barrett and his wife, Tess, helped her start up Dreamin' Beans after her husband passed away. Christine's daughter, Bri, and Barrett and Tess's son, Grady, are even closer. They're walking that fine line between friends and more than friends and from the sounds of it, not doing a very good job of it.

When I started working for Barrett and Josh, co-owners – and best friends since childhood – of the general contracting company I've been with for most of my adult life, it was simply as a summer job doing construction, but I found that I loved the work. Doing something with my hands every day, using my body, building someone's home, it made me happy. They've put trust in me and I run my own crew now.

Barrett and Josh's families are just that to me... family.

"Andy?" Christine's concerned voice snaps me out of my trance.

"Fine."

She looks at me closely but doesn't call me out on my surly attitude. "What can I get ya?"

"The last fifteen years back. No. I take that back. I want the boys, so let's go the last fourteen years."

She looks at me for a bit, blinks slowly before nodding her head once. Without taking her eyes from me, she hollers, "Hey, Emma? Can you cover the front for a while?"

"You got it, boss!"

Christine fills two to-go cups with black coffee, grabs two plates and something out of the pastry case, then places the cups on top of a tray along with the plates, and winks at me. She nods her head in the direction of the back room then turns on her heel and starts walking.

I follow her, even though I have no idea why, and less than two minutes later I'm settled on the plush tan-colored couch in her office. She hands me a plate holding an enormous piece of lemon pound cake, my favorite. She removes the lids from the coffee cups, reaches into one of the drawers in her desk, and lifts a short square bottle out, pours a shot of brown liquid into each, smiles at me then places the lids back on the cups and hands one to me before sitting on the other side of the couch and taking a sip of her own.

I raise my eyebrows at her, and she simply shrugs.

"Emergency purposes only. I promise."

Good enough.

Irish coffee it is. I think I'm probably going to either feel really good by the end of our chat, or really bad, depending on how many more of these she pours me.

She tucks her legs under her, places an elbow on the back of the couch and rests her cheek against her fist. "Where're the boys?"

"Football practice. My mom is picking them up today. Thank fuck."

She doesn't even flinch at my use of the harsh word, or the anger in my voice. "So, Mr. Simpson. Wanna talk about it?"

"Would you wanna talk about it if you saw your wife — or husband in your case — having sex with another person on your bed?"

The second the words are out of my mouth, I wince because it's such a dick thing to say, considering her husband passed away. But her response isn't what I expect it to be. She looks at me for several long beats and then shakes her head.

"No. I didn't want to talk about it either."

Her words make me choke on the sip of coffee I'd just taken. Didn't, not wouldn't. Oh shit. I look up at her slowly, and she just nods her head, the jet-black locks with a strip of shiny red, the diamond stud in her nose twinkling. She shrugs her shoulders as if to say, 'What are ya gonna do?' but says no more.

I settle back on the couch, take a long slow drink of the Irish coffee, wishing it weren't tainted with coffee in the moment, and lick my lips. I take a couple of bites of her *unbelievable* lemon pound cake, and she does the same.

For five minutes, we sit in silence — me digesting more than just the food she's given me. Her giving me the time I need to do so. I set the plate down on the table in front of me.

"So..."

"It was right before we found out he had cancer." She answers my unasked question, which I'm grateful for. I don't mean to be like Josh and Barrett and seem nosey, but holy shit. I didn't have any plans when I walked in here today. But if I had, laying it all out there and getting it in return wouldn't have been one of them.

I nod, still in shock. From what I understood of Christine's late husband, Todd, he was a pretty stand-up guy. Hell, he's the reason Dreamin' Beans even exists. He had surprised Christine and set aside a large chunk of money for her to invest in starting her own coffee shop. Something that had always been her dream, hence the name. Unfortunately, Todd lost his battle with cancer and passed away.

"How did..." I clear my voice because I don't know how much to ask, or if it's something she even *wants* to talk about. "You found them?"

She wrinkles her nose like she just ate something gross. "I walked in on her stark naked body straddling him, his pants around his ankles. Though, luckily, it wasn't our bed. It was the couch. I burned the couch." She smirks.

"Damn. When was this? How did I not know about it?"

She shrugs her tiny shoulders. "I never saw the need to tell anyone. And we found out about the cancer so soon after. Well, *he* had just found out that day. It just seemed less important in light of the whole C word being thrown at us along with his diagnosis."

"How did you stay with him? After that? And care for him when he needed it? My gosh, Christine. You must be the best person on this planet."

"Nah, I'm just a mom. Y'know? Bri was only twelve years old at the time. I wasn't going to have her *last* memories of her dad be of him cheating on her mom. And I didn't want to be responsible for her having the wrong idea of what a husband is like. He was a great father and aside from that, he really was a great husband, too. Despite it all, I still loved him. He screwed up — literally — but that didn't change the fact that he was my husband and I loved him. Might make me sound weak, but sometimes forgiveness is harder to give, and forgetting doesn't happen, but it's something that will eat you alive if you allow it to. I wasn't willing to let that happen."

"That's the furthest thing from weak you could get, Christine. Seriously. Giving someone forgiveness for something they don't deserve forgiveness for is the bravest, strongest thing you could do."

"Thank you." Her voice is soft, and a slight tinge of blush colors her cheeks.

"Do you... I guess, do you know who the woman was?"

She looks at me briefly and looks away again. "Yeah, I do. She wasn't a friend of mine, if that's what you were wondering."

I take a deep breath and lean forward, my elbows on my knees, hands clasped together and head lowered. "So now what do I do?"

"What do you mean?"

I raise my head to look at her. "I've given her my life, Christine. I don't know where to go from here. What my next move should be. What I'm gonna tell the boys."

"What is your gut telling you?" She leans her side against the back of the couch, again her head resting on her hand, and I follow her lead but don't turn to her. Instead, I rest my head on the back and look to the ceiling.

"My gut... my gut is telling me to stay the hell away from her."

"And your heart?"

"My heart is telling me to stay farther than the hell away from her."

She giggles, this light and tinkly sound that has me smiling, lolling my head to the side to look at her, despite the events that have transpired over the last few hours.

"Well, Andy, you're what? Thirty-four? Thirty-five?"

"Thirty-five," I tell her, though I don't really know why I clarify when I could have just nodded.

"Dang, you're young."

"Oh, please. How old are you? You're about my age, yeah?"

"Oh, you're good." She smiles shaking her head, her dark hair falling over her shoulder in the process.

"What?" I ask, not being able to hold back the smile that's overtaking my face.

"I'm forty-one!" she exclaims, pointing to herself.

"No way!" My eyes widen. There's no way she's that old. Not that it's old, but I truly thought she was younger. Though, I suppose, since her daughter is a senior in high school it would make sense. But still... she looks younger than me. I take a few moments to look closer at her. She resembles Mila Kunis. Long dark hair, beautiful round face, flawless skin, her only difference is the eyes. Hers are a much brighter green, huge and sparkling with happiness.

"Whatever. I'm old — just don't go spreading that around. Anyway. Like I was saying, you're young! You're only thirty-five. You have your entire life ahead of you, dude."

"Dude?" I smirk, and she reaches over to punch me lightly in the shoulder.

"Stop interrupting me!"

"Sorry," I tell her with my hands raised, smiling in her direction. I lean back farther into the couch and take another sip of coffee.

"I never imagined being here," I scoff, scrubbing a hand down my face.

"You seriously didn't know?" I can hear the disbelief in her voice.

"Oh, I knew. Trust me. She's not very sneaky. This wasn't her first time, I'm afraid. But I know what you mean when you say you were keeping it to yourself for Bri's sake. I kept quiet, not wanting the boys to be affected. I knew it would come to a head at some point, but I just never imagined having to *see* it. Know what I mean?"

"Yup. Unfortunately, I do."

"Man, this sucks."

"It definitely ain't no picnic," she says, chortling.

"How did you not always think of it when you saw him? Dang, Christine. How did you *forgive* him? Still drop everything to care for him when he was at his lowest?"

She looks at me long, assessing. "You really want to know?"

"I do."

She studies me for a few beats and looks away. "Why? Are you thinking of getting back together with her?"

"No." My response is instant, without question, earning the return of her pretty eyes to me. "I have no desire for that. But, I need to know there's a chance of..." I shrug my shoulders, "... moving on, I guess."

"Fair enough." She finishes her coffee. "I don't know how I forgave him. By the grace of God, I guess. He and I talked — a lot — about it, and he promised me that it was just the one time. I guess I believed him. I can't tell you why, but deep in my gut I feel like it was a one-time thing. The girl he was with — she stopped by the house that day. He didn't seek her out. They met, well it doesn't matter where they met, but they met and for a few months, she would come around. His work, the gym where he was a member. She'd stop by when he was playing a pick-up game of basketball on the courts. She was basically pursuing him." She pauses and picks a piece of lint off her pant leg, flicks it to the floor, clears her throat, and licks her lips before continuing.

"Not that it takes away from his involvement or his own fault in it, but I guess a part of him needed that. He had been feeling so shitty, had just gone in for testing to see if he had cancer, and we were waiting on the results. It was like a mid-life crisis on crack. She showed up at the house one day and..." she shows me her hands, palm side up, "...that was all it took. He was upset, scared, vulnerable. He was supposed to wait for me to go to the doctor to find out the test results, but he didn't want me there if it was bad news. He had just found out he had cancer. A cancer that, unless a miracle occurred, was going to kill him." Her voice cracks, and I have to war with myself not to reach over and hug her.

"He came home, had a few drinks to calm down, and she was just there. It was like she knew the timing would be perfect for her. I blame him. I promise you, I do. I always will. Forgiving is different than forgetting. No one can go without fault for sleeping with someone other than their spouse, but the circumstances surrounding his affair, if I consider it that, are a little different than most, I would imagine."

I get what she's saying. I can't imagine finding out I had a terminal illness. It's no surprise that he lost his head for a little bit. Still... "I agree with that. Still though, Christine. It doesn't make it right."

"I know. But... he's gone." Her voice is sad, eyes filled with tears. "I can't dwell on it. The last years of our marriage were good, even though he was sick. Doesn't make me forget what I saw, but it does give me something else to focus on."

Strong doesn't even cover what she is. Amazing. Incredible. One of a kind. How Todd stepped out on her is beyond my understanding. No matter the circumstances surrounding it.

I reach across the cushion and grasp her hand in mine, squeezing once. "I'm sorry you went through that."

She squeezes my hand once in response. "I'm sorry you're going through it now."

"Thank you."

"So, want some advice?"

"Eat more lemon pound cake?"

She releases my hand and sits back, giggling, and again I'm hit with how much I love hearing the sound of her laughter. "Well, that, too. I could even say it's healthy because it's made with Greek yogurt."

"You trying to tell me something?" I tease her, patting my flat stomach.

She smiles, a cross between sad and sort of resigned.

"My advice? Be happy."

"What's that?"

"Be happy. I promise you. First of all, it will drive Heather *nuts* knowing you are moving on without her." She winks and I can't help but laugh. "But second of all, and this is the most important part of it."

I lean a tiny bit closer and she does the same.

"What's that?"

"You'll be happy."

"You make it sound so easy."

"I've had a lot of practice. When Todd was at his sickest, we practiced a lot of happiness. Happiness because we had good days, or we had quiet moments to spend as a family when he could barely get out of bed. Happiness when we were able to celebrate holidays. After he cheated, one of the things we discovered was that we could either give in to the ugly that it brought on, or we could move on. We moved on. And he had to do the same. We both had guilt. Guilt for how we got there. I questioned if I wasn't giving him what he needed. He questioned *everything*. I'm not going to lie... it's hard, and most days you'll have to dig deep, but you'll get there. Trust me. The light is always better than the dark."

I lay my head on the back of the couch and turn to look at her. She's so gorgeous it almost hurts to look at her. I've always thought so, though I would have never done a thing about it. She has always been the mom who turned heads.

"What was he thinking?" I murmur.

"Pardon?"

"Todd. What was he thinking?"

"You mean..."

"When he stepped out."

She doesn't respond, just simply smiles before biting her lip and looking away, her long, dark, silky hair falling over her shoulder. She ducks her head and tucks a lock of hair behind her ear.

"I'm sorry," I tell her, though I don't know what I'm apologizing for. Almost admitting how gorgeous I think she is? Her husband cheating? Her husband dying? Me laying my shit out for her? All of it, probably.

"I'm sorry Heather's such an asshole," she replies with a shrug.

I bark out a laugh. "She is definitely an asshole."

"She forgot rule number one."

"What?"

"Never mind... it was in a book I read."

"Ahh. Good book?"

"More than good." She gives me a ghost of a smile and

reaches over to grip my hand, squeezing once before letting go. "So, what are you going to do?"

"Honestly? I have no clue. I need to find a place for the boys and me to stay, talk with a lawyer... that part I know for sure. I can't stay with her. As sad as it sounds, and maybe it's kind of a little mean, but I think we fell out of love a long time ago. We've been hanging on by a thread for years. I'm sure part of it was my fault, but still..."

"It's no excuse. This has nothing to do with you, Andy. This is all Heather. You're a great guy. It's Heather's loss."

"I appreciate you saying that."

"It's the truth."

THREE
CHRISTINE

My eyes track Andy's back as he walks out the door and into the cool early fall temperatures of the evening, knowing that everything I've held tight for the last several years is now loosening its grip on me.

I can't decide if it's a good or bad thing. Todd's affair was something that I never wanted to get out. I trust Andy that he won't tell anyone, but it feels weird knowing that someone else knows this giant secret I've kept hidden to myself all these years.

Part of me feels like it's a giant relief to have the burden lightened from my shoulders.

Part of me is terrified.

When I found my late husband, looking more broken than I'd ever seen him, with a naked woman straddling his equally naked body — and did I fail to mention the lovely picture of his hands being handcuffed around her waist? — on the couch in the living room of the home that we shared, I thought my world had simply crumbled around me.

It's funny. When hit with the impossible, sometimes it's easier to see clearly. Or, at least, a new side. It was his eyes.

A woman knows her husband's eyes, what they're saying in

each moment. Whether it be in bed, or when they're having a disagreement, when he's happy and telling a joke or upset or grumpy.

The day I opened the door and came face to face with emptiness — and a bit of drunkenness — in his eyes; he shifted his focus to me, and I knew. It only took a second. A brief flash, but I knew it was deeper than him sleeping around on me. I knew he'd gotten his results. And they were exactly what we feared. He was supposed to wait but in true Todd fashion, he probably didn't want me to have to sit there and listen to the news if it was bad.

"Christine," he croaks out, eyes on me, his hands gripping her hips as he tries to move her away from him.

She digs her knees into the couch on either side of his legs and lifts her pitiful, unapologetic eyes to me before looking down at Todd.

She trails a fake fingernail down his cheek. He flinches and jerks away from her touch. "Todd, baby, what's the matter?"

"Get the fuck off me. Now," my husband growls, empty eyes now being replaced with angry ones, hands pulling at the metal cuffs around his wrists. I don't even want to know details on that particular adventure. We've never had a perfect marriage. It simply doesn't exist in this world. Two people? Two personalities? They're meant to argue. It just happens. *And it's okay. It's what makes marriage what it is. Working together, fighting for your love. It's damn near impossible some days. Today seems like one of those.*

But in all the years we've been together? I've never seen those *eyes.*

He turns his head, looking directly at me, and I almost stumble.

Eyes filled with despair.

Sadness.

And rage.

But I know my husband.

That rage?

It's by no means directed at me.

At her.

At the results.

At life.

At cancer.

Fuck. Cancer.

"Baby?" She says the name like she has the right to.

She's wrong.

He lifts his hands and pulls on her back trying to get her to move. "Don't call me baby," *he growls.*

"But..."

"I'm not your baby. You're not mine. I don't know what the hell I was thinking."

"I can be here for you."

"You have about three seconds to dismount my husband before I take you by your cheap ass extensions and pull you off him. And, just so you know" —I point to the cell phone in my hand recording her— "whether he's in this video or not? I'll have no qualms posting this for the entire town to see, so everyone knows what a cheating, lying skank you really are. Not that anyone had any misgivings on that, anyway."

"See, Christine? This is why Todd came around looking for me. Because you're such a bitch."

I raise my eyebrows at her insinuation. First, that he came looking because — one glance at my husband tells me what I assumed in the first place. That she chased him down like the shameless whore she is. And second, because I'm not a bitch. Probably one of the people furthest from it. I'm... nice. *A bubble of laughter bursts out of me, and I scoff.* "I'm a bitch? Oh, that's rich coming from you. The town bicycle."

She narrows her eyes at me then smirks, the devil in her eyes shining with fury, then she twists her head and places her stupid breasts in my husband's face, all the while he's trying to twist and turn to get away from her, his hands bound, and his body weak. The reason for the weak body we were supposed to get when we went in for his appointment in an hour. Clearly, he had other ideas.

Cancer.

When we went to the doctor I never imagined that's the word we'd be leaving with.

Up until a few months ago, my husband was healthy.

Still rocked hard abs and strong arms and shoulders.

Helped coach Bri's traveling volleyball team.

Played basketball with his friends.

Then one day.

He just started to fall apart.

His illness hit him like a ton of bricks.

Hit us like a ton of bricks.

He no longer had energy.

His body was filled with pain.

Dwindling away like his body was being eaten away from the inside out.

And we were floundering.

Are floundering.

She places her lips next to his ear and says, "You always know where to find me, baby."

Then the whore slithers her gross body down, stopping at my husband's non-existent hard on, turns those snake-like eyes to me and licks, from bottom to top.

Todd continues to writhe under her to get her off him, all the while cursing a blue streak. I stand watching, oddly amused at her desperation and his stupidity.

He probably wants me to step in to help him, but if he's dumb *enough to get into this situation then he's going to have to deal with the consequences of his idiotic actions.*

"I said, get out of here!" he roars, and even I jump. She jerks to her feet after crawling out of where she had wedged herself, picks up discarded clothes, and starts putting them on, taking her sweet time.

"You're pathetic," I sneer once she's righted and standing in front of me.

"Oh, please. I'm pathetic? Right. Look in the mirror, honey. I know your type. Ignoring your husband, especially at his time of need. You're just jealous that I can be there for him. That I'm willing to be there for him."

"Oh, and your husband? Your children? What about them? Who's going to be there for them in their time of need? What about when they recognize you for the absurd, wretched, useless woman you are? Are you going to step aside when some other woman comes around?"

She clenches her jaw then scoffs, flipping her fake hair over her shoulder and stomps out.

As soon as I hear the door slam, I giggle. "She's got the best comebacks."

"She's also got the key to these things." He lifts his hands, showing me they're still cuffed.

And that's when I completely lose it.

Laughing uncontrollably like the lunatic that I feel like I am.

Because I just caught my husband having sex with another woman.

On the day he found out he has cancer.

Maybe I'll never fully know why he chose that moment to give in to temptation. Maybe I'll never understand why she continued going after married men and stepped out on her own husband.

But one thing I do know, is that Andy doesn't deserve what

he's been given. Not that anyone deserves that kind of disrespect, but with Andy? He's one of the good ones. The guy who would bend over backward to make sure that his loved ones are happy. The guy who would give up his life plans, dreams, in order to allow someone else to follow theirs.

Heather doesn't deserve Andy.

I just hope Andy realizes it.

FOUR

ANDY

THREE MONTHS LATER

"**D**ad. He didn't try to. It was an accident," Reece pleads with me in his brother's defense... all for me to calm down.

When Aidan came home with yet *another* cracked screen on his cell, I lost it. And the sad part is? It's not even the broken screen that's the problem. The fact that Heather *still* hasn't checked in on the boys in the three months she's been gone, that's really got me pissed off. But the cracked screen just pushed me over the edge of my already angry attitude.

"I don't care if it was an accident!" I roar, pacing through our living room like a caged lion. "I'm sick of you boys being so careless with your stuff! It's not like money just grows on trees!"

"Oh, my gosh, Dad! I can't *believe* you just said that," Reece groans, moving from his position on the couch to stand in front of Aidan, like he's protecting him from my wrath.

"What?"

He laughs, breaking up the constant tension in our home. "You sound like an old man."

I chuckle, despite my pissed-off attitude that doesn't seem to want to go away.

One would think I was a woman about to get her period.

I just can't get over the fact that she's just... vanished.

No phone calls.

No Happy Thanksgiving message.

No cards in the mail when they turned fourteen.

Nada.

Zip.

Nothing.

And I'm the one who gets to see the hurt lingering in their eyes every single morning after they try to go to sleep at night, wondering why their mother didn't love them enough to get over her own shit, suck it up, and stay around. I told her they were staying with me, but she didn't even try.

Just like they go to bed every night wondering, I wake up every morning hoping — but at the same time not hoping — to see a message waiting from her for the boys.

I don't want her back — I also don't really even want her back in the boys' lives if I'm being completely honest, but they deserve an explanation. None of what's happening is their fault.

They didn't ask to be born to a woman who didn't want to be a mother.

"I'm sorry, Dad. I was pulling my stuff out of my locker, and it just fell. You know we're not supposed to have our phones with us in class."

"So why wasn't it in the case?" I ask, trying to keep my temper at bay.

He shrugs and looks down at the ground, mumbling an apology and something about it needing cleaned.

I take a deep breath and blow it out then look to the ceiling, placing my hands on the back of my neck.

It's December, and my mood is shit.

The weather is gloomy.

Work is slow, which allows my mind way too much time to wander.

I think about life with Heather and how shitty of a wife she was.

I think about how the first place I went after finding Heather with another man was Dreamin' Beans and how I can't seem to get Christine out of my thoughts either.

And what she confessed.

That she understood what I was going through.

Probably better than anyone else.

I think about how I just can't seem to get out of this damn funk I'm in and how Christine told me to choose happiness but for the life of me, I just can't seem to do it.

The other day the boys left their wet towels on the carpet in their room, and I *completely* lost it. Couldn't even control myself.

One day they didn't get the dishwasher unloaded before I got home from work and by my reaction, you would have thought they had been caught smuggling drugs at school.

It's not just things that the boys — typical teenagers — are doing or not doing, though. It's when the guys at work look at me with pity in their eyes or someone on my team asks me a question about something they should have known easily; I don't handle anything well. My entire demeanor is shit.

I feel like I'm a live wire. My entire world has just imploded, and I can't think where to go next.

I never expected to be a single parent, raising the boys on my own.

And even worse, the resentment that's building over knowing that I was stupid enough to stay with her long after I suspected something was happening is becoming dangerous.

"Dad." Reece's voice interrupts what was brewing up to be another anger-filled rant. "It's a phone, Dad." His small reminder of what's truly important in life jars me back to reality.

And considering that we've had a hell of a go at *life* over the past few months, he makes an incredibly valid point.

"I'm sorry."

"What?" the boys ask in unison. They don't even try to hide the shock on their faces or confusion on their voices.

"I've been a shitty father. I know. You boys? You're everything to me. I'm sorry for letting my anger and frustration lately show and filter to you guys. You don't deserve that, and I know it. I promise. Right now? It ends. I'm going to do what I have to do to get through it, okay?"

"You haven't been a sh... bad father, Dad. Just..." Aidan looks to Reece who nods his head like he's encouraging him to say what they've both been thinking for a long time now. "...your temper is getting bad. It's hard to live with."

I close my eyes briefly and drop my head before I look at their faces, both so broken and upset by walking on eggshells lately. "I know. It's not right. I'm not pissed at you guys. I promise. You boys? You're incredible, and I couldn't ask for better kids."

"Why are you so mad all the time, then?"

If that isn't a kick to the nuts. I knew I hadn't been hiding my irritation well, but to actually hear it come out of my son's mouth? Well, that's a big awakening. I take a deep breath and give them my real. Because they deserve it more than anyone.

"Because I hate this. I hate that you question why you're stuck with just a dad. I hate that your mom hasn't called you. I hate that you turned fourteen and she missed it. I hate that you wonder anything about how amazing and awesome you both are and how blessed I am to have you."

They both blink at me, and I realize they need to hear it all. "Boys, I hate that I saw your mom was unhappy and I didn't step in sooner and help her sort it out. I *really* hate that your mom couldn't get over her own crap and realize that you're worth it all. You two are so amazing. The best thing that ever happened to me. I wouldn't trade a single moment of your lives for anything because you two are the only good I have."

And that's the moment where I see the boys break. Whatever they've been holding onto, crumbles before my eyes as both boys break down into tears. Crying, wondering why they're not good enough. Voicing the worries and concerns I was afraid were plaguing them the entire time.

And the only thing I can do?

Is sit on the floor right along with them and hold them.

Letting their tears fall and their own anger win out.

FIVE

CHRISTINE

Ever since Andy walked into Dreamin' Beans the day he found Heather with another man in their bed, I've not been able to get him out of my head. The anger I could almost feel coming off him in waves. The dejection and sadness was so palpable, I knew I had to give him a glimpse of my story. Help him know that he's not alone.

We haven't spent any time alone, but we have seen each other quite a bit.

At the high school football games.

Chatting briefly when he's come in to get coffee.

Soon after he left Heather, he stayed with Barrett and Tess for a week before finding a place more permanent.

I know he went over to their house for Thanksgiving.

And his boys had a birthday recently.

Andy had posted some stuff about their big day on his social media pages and it wasn't hard to notice that Heather wasn't present or even commenting on any of it.

Because I suddenly can't get the man out of my head no matter what I do.

Christmas is just around the corner, the weather is cold,

and the coffee shop is busier than ever. It's about thirty minutes from closing time, and it's finally died down for the night, giving me a few moments to clean up behind the counter.

The door opens, allowing a cool gust of wind in along with Andy. His black beanie pulled down low makes his already dark-rimmed eyes look even darker. Even covered by the beanie, I can tell that his hair has grown out some since the last time I saw him, the almost-black strands softly curling out from under it.

He stomps off the snow stuck to his brown boot-covered feet, strides over to the counter, eyes on me the entire time. His jeans hug his thighs as he walks toward me.

I realize it's not the right time to be having these thoughts, but holy crap he looks good.

"Hey, Christine."

I swallow at the intensity of the look on his face. "Hey Andy, how's it going?"

He stares at me for a few beats, not answering.

"Andy?"

His hands spread across the counter, and he leans in close. "Wanna get out of here?"

His question stuns me, but only for a moment.

"Sure."

He raps his knuckles on the counter twice then nods his head toward the door.

"Emma, I'm out of here for the night!" I holler to the back room without taking my eyes off Andy. "Can you finish up here?"

"Sure thing! See you tomorrow!"

Without another word, I follow Andy out the front door. It's December in Michigan, but I don't even take the time to grab my coat. For reasons I don't understand, I know that he'll not leave me out in the cold, so right now it's the least of my concerns.

He holds the passenger door open for me, and I climb in, but before closing it he stares at me again. I let him for a moment before wrapping my fingers around his hand that's resting on the door.

He looks at my hand on his and swallows hard. His Adam's apple rising and falling.

"Hey. Let's go for a drive," I tell him quietly.

He slowly nods his head a few times before closing the door and rounding the hood.

Once he's in the seat and we're both buckled up, he backs out of his parking spot and heads out of town.

He reaches over and pushes the button that looks like a seat warmer on the dash to switch on my heated seat and turns the channel on the radio. It's set to a country station but the music is turned down so low I can barely make anything out.

The near silence should bother me. Make me nervous.

It doesn't.

"The boys gone tonight?"

"Spending the night with a bud."

I relax into my seat, resting my head on the headrest, and look out the window. We pass through the town slowly, admiring the Christmas lights that twinkle both inside and outside of homes. A few snowmen are proudly on display in front yards from the early snowstorms we've received.

We drive past my best friend Carly's house. It's lit up beautifully. Classy. Tastefully. Just like her.

"She did a nice job," he comments.

I hum in agreement. "She had help."

Out of the corner of my eye, I see him nod his head thoughtfully.

"James?"

"Yeah. They're getting close. I like him for her. He's breaking down some pretty thick walls she's built up."

"From what Barrett has said, he's fallen pretty hard for her." His voice sounding much lighter than his actions are showing.

A few months ago, Tess had her brother James stay at their house while they spent a week in a cabin. While they were gone, their seven-year-old daughter Harper fell from the horse she was riding during lessons. James brought Harper to school the next day to make sure her teacher was aware of what happened, and that's when he met Carly. To say he became immediately smitten of Harper's first grade teacher is a little of an understatement.

Andy's hand is wrapped so tightly around the steering wheel, it's causing his knuckles to turn white, and the rigid way he's sitting in his seat can't be remotely comfortable. I want so badly to reach over and release his hold and help him relax, but I don't feel it's within my rights. We're just friends.

"She has too," I admit on her behalf. "But she's scared. Not even sure she's fully admitted it to herself yet. I don't know why, but I think he'll wear her down, figure out why she's so guarded."

"If he's anything like his sister, he won't stand aside for long. He'll bully his way in," he chuckles.

I giggle. "In the nicest way possible, so she doesn't even realize it. They're good people."

"They are."

He turns into an empty parking lot and puts the pickup in park, the lake a wide-open blanket of darkness in front of us, just the moon glistening off the water.

"Barrett told me this is a good place to sit and think."

"It's beautiful." I look around us. Trees line one side of the parking lot, the lake two sides, and the drive entry we came in the other.

The docks are pulled onto the parking lot, not that many people have a desire to put their boat in the frigid water this time of year.

He doesn't turn off the pickup, but he unlatches his seatbelt, and I do the same.

We sit in comfortable silence for about ten minutes, listening to the low crooning sounds of the music in the background.

Andy clears his throat and looks at me, adjusting in his seat nervously.

"Speaking of Barrett... I'm a terrible friend, Christine. How are you doing with everything?"

He doesn't need to explain what he's talking about.

Shortly after all his crap went down with Heather, I had my own family drama occur. Bri was at a field party with Grady, not too different than any other weekend.

Except this weekend?

Everything was different.

Another kid in their class, Dawson, decided he'd had enough rejections from Bri and thought he'd push his luck.

That luck though? Not so great.

Considering Grady's friends saw how Dawson got physical with Bri. Unfortunately, Grady ended up going to jail for beating the ever loving shit out of Dawson, rightfully so.

Bri's decision to not press charges against Dawson was something both Grady and I fought her on. She made a deal with the devil, so to speak, and told Dawson that if he didn't press charges, neither would she.

Something good did come out of it, though.

Grady finally stepped up, and they've been dating ever since.

"I'm... okay. And you're far from a bad friend, Andy. We both had our own junk going on when that happened."

"Still, I should have called, or something."

"Please. No guilt, okay? Not worth it. I didn't think a thing of it. We're good. Bri's moved on, and she and Grady are finally dating and happy. Dawson hasn't even so much as looked in her direction, either. I think Grady made his point." I laugh quietly.

"I bet he did," Andy murmurs.

Once again, we settle into the silence. The warmth of his pickup cab wrapping around me. I snuggle into the seat and sigh. Not out of annoyance but out of contentment.

"Does it still bother you?"

His voice is so low, so quiet, I almost don't hear him. If I hadn't been so attuned to his presence next to me, I probably would have missed it. He doesn't specify what he's talking about, but it doesn't matter. I understand.

"Him stepping out, you mean?"

"Yeah."

"I don't think I'll ever *not* be bothered by it. Right when it happened, it almost got swallowed up by our new life. Doctor visits. Chemo. Radiation. Knowing that no matter how hard he fought, the end would still be the same. I didn't allow myself time to really digest the fact that he was with another woman. Didn't really feel the sting of his betrayal."

He scoffs. "Betrayal."

I nod my head. "It's hard, you know? Not knowing what would have happened if I hadn't walked in on them. If it would have continued or been a one-time thing. Of course, he assured me over and over again that it was a stupid mistake — which, obviously..." I breathe out a laugh and roll my eyes.

"Well I guess there's a bright and dark side to everything."

"There really is. It's part of why I had such a hard time opening Dreamin' Beans. It was guilt money. You know? Or, that's how I looked at it. It was just hard to take, but when I got to thinking about it, I thought, well hell yeah, I'll take it. I mean, I deserved it. Bri deserved to have some sort of legacy."

He thinks for a moment on everything I just told him.

I like that he's not yelling in my defense or getting angry. He's just listening.

"When Heather cheated, I couldn't see any future where I wasn't riddled with hurt and anger. Honestly, I thought I would die a bitter and pissed off old man, yelling at kids from my front porch and stabbing people with my cane," he tells me grinning, and I laugh lowly. "But soon I started to realize that life is a bitch. We were never guaranteed this life here to be easy. And as much as I would like to blame her, be pissed forever, keep my boys from her, it's just not in me. The bitterness has been taking over my life, Christine. Just like you said it would, and I realized that it was hurting me more than her. And the boys. I'm becoming an ass to live with."

"Andy... no. That's not true."

"Oh, it is," he says, nodding his head and scrubbing a hand down his face. "The boys even asked me why I was always so mad, and the guys at work? They're on pins and needles around me."

"You've been through a lot." I nod my understanding.

He leans his head back against the headrest and taps his thumb on the center console of his pickup. "It's not easy to move on though, is it?"

I slide my feet out of my dark brown Uggs and tuck one leg under the other, turning to face him. The side of my head rests against the back of the seat, and I keep my voice quiet. "No, it is definitely not."

"But when you do, man it's like the most freeing thing in the world. To be rid of that anger, that hurt, and... her."

I swallow and roll my lips together before asking, "So if she came crawling back?"

There's no hesitation in his answer. "I have no desire. I mean, what's that teaching my boys? I know forgiveness and all that... blah blah blah... but honestly? Is that only teaching them that it's totally okay to screw over the ones you love most and just beg for forgiveness later? It's like that old crappy saying, I'd rather ask forgiveness than permission. What kind of bullshit is that? It's awful, the worst saying in the world. Yet that's what we seem to live by because, yeah, we need to forgive. I get that. I've forgiven. Or, almost, anyway." He smirks before continuing. "I've moved on. I've not forgotten, and I never will. I also know that I deserve more than that. I deserve a wife who's willing to give me exactly what I'm willing to give her. Everything. It just is what it is, you know?"

"And the boys? How do they feel about everything that's happening? Do you think they want her back home?"

"Oh, they would probably kick my ass if I even dreamed of taking her back. I hate that for them. In the beginning, she was a good mom. I'd never deny that. For a few years, anyway. She turned, though. Nothing was ever enough for her. She felt stuck and in feeling that, she hurt my boys."

The words he just quietly admitted have me gasping. "Wait. They knew?"

He winces slightly then lifts one shoulder and drops it. "She wasn't good at hiding her discontent. It wasn't lost on them that they were more of a burden than a blessing to her."

"Oh, Andy..."

"She dug that hole, and I'm not throwing the dirt on her or anything, but she's gonna need to be the one who picks up that shovel or builds the ladder to get herself out of it. They deserve a mom who's willing to throw everything in to get them back and right now, she's just simply not doing the work.

"I don't know — maybe she doesn't give a shit. But if she doesn't, then I want her gone. Even more than she is already.

She left without even looking back. We'll see what she says when we meet for the divorce proceedings."

My head jerks up at his mention of divorce and he notices. "Yeah, my lawyer is drawing up the papers now. She hasn't come around, Christine. She hasn't called. Doesn't seem to even give a shit. Who does that? They turned fourteen and not even a text was sent to either of them. It blows my mind. She lost her right and, as shitty as it sounds, we've been better off. Even with my anger that can't seem to dim, the boys seem happier without her. Still sucks, though."

"I hate to break it to you, but it's gonna suck for a while. Those boys—"

"Need a woman in their lives who is going to teach them the things their dad can't," he finishes for me. "Every boy needs a mama. Just like Bri needed to have that fatherly figure, and thank God for Barrett, right?"

I smile at the thought of how much the Ryan men have meant to us, what they've done in our lives. "Oh man. Right? He's been so good for her, and having Grady and Cole around is amazing. Obviously, Grady's role is a tad different." We both laugh, knowing that Grady and Bri were friends for many years before recently bridging the gap into a relationship. "We've made it fine. That's not to say she doesn't still and won't always miss her dad. No one can replace one's parent, you know? But, I think in some cases, that's not an option."

He turns in his seat, facing me. My head rolls to the side, looking back at him. It's a position we find ourselves in often, I'm noticing. It feels intimate, especially with the soft looks he gives me. When he finally speaks, his voice is filled with compassion and curiosity, not pity. "Do you ever think about what would have happened if he hadn't gotten sick?"

I press my lips together and close my eyes briefly, remembering the nights I lay awake thinking that exact same thing.

Sometimes crying myself to sleep. Sometimes angrily stomping through the house cleaning on a rampage. "I used to. I don't anymore."

"Why?"

"The only thing I have keeping me from going there is knowing that whatever he had with her was over before it really got started. At least on his end. He had made it clear to her that he wanted to cut ties. I know it makes me sound weak or gullible, but I believed him when he told me that it meant nothing to him. And I don't want to wonder if it would have happened if he hadn't been worried about the diagnosis he had just received."

"Doesn't make you sound weak. You trusted your instincts. Still, though, that's rough," he mumbles.

I shrug my shoulders but can't deny that. "No rougher than walking in on him with someone. Or her, in your case."

"That did suck, gotta admit." He grins and shakes his head. "Dunno. I'm glad I did. The image is burned into my head, so that part sucks, but seeing is definitely believing, I'll just say that. I was living too much in denial until I saw it."

"No one blames you for that, though. And you shouldn't blame yourself. You were living that way because you cared about your boys. I had a lot of denial afterward, too. I was so worried about Bri finding out and threw myself into caring for him during his illness. There's not an instruction manual on how to handle it, Andy. The boys are happy and adjusting well, from what I understand."

He nods in agreement and rests his head on the headrest, mimicking my posture.

For long moments, we sit in silence before he reaches over the center console and wraps his hand around mine, the only sound in the cab of the pickup our breathing. Our fingers naturally link together, and he stares at them resting on his console for a moment before lifting his eyes to me. "Can I ask what changed?"

"What do you mean?" he asks me, eyes bunching up.

"You said that you decided not to let the bitterness take over."

The way he looks at me, like he's examining me, taking everything in, almost makes me squirm in my seat. He bites his bottom lip, and I see the white of his teeth.

"You really wanna know?"

My heart rate picks up at the way he's looking at me. The way his thumb is brushing across the top of my hand. I bite my lip, and his eyes drift to my mouth. "I do."

"You."

I take a deep breath, letting that simple statement wash over me. "Me?" My voice is barely above a whisper.

"You," he repeats quietly. "When I walked into Dreamin' Beans that night, you told me to be happy. And every time I'm around you, I feel this lightness. When the boys asked me the other night why I was so short with them, I realized that I was letting her win. She doesn't deserve it. And my boys definitely don't deserve it."

He releases a shuddering breath and squeezes my fingers. I try not to wince at the pressure.

"Andy..." I try to keep pity from my voice, but everything about this is breaking my heart.

The fact that he feels so lost, like a failure to his boys.

"I'm fine, sweetheart. It's just... the holidays and everything. I guess life is catching up to me. Too much time on my hands to think when we're in our slower season at work, too. I'm sorry for dumping this on you."

I try not to dwell on the fact that he called me sweetheart. "Don't be. I'm glad you stopped in tonight."

"Me, too." He pauses then smiles at me, seeming to snap out

of his sullen manner. "So, how long do you think Carly plans to leave James in the friend zone?"

A laugh bubbles out of me unexpectedly. He does the change in subject thing amazingly well. "He has it bad, doesn't he?"

"Sounds that way, though I haven't spent much time with the guy. But, of course, Josh and Barrett talk about it all the time like a couple of high schoolers."

I burst out laughing. "They're so nosey."

He smiles my way, and I know.

The boys are going to be just fine.

Because Andy is going to be just fine.

Better than fine.

And hopefully.

One day.

He'll be happy again.

SIX

ANDY

"Say what now?" I ask, choking back a laugh.

I'm out to dinner with the guys — Barrett, Josh, and James. Tonight's dinner has been a good distraction from life in general. But when James informs us that the owner of El Charro, the local Mexican restaurant in town, just called to inform him that his sister and her friends are three sheets to the wind drunk, my ears perk up.

"Well, boys, looks like we have a rescue mission."

"Oh boy, now the whole Captain America thing is going to your head." Barrett lightly shoves James, and we all laugh.

Of course, I hope that Christine is included in that group of friends because I want to see her. Any chance I can get anymore, it seems. A week ago, I was in a bad way and all I could think was *I need Christine.* And she was there. Immediately. No questions asked.

I can't get her out of my head. Not for a while now but especially not since her scent overwhelmed the cab of my pickup as she listened to me ramble on. She's everything Heather was not, which is only *part* of the appeal.

The next morning after our talk at the docks, I walked in to

Dreamin' Beans for a coffee, and the smile she shot my way nearly buckled my knees.

That afternoon, I just so happened to offer to get coffee for my crew.

Such a burden having to see her twice in a day.

"Well, what are we waiting for?" I slap Josh on the back, and he chuckles.

A few minutes into our dinner tonight I may have let it slip that Christine and I had been talking, and there's no way this nosey group of buggers didn't pick up on it. In fact, they promised me we would be coming back to that conversation later.

Luckily, their plan was thwarted by learning that Tess and her friends are making a scene at a Mexican restaurant.

When I pull into the parking lot of El Charro, I look around for Christine's car, pleasantly surprised to see it sitting there. But when we get inside? That's a horse of a different color. Surprise doesn't even begin to express what I'm seeing.

Tess and Lauren, Josh's wife, are slow dancing together while Christine has her phone in the air, swaying back and forth with a blissful smile on her face, encouraging every odd moment that's happening. Carly has her head on the table, looking like she's well past her limit. The four of us stand there, staring at the odd performance in front of us, before we individually jump into action.

Tess is in Barrett's arms in a flash.

Lauren runs to Josh just as quickly but trips over her own two feet along the way and face plants into his chest.

James moves to Carly's side, his head bent toward hers as she mumbles something. But me? My sole focus is on the curvy, petite, dark-haired beauty before me.

"So. How's your night?" I ask, a teasing smile on my lips.

"Hi, Andy." Her voice is quiet, her lips a glossy pink, her

eyes sparkling. Everything about her is pulling me to her in this moment.

"Did you guys drink your dinner?"

"We aren't that bad!" She tries protesting but stumbles into my arms instead.

I catch her, willingly.

"Thanks," she mumbles into my chest, but I simply tighten my arms around her.

"Anytime," I murmur and inadvertently press my face into her hair, inhaling deeply.

"Did you just sniff me?" She shifts, looking up at me.

I smile at her. "I did."

"And? What's the verdict?"

"You smell like a tequila factory at the moment." She laughs so hard she folds herself in half. I have to work to hold her up and bring her closer. "But I have no doubt under normal circumstances that you would smell incredible."

When she finally stops laughing, she says, still smiling, "How do you know that?"

"Because someone as gorgeous as you are couldn't possibly smell bad."

"You think I'm gorgeous?"

I cock an eyebrow. "You're the definition."

"I hope I remember this in the morning."

"Me, too," I admit.

"What are the chances of that happening, do you think?"

I hold up two fingers spaced barely apart. "Probably not very likely."

She squints and huffs out an angry breath. "Remind me?"

"Of course."

And that it isn't a lie. I have no problem reminding her every single day that she's gorgeous. That realization should have *me* stumbling. I'm not divorced yet, though the papers are ready to be served. I shouldn't be having these types of thoughts and feelings for another woman. But they're there, and I can't deny them.

"Come on, let me drive you home. I'll come get you in the morning so we can get your car."

Fifteen minutes later, we're pulling into her driveway. Christine is snoring in the passenger seat of my pickup, her head resting against the window. No doubt she'll be hurting in the morning. I reach across the console, jostling her arm a little, hoping to wake her up.

"Christine, we're home."

She mumbles, shifting in her seat, and brings her hands up under her head while pulling her legs up under her, getting more comfortable.

I bite back a laugh while I continue to try waking her up.

"Sweetheart." I nudge her on the shoulder. "We're at your house. Time to get up, sleepyhead."

She sits up quickly, looking around like a frightened puppy. "Where the hell am I?" she shouts then grabs her head and groans.

I chuckle at her confusion. "I drove you home from El Charro. You had just a tad too much to drink tonight."

She looks over at me, clarity seeming to take over. "Oh."

"Oh?"

She wipes at the bit of drool on her face and smiles sheepishly. "I'm sorry."

"Did you have fun tonight?"

"I think so. I'm fairly positive I'll never be able to set foot in El Charro ever again, though. Did we get kicked out?"

"Nah. The owner called James and just let us know you guys needed rides home."

"Well that's embarrassing."

I chuckle. "It was entertaining to see, that's for sure."

"Well, thanks for the ride." She tries getting out of the pickup and can't even find the door handle. I put a hand on her arm, stopping her lack of progress.

"Not a chance. I'm walking you in."

"What about the boys?"

She always asks, and something about that makes my heart feel pretty damn good. Knowing that she cares, has concern for their well-being. Even in her drunken state of mind, they're on hers.

"They're old enough to be home by themselves for a bit. I won't be able to sleep tonight if I don't know that you're okay."

"Andy Simpson. You could charm the panties straight off just about anyone, you know that? You're like the hottest guy everrrrrrrr."

I choke on my tongue, not expecting those words to have come out of her mouth.

"What did you say?" I ask her, laughing.

"What?"

I honestly don't think she realizes what she just said.

"Nothing," I murmur, a grin taking over my face. But it's not nothing. In fact, I'll probably be reliving those words for quite some time. Possibly later tonight. Alone.

Damn I'm pathetic.

"Bri home?"

"Nope," she ends the P with a pop. "She spent the night at a friend's house. Why? You wanna come in?" she asks, voice slurring and trying, but failing, to wiggle her eyebrows.

I chuckle again. "Alright, Don Julio, let's get you inside." I climb out of the pickup and walk over to her side, helping her down.

"I would make a snarky comment about your nickname, but you know what? I think the tequila sucked up all my brain cells."

"It does seem as though you all had plenty of it."

We're about two steps from the bottom stair of the porch in front of her house when she stops dead in her tracks. "Oh no," she mumbles and rushes over to the snow-covered bushes before getting rid of what sounds like everything she ate this entire year.

I slowly walk over, knowing my own gag reflex is going to be tested by getting closer. I don't do well with vomit. I can't imagine anyone does, but still... it's *really* gross.

I pat her lower back, standing back as far away as I possibly can. I wish I had a broom, or stick, or something to touch her with, but that would probably come off as rude.

"There, there," I say awkwardly, gagging and turning my head while covering my nose with my sleeve when I not only hear her get rid of some of the alcohol, but *smell* it too.

She laughs at me. "You don't do puke well, do you?"

"What was your first guess?" My voice is muffled being that my mouth is covered by my coat sleeve.

Gag.

"The fact that you're not coming very close is a good indicator." She laughs, standing from her spot and wiping her mouth with the back of her hand.

Gag.

"I'm sorry. It's just..."

She waves me off. "No worries. I don't blame you."

"Let's get you inside and" —I gulp, trying not to, but failing miserably, gag again— "cleaned up."

She bursts out laughing then groans, doubling over again and holding her head. "Are you sure you can handle it?"

I swallow and nod my head resolutely. "I can."

"Ha! You sound really" —hiccup— "convincing."

"I can! I promise. Or... I'll try."

We make our way inside, and she fumbles for the light

switch against the wall. As soon as she flips it on, she leans against the wall.

She moans then slides down the wall and lands with a thump.

"Bri is going to be sooooo disappointed in me," she mumbles.

I chuckle, looking around her living room. I spot the kitchen and move to it, opening a couple of cupboards until I find the glasses. I fill one with water from the tap and walk back into the living room to find Christine slumped over completely on the floor.

I bend down close to her, her head lifting as she looks up at me. I press the glass to her lips, and she tips her head back, allowing some of the liquid to wash down her throat. After she's taken a few drinks and seems satisfied, I place the glass on the floor next to her and help her to stand.

"I'm kind of embarrassed."

"You should be. I've never gotten drunk before."

I hear her scoff. "No one likes a smart ass, Andy," she teases.

Now it's my turn to scoff. "Of course, they do. In fact, I'm pretty sure it's the opposite. Everyone loves a smart ass. We keep conversations entertaining."

She gazes up at me, looking pathetically beautiful. I swipe a chunk of her hair off her sticky forehead, trying not to imagine why it's sticky in the first place, and tuck it behind her ear.

"You're gorgeous," I remind her, wondering if she'll remember in the morning.

"Right. With puke on my face and in my hair and uggghh..."

"I've always thought you were gorgeous, Christine."

"You have?" she asks, her voice quiet and unsure.

"I have."

We stand, staring at one another for a few beats before her

cheeks puff out and she bolts from my grasp, running down the hall to what I hope is her bathroom.

I take a moment to text the boys and let them know that I'll be a little longer than I expected before I get home. Their reply is instant, telling me that they are fine and heading to bed.

I stare at my phone, wondering how I got such good kids, willingly going to bed on their own.

I don't have long to sit and ponder it before I hear some awful noises coming from the direction that Christine just bolted. I pop a piece of cinnamon gum in my mouth, sigh heavily, and head into the battlefield.

SEVEN

CHRISTINE

I t's been a week since Andy saved me from Margarita Madness. A week of random pop-ins at Dreamin' Beans, shared texts, and phone calls. We began checking in with each other after the night at the docks. He opened up to me and I know his main concern was how bitter he was getting. I'm not sure either of us even realized we were checking in so often.

At first, it was just a common courtesy call thanking him for helping me get home safely after I had stupidly gotten wasted at El Charro. I don't know what any of us were thinking. We hadn't made a plan for how we would get home, and considering every single one of us were three sheets to the wind, it was not only stupid but incredibly irresponsible.

Andy being Andy had just shrugged it off, laughed about it the next day, and told me that he and Josh had gotten all our vehicles home. I didn't even remember giving him the keys to my car, but apparently I had when I was bent over, heaving out mountains of chips and salsa and tequila, all while Andy stood back, gagging but being the supportive friend that I've come to... I don't know. Like?

But then I realized it wasn't just me doing the checking in. It was Andy popping in often at Dreamin' Beans. So often, in fact, that if I didn't see him by noon I wondered what was wrong.

When my phone pings with a text, I look down and mutter, "What in the world?"

Andy: *Mayday! Mayday!*

Before I can even type out a response, my phone starts ringing.

"Yes?" I answer, trying not to laugh.

"Do you have any idea what the date is?"

"Uhh."

"December twentieth, Christine. December. Twenty," he says, drawing out the word twenty.

I giggle. "And?"

"And? Are you kidding me right now? Do you *realize* that Christmas is in just a few days?" His voice is coming out higher than I've ever heard it before, which almost makes me laugh, but I hold it back.

"I'm aware."

"Are you also aware that I have nothing ready?"

I gasp. "Andy!"

"Christine!" he mocks.

"Hey, don't mock me, procrastinator."

"Are you ready?"

I hear a car door shut in the background, followed by an engine starting up.

"Ready?"

"For Christmas! Come on, keep up!"

"Keep up with *what*?"

"Shopping! We need to shop!" he shouts, panic clear as day in his voice.

I lean back against the counter, still facing the front of the shop so I can see if someone needs refills, or be aware of new customers coming in.

"Shopping, huh?"

I hear him blow out a breath. "I'm so glad you get it. We need to shop. We need to Christmas!"

"I don't think saying we need to Christmas is at all correct."

Clearly, I've been spending too much time with Carly now.

I can almost *hear* him rolling his eyes at me, if that were even possible.

"I need your help."

I bite my lip to keep from doing a girly giggle because, *hello,* I'm a *grown* woman and I'm getting butterflies and fighting back twirling in the middle of the business that I *own.*

Ugh.

I'm almost annoying myself.

But I challenge anyone to not totally crush over someone like Andy. He makes me feel young again.

"You there?"

"I'm here."

"So, you'll help?"

"Honestly I don't know how much help I'll be. I only have a daughter, you know?"

"No. I know what I'm getting the boys. But I need help getting something for my mom, and Tess and Barrett helped so much after we left Heather so I want to get them something and... shit. I'm screwed. Do you have any *idea* what the crowds are going to be like? I can't ask you to do this. I'm sorry. Ignore me."

"No!" I shout, all too eagerly before he can just hang up. "I'll help! I have to get a few things anyway."

I don't. Unlike most men, I've been done shopping for a while.

But, he *needs* me, and I literally have zero ability to say no to him.

"Are you sure?"

I nod eagerly, my hair brushing against my cheeks in the process.

"I'm sure."

"Thank you. When can you leave the shop today? I feel bad. I'm always pulling you away from there."

"Today? It's Monday. Don't you have to work?"

"Nah. It's slow."

"It's slow here, too."

The bell above the door jingles, alerting me to a new customer.

"I see that," Andy says, a smile in his voice.

"Yeah," I say, my voice barely above a whisper when my eyes connect with his.

He's wearing that damn black beanie again that does funny things to my insides, a denim shirt, and slim black jeans. He has a thick layer of stubble on his face, and when he smiles, the white of his perfectly straight teeth gleaming, I almost stumble forward.

Good heavens above, he's *gorgeous*.

I slowly slide my phone down from my ear, hitting the red button before slipping it into my back pocket.

"Hey."

"You're anxious to get this shopping over with, huh?"

"Or maybe I was just anxious to see you."

A million butterflies flutter around in my stomach.

I smile, not trusting my voice.

We're staffed well... a few of the college kids who worked for me this past summer are home for holiday break, wanting hours. And, I know Emma is here to handle things in my absence. She's more than capable. And now that I've seen him, I don't want to wait to get our shopping excursion going.

"Give me five minutes?"

"Of course," he murmurs.

I reach down and grab him a slice of pumpkin bread out of the front case and fill a to-go cup of coffee for him, then slide them both across the counter.

"The way to a man's heart." He winks. And the butterfly farm might as well have exploded.

"Staying out here or coming back?" I ask him, nodding toward the office.

He looks that direction and back to me.

Rather than answer, he picks up his bread and coffee and moves in the direction of the backroom.

When I meet him at the end of the counter, he moves closer to me, reaches out and places a hand at my lower back.

I look at him from under my lashes and he grins, a small side grin that's adorable and endearing and all things Andy.

We're moving forward into a territory neither of us are sure of. Well, I know I'm not. Shaky ground to say the least.

I don't know if he's feeling the things I am.

But *having* feelings and *acting* on them are two entirely different things.

I remove my apron, hanging it on the hook on the back of my office door and sit at my desk, bringing my laptop to life.

Andy takes a seat, bites into the pumpkin bread and groans, deep and throaty, his head falling back.

My fingers stay suspended above my keyboard while I sit transfixed, not being able to pull my eyes away from him.

"Good God, woman."

"You like?"

"Love," he corrects me.

I flush at his words, happiness and pride filling my chest.

I bite my lip and finish what I'm working on, closing out the programs on my computer before shutting it down for the night.

I stand up and make my way to the door, Andy's hand

catches mine on the way, sending tingles through me when he rubs his thumb on the palm of my hand.

It only takes a single touch for my body to react.

"Where're you goin'?" His dark brown eyes boring into mine.

"Need to tell Emma I'm leaving," I explain.

"Oh. Hurry?"

I nod, and when he bites his lip I feel a quiver roll through my entire body.

He releases my hand, and I move into the kitchen where I know I'll find her.

"Hey, girl. I'm out of here."

"Gotcha."

"You're okay with that?"

She smiles knowingly. "I saw who came in. It's all good, Christine."

"I... are you sure?"

"How long have I worked for you?"

I scrunch my eyebrows. "Since I opened?"

"That's right. And want to know something?"

"What's that?"

"I've never seen you happier than I do when he walks into this building. Go."

I stand stunned for a few beats before I give her a hug. She laughs and shoves me out the door.

I make a pit stop in the employee bathroom, where I keep a few makeup essentials stashed in the small closet Barrett built for me when we opened the shop.

I freshen up, adding a little blush, some lip gloss, and brush through my hair.

I smooth down my dark green and blue plaid button down shirt, one that I actually stole from Andy the night of Margarita Madness when he took it off after he panicked, thinking I got vomit on it. I offered to wash it and never returned it. No shame. I fix my dark gray camisole, also not ashamed to realize that I have a tiny bit of cleavage and check out my ass in my jeggings.

Don't judge me.

Everyone does it.

And it's Andy.

My feelings for him are growing to scary levels.

Satisfied, I walk back into the office.

Andy's fiddling with his phone, one leg crossed over the other, ankle to knee. He has his bottom lip pinched between the thumb and forefinger of the hand not holding his phone and his knee is bobbing up and down.

The moment he hears me walk in, he lifts his eyes to me, does a slow perusal of my body, and slowly stands, sliding his phone into the pocket of his jeans.

"How is it that you're always so beautiful?" he says, reverence in his voice, tucking a piece of hair behind my ear, his palm resting on my cheek.

The breath catches in my throat.

Then.

"This divorce can't happen soon enough." His voice is low, husky and, *ohmylanta*, I want to crawl inside it and burrow down deep and never come up for air.

I *think* I know what he means but yet...

"What?"

"You heard me," he murmurs.

I did.

But I almost want to hear it again.

"You got a coat?"

I nod my head, his hand still to my cheek.

He smiles.

"Ready, then?"

"Oh yeah," I reply, my body swaying toward his.

"To shop," he says, his mouth a mere breath away from mine. I can smell the spices from the pumpkin bread and coffee.

Delicious.

"Yup."

"I think we need to get out of here before I do something I promised myself I wouldn't. Especially with you in my shirt."

I nod, though I feel like making a few bad decisions wouldn't be such a terrible idea.

"You want it back?"

"I'm thinking you make it look way better than I ever did."

He obviously hasn't looked in a mirror lately.

Thirty minutes later we're parking at the mall, the parking lot crowded from all the other last minute shoppers.

As we walk through the parking lot, our arms brush against each other. Having left my coat in his pickup so I wouldn't sweat inside the mall, I wrap my arms around myself to keep myself warm.

Andy notices and wraps an arm around me, pulling me in close.

"Cold?"

"Well, it's twenty degrees out and flurrying."

"I take that as a yes?" he asks, smiling down at me.

I don't know how to respond, the look in his eyes alone warming me.

I bite my lip and look away, focused on getting into the mall without slipping and falling on a patch of ice.

He rubs a strong hand up and down my arm once then squeezes me closer. I wrap an arm around his waist to make it less awkward walking and almost whimper when we reach the entrance, knowing there's no reason to be doing the walk/cuddle anymore.

It only takes us a couple hours to finish his shopping. As we were shopping for his mom, he mentioned that she raised him by herself. It made me fall for him just a little harder watching him shop for her. He knew the things she liked and wanted so much to get her things that would make her happy.

I also picked up a few more items to stick in Bri's stocking and give to my friends and Emma, especially for all the extra work she's been putting in.

When we were finished shopping, we stood on the upper level of the mall, watching the poor Santa fighting kids who don't want to sit on his lap, while their parents, desperate for a picture, stood by trying to encourage their child to sit still.

"Poor schmuck. I wonder how many times he's had a little boy or girl pee on him?"

I snort. "Probably more than he would care to admit. When Bri was three, she was determined to sit on Santa's lap. We waited in line for over an hour, and when her turn came, she crawled up there happily. Other kids kicked and screamed, but she was so excited. She sat on his lap for about ten seconds before I watched her eyes narrow at him. Her tiny little hand reached up, and she poked at Santa's beard before she tugged and pulled. The beard came off, and when she released her hold, it slapped the poor guy in the face, all cock-eyed. Then she pointed right at him and yelled, "You a fakewer!" in her cute little three-year-old voice."

"No way," he says, eyes twinkling.

"Oh, yeah. She was so mad that she had been swindled." I giggle, remembering the look of horror on the Santa's face as well as the elves'. "The kids still in line started screaming, and we had several parents walk up to us and thank us — very sarcastically, mind you. Although a few of them I think were genuinely thankful that they no longer had to worry about standing in that dreaded line again."

"Oh, man," he chortles, leaning over the railing that overlooks the center of the mall where Santa is sitting. "I think I love your daughter. That's the best thing I've ever heard."

"It was pretty awesome. Needless to say, she never asked to sit on Santa's lap again."

"I bet," he says, smiling at me.

We watch the line for a few more minutes before Andy turns to me. "I have an idea before we head out."

"Okay?"

He tugs on my hand as we head down the escalator, past the Santa and flustered parents waiting in line with their impatient children. We share a knowing smile but continue walking until he comes to the store he was apparently looking for.

"What are we doing here?"

"Trust me," he says, a twinkle in his eye.

"Good afternoon," the sales lady welcomes us into their tiny little nook in the corner of the mall. "Is there something I can help you two find?"

I start to shake my head, but Andy squeezes my hand. "Kind of wore the old mattress out so we're needing a new one."

My eyes widen as his suggestive tone, combined with the waggle of his eyebrows to the poor saleslady who can't take her eyes off him.

Not that I blame her.

We walk around the small store for a few minutes before he flops down on a mattress, flipping and flopping around like a fish out of water.

"Hear that babe? No squeaks! The kids won't hear a *thing*!"

I.

Could.

Die.

Of.

Embarrassment.

I groan, dropping my head into my hands.

"Mm hmm. I hear."

"Come on! Test it out with me," he says, grinning ear to ear and crawling over the mattress on his hands and knees to get to me before reaching out and pulling me down on the bed with him.

I lie there, my body bouncing around while he continues his test run of the bed.

I risk a glance at the saleslady, who's stifling laughter.

There are a few other customers in the store, the men laughing, the women staring at Andy.

The dork.

When he's satisfied with his fun, he rolls off the bed, me doubling over in laughter, needing his help to get off the bed.

"Fun, right?"

I roll my eyes.

"Right."

"Oh, admit it, I make for a good shopping date," he teases.

I can't deny it, though my heart is definitely caught up on the word date. He made battling the crowds of holiday shoppers fun and light hearted.

He tried on scarves and sweater cardigans that he was looking at for his mom, claiming that they had the same coloring so then he would know for sure if it would look good on her. He smelled candles and read the blurb on the back of about twenty books — out loud — before finally choosing one.

"I have to go to the pet store to get the boys their last gift but want to do dinner first? I'm starving."

He had told on the way to the mall that he was surprising the boys with a huge aquarium and a pet turtle. Something they've wanted for a long time now.

"Of course you are. You haven't eaten in like two hours."

"I'm a growing boy!"

"Mm hmm."

"So. Dinner? Then the pet store?"

"Good plan."

All in all, it was a great day. We were both able to finish our Christmas shopping, and we ended the day eating burgers and fries before we picked up a turtle.

Words I never thought I'd say tumble out of my mouth, "That turtle is actually really cute."

"Right? So ugly it's cute."

When he pulls up next to my car still parked behind the coffee shop, I hesitate just long enough for him to speak up.

"Thank you for coming along today."

"Thank you for asking me."

He blows out a breath and rests his head on the back of his seat, watching me watching him. "Lawyer drew up the papers," he says out of the blue, his voice low. He already told me, but it's obviously still on his mind.

"Are you okay?" I ask quietly.

"More than okay. Not that she gives a shit, but I'm asking for full custody. My lawyer doesn't think it will be an issue, considering she's all but abandoned her kids. But I don't have a place to serve her. Not until we figure out where she's staying."

"I'm sorry."

"Don't be. Starting to move forward. I want it behind me. *Her* behind me."

I reach over the console and squeeze his forearm, and he closes his eyes.

We sit in silence for a few beats until the back door to the shop swings open, Paul, one of the college students, bringing a bag of garbage out to the dumpster.

He notices Andy's pickup truck parked and still running and stares for a bit before he sees me waving to let him know it's me then waves a hand in return and walks back inside.

Andy and I climb out of the pickup, and he comes around to

help me place my bags in my car. I start it up so it has a few minutes to warm up before I head home.

"Thank you for coming along today," he repeats his earlier words.

"You already said that."

"It was worth repeating."

"I'm glad you asked me. I had fun."

"Told you I was a fun date."

I glance away then back to him. "Christine?"

"Andy?"

"I won't ask you now. But you gotta know, when I'm free of Heather?"

"Yes?"

"Be ready."

EIGHT

CHRISTINE

It's New Year's Eve, and my pathetic self is sitting cross legged, a tray of junk food sitting on the right side of the bed, the ball dropping in New York City on my TV screen.

My phone vibrates on the tray, buzzing around like an angry hornet.

I lift it up and smile, seeing Andy's name lighting up my phone as confetti rains down on everyone in Time's Square.

"Andy."

"It's midnight."

"It is."

"New year. New beginning."

"Yeah."

"New beginning," he repeats.

"You drunk?" I joke.

"No. Needed to be sober so I could get my boys from the party they went to. Which I haven't picked them up from yet. Because they have lives. And their dad does not."

"Oh, please. You have a life."

"This is partly true. The life I had? Not so great. The life I see coming? It's pretty damn great."

A shiver rolls through me at his words.

"And what do you see coming in your life, Andy Simpson?" my voice is barely above a whisper.

"You."

SINCE THAT MIDNIGHT PHONE CALL, we've talked every day. It's been over a month, and there hasn't been a single day that we haven't spoken, texted, or seen each other.

One night when the boys were at a friend's house for the evening, he called and by the sound of his voice, I knew it was going to be different from our lighthearted calls. We talked for hours about nothing and everything. And in those quiet moments over the phone where we both admitted we were lying in bed while talking, he confessed things that I can only imagine were bothering him for a while.

The admission that had me sitting up straight in bed, flush and thinking things I had no business thinking, was that he hadn't had sex in almost a year. *They* hadn't had sex in almost a year. *She* had. Obviously.

And what shocked me even more was that he said it didn't bother him.

He lost all sense of affection toward her years ago and had simply lost the desire.

At least with her.

His quiet murmur that his desire was back again had me aching for him to be near me.

After that, our late-night confessions became our thing.

Some were silly and at risk of a teenage sleepover truth or dare.

Others were pushing the boundaries of friendship.

Celebrity crush: Teenage sleepover. (Though, when he told me Mila Kunis was his, I was glad we were on the phone so he couldn't see my blush, considering that he's told me more than once I resemble her.)

What we wear to bed: Boundary pusher.

What's the most embarrassing thing that ever happened: Teenage sleepover.

Song that turns us on: Boundary pusher.

First kiss: Teenage sleepover.

Our favorite sexual positions: Boundary pusher.

And on and on they went. Admitting our deepest, darkest insecurities to making each other say what we liked about ourselves.

It was a combination of a therapy session and friendship building.

And I loved every single minute of it.

A few times he would call when Bri wasn't home yet from a date with Grady and she would see me talking to him when she walked in the door. The first few times she simply smiled, kissed me on the cheek and went to her room.

The third time it happened, she walked over, leaned close so Andy could hear through the receiver and said, "It's almost past her curfew, young man." He laughed in response, and she giggled at herself, kissed me, and said good night.

The next morning, she told me she liked seeing me happy again.

When I hear a ringtone that I know *I* didn't set for myself, I scramble to answer it.

"Hey, Andy," I answer after sliding the phone out of my apron pocket, continuing to work the cinnamon roll dough.

"What's up, buttercup?"

I laugh but still respond. "Not much. What's shakin' bacon?"

He chuckles. "Nice one."

"Thanks. Nice ringtone, by the way."

"How'd you know I had anything to do with it?"

"Uhh, who else would have changed my ringtone to *Pillowtalk*?"

His answering chuckle has me blushing. Again.

Funny how I'm a grown woman and blush like it's my first crush.

Which yeah, I've finally admitted to myself having.

An enormous crush on Andy.

He clears his throat. "So, I have a question."

"Shoot," I tell him, adjusting the phone on my shoulder while I knead and roll the dough.

"Would you be up for meeting the boys?"

I drop the phone on the counter into the dough and rush to pick it up, flour covering my hands. As soon as I have it back to my ear, I grab the closest towel and wipe my hands clean then motion to Emma to finish the cinnamon rolls for me.

It seems like she's always picking up where I'm leaving off lately. Especially when Andy is on the other end of what I drop work for.

She looks at me funny before I mouth *Andy* to her as I point to the phone.

She makes a kissy face at me, and I hip bump her while I'm making my way past her, to which she replies by cackling in return.

Brat.

Obviously, I may have been denying it to myself that I had a super crush on Andy — but I was doing a shit job at hiding it from those around me.

I knew good and well that's what was happening, but I didn't realize the extent of which it had built to.

"What?" I ask while I'm walking to my office for some privacy.

"Did you really not hear me, or are you just confirming what I asked?"

"Just confirming," I murmur.

He laughs, which has my body warming.

"So, would you?"

"Now?" I ask on a shriek.

"Uh, kind of figured you could come over tonight. Not like this exact instant. And bring Bri. I think it's time I meet her also. At least, officially."

"Really?"

"Why not?" he asks, hurt in his voice.

I shrug even though he can't see me.

"I'm not fighting it, Andy," I promise him.

"I want my boys to know you, Christine. And I want to know Bri."

"You're not divorced yet," I remind him.

"You think I give a shit about Heather?" His voice is a cross between shocked and angry, and I feel a little guilty, but he needs to be thinking clearly.

"You should. If she catches wind that you and I are..."

"Are?" he asks, prompting me with a teasing lilt to his voice.

"Well, um..." I stumble around for words. "That's we're..." I don't know what we are. I know what I want to be. But I'm much further along in my single status than he is.

"Christine. I like you."

I suck in a breath and spin around in my office chair.

"Do you like me?"

"Did you want Carly to pass me a note in class so I can check off yes or no?" I tease him.

He chuckles again. "I know I'm not divorced. Yet. But I'm not asking you on a date. Yet. Truth time?"

"Always."

"We're not dating but we're dating, yeah?"

I hum a response because nothing is official, but it's very clear there's something happening between us. Him asking me to meet his kids just solidifies that.

"Right. We're not official, but I want to be with you. I want you to meet my kids, and I think it would be nice for all of us to get to know each other a little better. The five of us. It's time, Christine."

"Okay," I find myself saying, though knowing that I would have said yes anyway.

He doesn't hesitate or gloat that he got me to say yes so easily. "Seven o'clock. Just bring yourselves."

NINE

ANDY

"Come on, boys! They'll be here in just a few minutes."

"Dad. Calm down. We've met Christine before," Reece says with a roll of his eyes.

They don't understand the significance of tonight. Hell, maybe Christine doesn't either. But I served Heather divorce papers today, and now that the ball is rolling, I'm not willing to back off on setting my sights on something I want.

And I want Christine.

Not even knowing my boys, she worries over them.

Asks about them.

Wants to know what's happening in their lives.

And me not knowing Bri, I feel the same.

We talk every day.

Multiple times.

I know that Bri is looking at colleges near home and that she and Grady are growing closer by the day.

I know that she wants to go to school for Communications and is both nervous and excited about the change, much like Christine is.

Christine knows that the boys play basketball and knows how their season is going.

She knows how they're doing in school, asks how tests or certain projects and assignments went after I had mentioned them.

She knows their favorite foods and what vlogger they're currently following and, even though they're boys and she only has a girl, knows that puberty is a son of a bitch to deal with, especially as a single parent, and helps me understand that my kids were not, in fact, abducted by aliens.

But it's more than just our mutual single parenthood that has me wanting to find out everything I can about her, and get to know her better, and... yeah, eventually *really* get to know her better.

It's the fact that she's kind and gentle and her genuine smile lights up my day.

It's the happiness that radiates from her.

And it doesn't hurt that she's the most gorgeous woman I've ever met.

So, yeah.

I want more with her.

I want everything with her.

But I'm not jumping into anything.

What we have already is great.

I'll take the rest as slowly as we need.

But when those divorce papers are signed, I'll have a hard time not speeding that timeline along.

I won't do a thing until the divorce is final, though. Even if our marriage ended long ago, I won't do that to Christine. Or me, for that matter. I'm not a cheater and having the ink dried on the papers is just something that I need to have before I move that one final step forward.

I blink at the boys and look around the house.

The house we've turned into our home over the last few months.

No sign of Heather anywhere.

They won't let me put up any pictures of their mom.

Tess came over and helped make it, in her words, not a stinky man cave, but otherwise it's all us.

Our living room is simple.

Chocolate brown oversized leather furniture.

Large flat screen TV with a sound system set up.

Video game console on the rustic wooden TV stand I built below.

On the wall, there's a collage of pictures of the boys.

In the corner is the stand for the aquarium that houses the boys' turtle, Harry. How ironic his name is, is not lost on anyone, trust me.

Something Heather always said no to, but they had been wanting for years.

Their wish came true on Christmas morning, and the joy on their faces was worth it. I had been dreading that day since their birthday came and went without a single call from their mother.

Having Christine help me get the final touches of Christmas gifts ready helped more than I think she would ever know.

Christmas Day proved that they were moving on when they were happy, laughing. Despite her absence. When neither of them asked for Heather.

And I could do the same.

"Yo! Dad!" I hear Aidan's voice interrupt my thoughts, laughing at me.

"What's up?"

"What's up with the weird looks you've been getting on your face lately?"

I decide not to tell him that on more than one occasion they've caught me daydreaming about Christine.

"You ready?" I ask them both instead.

"Yup."

That's when I really look at them. I do a double take and have to press my lips together to suppress the laughter threatening to bubble up out of me.

Reece has on khaki pants and a tucked-in button-down shirt, his hair gelled up with what looks like an entire bottle of hair gel. The strands of his dark blond hair sticking up in what I assume he thinks is stylish but because of the amount of gel looks more like he stuck his finger in a light socket.

Aidan looks similar, but his hair doesn't have the same amount of gel in it. Probably because Reece used it all up.

And then I get a whiff of them.

"Boys? Did you happen to put on some cologne?"

Aidan nods, but Reece shakes his head. "It's not cologne. It's body spray."

"Is there any left?" I dare ask.

He shrugs. "I think so."

Not reassuring at all.

"You know that you don't need to use a lot, right? A little bit goes a long way."

"Right. But we figured we didn't want to stink for Christine and Bri."

Mission not accomplished there.

"Just to say, boys, you may have overdone it. And the gel" — I lift my chin in Reece's direction— "is a little much."

"We smell?"

"Not in the B.O. kind of way but..."

Reece punches Aidan in the shoulder. "I *told* you it was too much! Ugh! Why do I always listen to you?"

"It's not my fault! It's *body* spray. It's meant to go over your body. Duh!"

"But with just a small amount," I remind them.

"And the hair gel thing was *all* on you." Aidan glares at his brother.

"What are we supposed to do now? They're gonna be here any minute, and they're gonna think we look stupid, and smell stupid, and act stupid..."

I cut off Reece's rant and ensuing panic attack moment with a hand in the air.

"Boys. Calm yourselves. Go throw your clothes in the laundry room, take a quick shower and scrub down. One of you take your bathroom, the other take mine so you get it over with quickly. Then get into some *normal* clothes. T-shirt. Joggers. Jeans. Hoodie. Whatever. They'll love you more if you're yourselves, got me?"

They nod eagerly and both jet off to do as told, leaving a cloud of body spray in their wake. I have half a mind to open a window to air the house out but decide to check on supper instead.

I'm admittedly not the best cook but being a single dad of two growing boys, boys who are active and can't live off frozen food and boxed meals, I'm learning. Slowly but surely getting this whole cooking thing down.

I check the chili, one of the few things I make that I'm proud of, and double check the cornbread in the oven isn't burning.

I had the boys help me set the table before their run-in with a gallon of body spray and hair gel. I place the bowls of shredded cheese, diced onion, and crackers on the table while I wait, impatiently, for the doorbell to ring.

"Better?" I glance over at the sound of the Aidan's voice, who looks like himself again, and over to Reece and smile.

"Much."

And then the doorbell rings. Their eyes widen, and they both take off to answer the door at the same time.

"Welcome!" Aidan shouts, and I chuckle.

Five minutes ago, they were in panic mode over what they looked like for Christine and Bri, and now they're welcoming them with open arms.

Not that I mind the change.

"Boys!" I hear Bri's voice cry out.

"Hey, Bri," they say in unison.

Knowing my boys. My *fourteen*-year-old boys, there was a reason they were so focused on how they looked — and smelled — for tonight's festivities.

And the one who just greeted them is it.

I chuckle to myself as I round the corner and stop in my tracks.

In the doorway of my home stands Christine, an arm on each of their shoulders, looking up at them and smiling.

She's short enough that they're both already taller than her by a few inches. She looks gorgeous as usual, her dark hair down. She's wearing a pair of skinny jeans and a big chunky mustard yellow sweater, Bri wearing something very similar, but her sweater light gray. They both step out of their boots and continue greeting the boys.

Aidan and Reece are looking at Christine with giant smiles on their faces, and she's looking at them in adoration.

I hadn't seen those looks shared between them and Heather in so long, I forgot what it was like.

And it's in that brief glance that I know I won't stop pursuing this for our future.

I want this for them.

For me.

For all of us.

TEN

CHRISTINE

I didn't realize I was looking for something. I felt content in the life that I was living, and then Andy walked in and shook everything up, everything that I thought I knew. He's on my mind constantly, which is a bad thing. He's not even divorced yet.

I smile, resting my chin in my palm, feeling more content sitting at a table around empty bowls of chili, listening to the boys tell Bri about their lives. Neither can tell her stories or ask questions fast enough, and Bri is eating it all up.

"Want to watch us play Xbox?"

"Watch? Are you kidding me? Do I look like a sit by and watch kind of girl? Heck, no. I'm gonna destroy you. Tell me you have the new Halo game."

Both their eyes light up and they glance at Andy.

"Yeah, we got it for Christmas! Along with Harry."

We all laugh at the ridiculous name for their turtle.

"Go on. I'll clean up while you guys get your butts handed to you by a girl," Andy teases them.

The three kids jump from their chairs and all settle in on beanbag chairs on the floor.

"Do you have headsets?" I hear Bri ask.

"Oh, she just won some major points with them."

"It doesn't seem like she was struggling for their approval." I wink at him as I lean down to pick up some of the dirty bowls and he saunters over to me.

"They're like their dad," he says, his voice so husky it sends a shiver through my body.

"Yeah?"

"Mm hmm. Good taste, I must say."

"Andy..." I whisper.

"It's gonna happen, Christine. I served her papers today."

I sink slowly into the seat I had just stood from. "What?"

He sits down and pulls his chair in front of me so we're facing each other. He leans over and takes my hands in his. "I finally got a hold of Heather's sister and found out where she's staying. Lawyer had the papers ready to go, so he sent them over. Served her today."

"Are you... I mean. Wow. Are you okay?"

"Why wouldn't I be?" he asks, looking back and forth between my eyes, thumb rubbing against the back of my hand.

I bite my lip, and his eyes drift briefly to the movement. I look down at our linked hands and take a deep breath then lift my eyes back up to his. "Have you heard from her?"

He shakes his head and shrugs his shoulders. When he leans back against his seat, our hands separate. The loss of his touch against my hand is felt immediately, and I have to fight to not reach out and grab his hand in mine again, wanting and needing the calm it brings me. He rakes his hands through his hair as he looks into the living room and back to me again. It's grown out so much since that first day he walked into Dreamin' Beans. Sometimes he even wears it in a man bun, something I never thought I'd be attracted to. Until now, that is. Before I can stop myself, I reach up and push some strands out of his face. The curls are soft between my fingers. He closes his eyes briefly and leans into my touch.

"I don't expect to. She's... well, she's not the same person I married. Or at least, not the same person I thought I married. I figure we'll hear from her again when she empties out the house. We have an offer, so she needs to get her shit unless she wants it all to go to the thrift store."

"I'm sorry," I whisper when I don't know what else to say.

He shakes his head back and forth a few times. "Don't be. I'm not. She's not worth it, right?"

"I just want you to be happy," I tell him.

"I am." He leans forward again, bracing his elbows on his knees and cocks his head sideways. "You're part of the reason for that. A huge part."

I smile and look away. "Let's get this table cleaned up so we can join the kids."

"Sounds like a good plan."

We clean up quickly, putting away the leftover chili in the fridge and loading everything we can into the dishwasher and start it up.

He pops some popcorn, and I raise an eyebrow at him, considering we just ate.

"They're fourteen-year-old boys, sweetheart. They both have hollow legs."

I giggle and grab the bowls from the cupboard he motioned to, fill them up with popcorn, and make our way into the living room only to stop dead in our tracks.

Bri is sitting on Aidan's back while he keeps switching his controller from one hand to the next while Reece sits on his beanbag chair laughing and recording it with his phone.

"It's my turn!" Bri shouts at him, and from the sound of it, she's only partly teasing.

"No, it's not!"

She sticks her finger in her mouth and pulls it out with a loud pop. "I'll give you a wet willy!"

I share a look with Andy, and we both laugh hard enough to double over. "I take it they're getting along." I smile at him, and he pulls me in for a hug with his arm around my neck. Andy kisses the top of my head, and I sigh contently.

"Gross! Don't you dare!"

"Then give me the controller, you twerp!"

"No way! I thought girls were supposed to be nice!"

"Don't call me a girl!"

Clearly, she grew up with a boy for her best friend.

Boy turned boyfriend, but still.

Andy guides us to sit on the couch together, him planting me right next to him, watching the three of them argue and fight over controllers. Bri finally wins the battle, boasting by doing a little dance. Reece laughs so hard he falls on the ground, abandoning his phone from recording the entire thing. After playing Xbox for a while, they eventually move to the basement to play foosball. Their raucous laughter from downstairs has warmth spreading through my body.

Andy pulls me closer, and I tuck my legs up on the couch next to me. "It's gonna happen," he murmurs, the same words he spoke earlier. "But I won't do this until I'm officially out, Christine. I won't put you in the position of being the other woman."

"Won't do what, though?"

"You really don't know?"

"Well, I know what I want," I admit.

"Hope it's the same thing I want... to keep moving forward with this, building what we have. Our friendship. Our relationship. And as much as it kills me, I have to push aside every instinct I have to pull you into my lap and kiss the stuffing out of you right now. Like I said, I won't put you in the position of being the other woman."

"I want you to kiss me, too," I whisper.

"Really damn happy to hear that."

"But do you really think keeping the physical part out of our relationship until you're divorced will stop people from talking? It's obvious we're getting closer, Andy. And not just to us."

"I don't care what people say. It's not about that. It's about the fact that you and I both had our spouses step out on us, and it feels shitty as hell. I don't care about Heather and her feelings, so don't even think that. This is about me respecting you, knowing that when we share that part of us with each other, we have nothing holding us back. Tonight meant a lot to me. Seeing our three together, getting along, happy, blending. It just proves that this is a good thing, and I don't want anything screwing that up."

"Thank you for being so wonderful. For respecting me that way, as much as I almost don't want you to. I suppose I agree."

He chuckles and pulls me close, kissing the top of my head.

Sigh.

"Is it weird if I tell you I was tested?"

I stiffen in his arms and turn to look at him.

"You did?"

"Yeah. She said I didn't need to be but, not really feeling a whole lot of trust in that woman. "

I laugh lightly. "Can't blame you there."

I let the silence drift between us.

"I was tested too," I admit quietly then rush to continue, "I don't think it was necessary but I couldn't sleep at night not knowing."

"I get that. Probably for the best. You were all good?"

I grin. "Yeah. All good. You?"

He nods, eyes darkening as he looks at me with an intensity that causes me to take a deep breath.

"I'm good," he tells me, voice husky.

Warmth spreads through my body, and I war within myself. The snarky, bitchy side wants me to just have those damn papers signed already so we can be together. So he can finally be rid of the disease that is Heather. The kind side of me fears what this will do to the boys. "It's been a good night, Andy."

"It's been a *great* night," he corrects me.

"Thank you for having us over."

"Thank you for coming over."

He looks at me for several beats before tucking a lock of hair behind my ear.

"TWD?" he asks, rather than leaning in and kissing me like I want him to.

But I respect his desire to wait.

And I agree with it.

"Yeah," I nod my head and shift so I'm facing the TV, oddly fascinated about watching zombies take over the world.

ELEVEN

CHRISTINE

I'm at Balance, going over what I needed with James to get my part of the kitchen set up the way we both need it. He had asked me to head up the desserts once he opened his new restaurant, and considering it's right next door to Dreamin' Beans, it works perfectly. I could make some of the desserts that didn't need to be fresh over at my place and train his chefs on how to make the rest. I think what I love the most about Balance is the fact that it's kind of a fusion restaurant. A combination of the southern foods James's dad grew up with, and the Italian and Asian meals he's learned to cook over the years.

I just finished taking measurements and wrote down everything for James and took a picture of it to keep in my phone, when I hear movement coming from the front that will soon be the dining area. I glance up just as Andy walks into the kitchen, covered in sweat and dust, white t-shirt pulled tight across his chest. Brown leather tool belt hanging low on his hips, well-worn jeans slung low beneath the belt. Dark brown work boots cover his feet, and a bright smile spreads across his face when he sees me. Even from where I'm standing, I can see a hint of red between his molars, the cinnamon gum he seems to be addicted to chewing making an appearance.

He lifts the hem of his shirt to wipe the sweat from his brow, and my mouth goes dry. I feel my jaw go slack and eyes widen. When he drops his shirt, he winks, letting me know he caught me staring but doesn't seem to mind one bit. I smile, not giving in to the blush that is trying to creep up my neck. I'm grateful for my olive-toned skin in that moment.

"What are you doing here, cutie?"

"Cutie?"

"Well, I'd call you beautiful, but James already has that one covered with Carly. Or maybe I'll start calling you gorgeous. Seems a little more fitting."

Then I do blush. And I know it's a deep shade of pink, given that his smile only broadens.

"So?" he prompted.

"Oh! Yeah. I'm just working on the dessert menu a little bit. Needed to do some measurements, make sure we had the space needed for the extra oven James is installing."

He nods his head.

"You got plans after this? Want to grab some dinner? I promised the boys I'd take them out to pizza. James recommended a place a couple towns over."

I'm shaking my head to the first question before I even have a chance to realize what he's asking.

"No, you don't have plans, or no, you don't want to come with us?"

He shifts his stance as he reaches around his back, removing the tool belt. Such a shame, too. Or maybe it's better this way. It only added to his hotness for some reason.

"No, I don't have plans."

"Pizza then?"

And against my better judgment, this time I nod my head.

Meanwhile, James is looking back and forth between us like we're a tennis match, a shit eating grin covering his face. One he's not even trying to hide. He should just pop himself some popcorn and settle in.

I grab my coat and Andy does the same, though he doesn't put his on. When we both head for the back door at the same time and Andy places his hand on my back, James hollers, "Have fun, you guys! Don't do anything I wouldn't do!"

"Son of a bitch," Andy mutters. "Barrett's going to be tweeting about this later."

If it wasn't for the movement of his hand from my lower back to the base of my neck, squeezing slightly and the twinkle in his eye as I peered under my lashes at him, I would have been a little hurt by his statement, thinking that he was embarrassed to be seen with me. But my insecurities quickly get squished, understanding that it was a lighthearted statement about how Barrett is, rather than anything to do with me.

And his actions?

Those speak much louder than words.

His constant affection, even though we aren't officially anything.

His texts and wanting to be around me whenever possible.

His desire for the boys to know me and me to know them.

"I'll follow you to your place to drop your car, okay?"

No room for argument, he's already gently guiding me to my car.

His hand is still on my neck, the heady combination of cinnamon and man overwhelming my senses, almost causing me to stumble. But he has a firm grip on me. I chance another quick look at him, the strong chisel of his jaw, the stubble covering his cheeks, a light smattering of dust in his hair.

He doesn't look like he belongs in this tiny little Michigan town. He should be on the cover of a DVD case, having just starred in a role of some movie where women would swoon and fawn over him. And probably men, too.

He walks me to my car as I hit the unlock button on my key fob. He reaches around me, his hand making a return trip down my back as the other opens my car door. The feeling lighting a fire I could feel even through my thick coat.

He leans in closer, squeezes my side lightly, and winks. "I'll follow you," he repeats when I realize that I never answered him the first time he made the suggestion. Though, it didn't sound like a suggestion in the least.

I swallow hard and nod my head. "Sounds good," I croak out.

"Bri around? Should we call her?"

I love that he asks. He always does, although she's usually busy. "Nah. She has a big group project she's working on."

He hums his understanding and fifteen minutes later, I'm climbing into the passenger seat of his pickup. He reaches over the console and grips my hand, a movement so natural. How we got to this place together, I don't know.

He releases my hand for a moment when he reaches into his pocket, leaning up onto one hip and hands me his phone.

"Can you text one of the boys and let them know we're on our way? I'll need to shower quickly when we get home, but I want to make sure they're ready."

"Okay," I say softly.

I do as asked then place his phone back into the console, and he immediately wraps his hand around mine again and murmurs a thank you.

My heart literally feels like it could explode from my chest, but the questions that are rolling through my mind are even more overwhelming. I'm a forty-one-year-old woman. A mother. A widow. A business owner. I should be able to have simple discussions like this, yet I find myself feeling so out of my element. I haven't dated anyone since Todd passed away.

A few men asked about a year after he was gone. But no one held my interest, even for just a date. One man pursued me for a bit, came to the coffee shop and asked me out at least three times a week for a couple of months. Eventually he got the picture. It truly had nothing to do with him, though it did feel a little weird since it was one of Todd's closest friends.

The only thing I know for sure is that whatever is building between Andy and me? It doesn't feel pressured. It doesn't feel forced. It feels natural. And it feels good. Great, even.

He pulls into his driveway and squeezes my hand again. I shift my focus to him, and he blinks, one side of his mouth curving up into a smile.

"We good?" he asks, voice confident, but the look in his eyes is a little unsure.

"We are," I tell him, squeezing his hand back in return.

His eyes search mine for a few minutes before he nods once and the smile I love stretches wide across his face.

Once we're inside, I'm assaulted by two rambunctious teenagers.

"Hey, Christine!" they both say energetically, rounding the corner from the kitchen to greet us as we come in through the garage entry door.

They each give me a teenage side-hug, not fully committing to the affection but not rejecting it, either.

"How are my favorite boys doing?"

They both beam at me, and Andy snorts.

"Hello?" he asks, pretending to be hurt.

I laugh it off, and his boys each puff their chests out, making all of us laugh harder.

"I'm going to go shower quick then we'll head out for pizza, got it? You boys ready?"

"Yeah, Dad. We got your text. We're ready when you are."

"Good." He winks at me then leans close, that hand blazing a trail around my waist again as he slides it around my back. "I'll be just a couple minutes, okay?"

I nod my understanding, not being of sound mind enough to speak the words. Between his choice of nickname and his physical affection, I feel like an atomic bomb could go off beside me and it wouldn't affect me as much

The rest of the evening goes about the same. His hand would find its way to the base of my back when we were walking. He positioned me so I would be sitting next to him in the booth at the little Italian restaurant James had referred us to, his thigh resting up against mine. We spend the night together laughing over shared pizza and wings, a pitcher of soda, and warm cookies with ice cream for dessert. When supper is done, he drives me home, telling the boys to wait in the pickup. After giving them my goodbyes, Andy walks me to the door, waits for me to unlock it, and follows me inside.

A butterfly garden just hatched in my stomach.

"Thank you," he says simply.

"You're the one who invited me, paid for supper, and provided me with entertainment for the evening," I remind him.

"You're the one who said yes."

He looks at me deeply, leans in, and kisses my cheek then my forehead, lingering in place for a few beats, his hand wrapped around the back of my neck.

He squeezes twice. "Sleep tight."

"You, too," I squeak out.

"I'll call you tomorrow, okay?"

"Okay, Andy. Good night," I whisper.

"Sweet dreams," he whispers and kisses me once again on the cheek before disappearing out into the darkness.

TWELVE

ANDY

"You're seriously leaving town? For good?"

Heather is in the middle of packing what looks like her last bag when I step into our old bedroom. The boys' and my stuff had been moved out for a while now, just two weeks after she left, but I haven't touched her things. Didn't care to. But now the house is sold, and she needs to get her shit. I still don't know why she didn't get it before now.

I'm a little surprised she actually showed up today.

By the look on the boys' faces when they heard her car pull up, they were surprised, too. And I'm not sure it's a good one.

"Well, what would you expect me to do, Andy? We have a meeting with our lawyers set up. You knew this was coming. Hell, you were the one who served *me* papers, not the other way around."

She shoves another pile of underwear out of her drawer into the bag then slams the drawer shut before moving over to the closet. I stay right behind her, not letting up an inch.

"Oh gee, I don't know. And what do I expect from you? Maybe... be a mom? Stay in town? Have a relationship with your sons? Realize that you were a selfish ass? Any of those would work. You missed their birthday. Thanksgiving. Christmas!"

She spins around with fire in her eyes and points an accusing finger toward me.

"You know I never wanted this."

I raise my eyebrows and fold my arms over my chest. "Uh, actually, no. I didn't know that."

She storms out of the closet with an armful of shirts on hangers and throws them onto the bed that I plan to donate. "It was always you who wanted the family, who wanted kids and the whole white picket fence thing."

"So, when you kept showing me rings and didn't bring your birth control pills on our honeymoon, that was all me?"

"You know what I mean." She grabs the last of her clothes out of the closet before moving on to the shoes, well the shoes that are left. I did touch those. In a desperate attempt at calming my rage one evening, I came to the house, took most of her shoes, threw them in a box, and took them to the Goodwill store. I wanted to burn them but figured someone else could actually get enjoyment out of them. And they're expensive shoes. Those damn red bottoms don't come cheap, it seems.

I came from nothing. I was raised by a single mom who struggled to put food on the table. Without the help of second hand stores, I would have gone to school naked. I can't bring myself to throw things out, even if I do all right for myself now.

"I don't know what you mean. Enlighten me."

She looks around the closet, and I know she's looking for her shoes, but I just stand there with my arms crossed over my chest, and ignore her silent questioning. "Andy, cut me some slack. All I've been for half my life was a mom and wife."

"Don't you dare pin this on me, Heather. You know damn

good and well that I would have supported you if you wanted to work outside the home. I would have helped out more here, been available more, not taken the promotion with Barrett and Josh. You never, not once, made mention of you wanting something different."

She lifts her bags off the bed, and if I were a gentleman I would take them for her. I am a gentleman, just not to her. Not anymore.

"You had to know things weren't great."

I follow her to the kitchen where she leans against the counter and twists the top off the bottle of water she brought in with her.

"Of course, I knew that. I didn't realize it was because you felt like you were stuck in some suburban hell."

Her eyes flash, and she slams her bottle down on the counter, a few drops spilling out. "I never said that."

"You didn't have to!"

I clench my fists tightly and take several deep breaths, trying to get control of my anger. It's not me who I'm angry for. It's our boys. Our boys, who are teenagers who need their mother, no matter how crappy she seems to have turned.

"Don't make this harder than it has to be. Besides, you have the boys. You have what you wanted. Why are you fighting this? Why do you care? You've already moved on with *her* anyway!"

"Harder than it has to be? You don't know why I'm fighting this? And what the hell do you care if I've moved on or not. You moved on from me years ago." She flinches at the tone of my voice, and I know she recognizes the anger that's laced in it. "And what the hell do you know about my private life? I haven't gone on a single date."

"That's not what I hear." She sneers.

"You heard wrong then."

She watches me closely, probably to see if I'm lying to her. When she doesn't get what she wants, she huffs and rolls her eyes.

"You told me you wanted the boys. I gave them to you. Why do you still want me around?"

I slam my fists on the counter, making her jump. "*I* don't want you around, Heather! I want the boys to have their mother! How do you not understand that? Do you know how it feels for them? To feel like they're worth nothing? That their own mother doesn't want them? You abandoned them!"

"I didn't *abandon* them." She rolls her eyes. "I left them with their *father*. You know — you, in all your perfect glory?"

"Oh, please."

"You know what? I almost didn't do this, but now that you reminded me that I so *graciously* gave you the boys..." She reaches around and pulls a tri-folded piece of paper out of her back pocket and hands it over to me.

I open it up, my eyes flitting over the words that I can hardly believe I'm reading.

I slowly lift my gaze to hers. She's smirking, inspecting her nails like she doesn't have a care in the world.

"What the hell is this?"

"My share."

"Your. Share."

"That's right. My share. You didn't think I was just going to walk away and not get anything out of being married to you, did you?"

"My family's cabin?"

She shrugs her shoulders.

"You know how much the boys love it there."

"Then I guess you'll have to find one to replace it."

I laugh, a bit hysterical and manic. When I finally get

control of myself, I blow out a breath and scrub a hand down my face. "Holy shit. You're the biggest bitch on the planet."

"Well that's not very nice," she chides.

"Nice? You lost the right to expect me to be *nice* to you long ago, you miserable, rotten, no good excuse of a human being."

I lean over the counter toward her when I can tell my words aren't getting through to her. Or maybe they are, and she truly is that selfish and doesn't give a damn. Either way, I'm done. So done. I take a deep breath through my nose and try to steady my racing heart and the heat that's coursing through my veins.

"You want the boys?"

"You know I do," I grind out.

"Then you'll give me the cabin."

"Why? It doesn't mean shit to you. You never wanted to go there."

"Aww, Andy. You know why."

"Explain it to me."

"What are you going to do for vacation without your precious cabin? You never wanted to go anywhere else. It was always there. No matter that I begged for you to take me places like Mexico or Hawaii."

"Places we couldn't afford," I add.

"Oh please. You could've found the money," she scoffs.

"What the hell did I ever do to you? You should be thanking me, getting rid of the 'baggage,' as you called them."

"They're my sons, Andy. They're not baggage," she says in the fakest voice I've ever heard with her hand on her heart.

"You walked away. What do you care?"

"If you want them so badly, why are you hanging on to the cabin?"

"Because it's means something to me, you bitch!" I roar.

I take a steadying breath.

"Make a choice, Andy. Your boys or the cabin? How ugly do you want this to get?"

She didn't even call them her boys, or our boys. I sit down, defeated but not out of the game. My family will hate it that it went to her, but they'd hate it even more if she was still in our lives.

"How did I ever love you?"

"Gee, I've wondered the same thing about how I ever loved you."

"Take the cabin. I want you out of our lives. You're signing away your rights to those boys. You're never going to be near them again, you understand me? I don't want your toxicity around them. I don't want you to be a part of their lives in any way. We've been away from you for months now, and you know what? We're better off.

"Here's how it's going to go down." My voice is so low, I hope she has to strain to hear me. "If you walk away, you walk away. This right here? Is your *only* second chance I will give you. You told me you're prepared to sign the papers the way they're drawn up, so this is me with an olive branch. That final decision is on you, but I'm feeling generous and am giving you this time to re-think how selfish you're being. But you don't get to come back here and screw with the boys' heads after this, giving them hope for you sticking around.

"You make this *final* choice, but you make it without me in mind, you got me? You know I think this is total bullshit. But if this is how you're gonna play it out? Then I want you gone. Forever. You don't get to be pissed if I meet someone and the boys love her and she loves on them like they're her own. That jealousy won't fly with me. You don't get to come back at their graduation. Their weddings. I won't send you updates on their lives. You don't come to any of their games or watch when they grow up into amazing adults, because guess what? They will.

They're already amazing kids. And I have no doubt that they'll be even more incredible as they get older. You're gone? You want that? That's fine. But..." I lean closer for my final blow. "You're telling the boys."

"What?" Now it's her turn for her voice to be a whisper. But rather than anger, it's filled with fear.

"You heard me. You wanna walk away from the two best things that ever happened to either of us? You plan to take away one of their happy places? You do it. But you don't pretend that it's on me. You own up to this, you make sure they know they've done nothing wrong. That you just can't handle it because *you're* the shitty one." She flinches again, but I carry on, smirking. "Truth hurts, doesn't it? I'm not the one who stepped out. I'm not the one who left immediately for a couple months, leaving you here to deal with the blowout and questions from our two boys. I'm definitely not the one who's taking away one of the places that makes them the happiest. I'm not going to lie for you. I'm not going to allow them to question if they did something that upset you and made you leave. You will not be allowed to fuck them up, you got me?"

"But—"

"You got me?" This time I do nothing to hide my frustration from her. My voice comes out booming, in a roar that I'm sure our neighbors heard, not to mention the boys who are hanging out in the back yard.

"I got you," she cries.

She looks at me with tears in her eyes.

It doesn't faze me.

Her heartache is no longer my problem to deal with.

"And Heather?"

She looks at me, eyes hopeful as she wipes away the wetness now coating her cheeks.

"Yeah?"

"You don't get the cabin until it's final. I expect to see you at the divorce proceedings. I want this shit done."

She drops her chin to her chest and quietly agrees, sniffling.

I walk outside and around the back of the house to the back yard where the boys are kicking around a soccer ball.

I lean against the side of the house before they've noticed me and watch them, so much worry taking over my mind I don't know what to focus on first. I scrub my hand down my face. Bitterness threatens to take over, its ugly fingers snaking around the soft places of my heart. I try to shake it off, not wanting the boys to sense my mood, though I know that's pointless.

I stick my forefinger and thumb in my mouth and whistle loudly. Both their heads pop up when they notice I'm standing there.

I lift my chin to let them know I want them to follow me.

Both their shoulders, slump and I see Aidan whisper something to Reece. Reece nods his head as they continue to make their way to me.

"Yeah, Dad?"

Gutted.

Their expressions tell me they know exactly what's happening.

"Your mom wants to talk to you for a bit."

"No thanks," Aidan says, his tone full of anger.

I feel my heart crack and twist around, hoping to see Heather standing on the back deck, but she's not there. If she left, I know I'll lose my shit.

"Come here." I hold my arm out as I sit on one of the chairs that are set around the stone fire pit in our back yard.

The boys both walk over, looking like their feet are full of lead.

"Just tell us." Aidan, the bolder of my two boys, the natural leader. He's a no-nonsense kid, always honest, sometimes to a fault.

I blow out a breath and lean my elbows on my knees.

"Your mom is inside. She wants to talk to you."

"No, she doesn't. She doesn't care." He looks away quickly and sniffs.

I can't lie to my boys. Does she care? Hell if I know. I stay silent instead of giving them a sense of false hope.

"Then why is she leaving? Why did she *already* leave? For him? She just cares more about herself than us, so why should we care to go in there and have her tell us that?" Reece angrily swipes at a tear, his voice strong, even for his age.

"She's—"

"Boys." Heather's voice cuts through, and all three of us turn to look at her. She's standing on the bottom stair of the deck. Mascara smudged under her eyes, a few strands of hair falling out of her sloppy ponytail.

Neither of the boys makes a move toward her. Her eyes connect with mine, and I lift my chin and nod, hoping that she'll be the mature one of the group and come to them. I stand up, grab another chair, and pull it near mine. I point to it while looking at her, and she takes a tentative step down off the stairs. I watch as her shoulders rise and fall with a deep breath and her hands holding a tissue twist together in front of her.

She makes her way over and sits down. No longer feeling a bit of empathy for her in this situation, I lean on the arm of the chair opposite of her. The boys take notice of my position, and I feel a twinge of guilt, but only for a moment.

She's making this choice. This is on her, not me.

"Get on with it, *Mom*," Aidan bites out, his eyes filling with tears that I know will only build on his anger.

"Boys..." She sniffles and reaches out to them. Neither leans forward to grasp her hand. She winces, apparently realizing they aren't going to let her touch them, and slumps lower in her seat. "It's not... I'm so sorry," she whispers.

"Sorry for what, Mom?" Reece says, not hiding the fact that he's crying. "Why are you sorry? Why aren't we good enough? Why did you leave? Why are you leaving again?"

"I wish I had the words, I truly do."

"Just go," Aidan doesn't even look her in the eye.

"Aidan."

"What? What do you want me to say? That I want you to stay? Why would I want you to stay if you don't want us?"

"I do!"

"No, you don't. You don't care. You never did."

"I care. I love you boys so much."

"Apparently love isn't what I thought it was, then." Aidan's words are well beyond his fourteen years and break my heart even further. The thought that this is what they think, that this is what love is, pisses me off.

"Boys, I just—"

"Your mom doesn't love me anymore." I blow out a breath and look over at the woman who I once thought would be my forever. Her eyes plead with me to save her. Just like I always did. But I'm done. I've done the best I can do, the best that I can even think of in light of this messed up situation.

"So, you just don't love Dad anymore? How does that happen? And why leave us all? We have friends whose parents are divorced, and their moms didn't just leave completely."

"Because..." She looks at me again, but I have no words to help her anymore. This is on her. "Because I'm not good enough."

"Whatever, you just don't want us!" Aidan cries out and stands up from his chair, knocking it over in the process. He points to her. "You're just a coward! A big baby selfish coward who cares more about herself than anyone else! You don't want us? Well, we don't want you, either! You've been gone for months, and we didn't miss you. Not a minute, right, Reece?" He turns to look at his brother then shifts back to his mom. "Not a minute. Because guess what. You can't miss someone who doesn't care about you! So leave. Go away with your jerk of a boyfriend."

She reaches for him, and her cries have turned to sobs.

"He's right." Reece nods his head and stands up, putting his arm around Aidan's shoulders. "We didn't miss you. Just leave and get it over with. And you were right, too. You *aren't* good enough. You're nothing like a mother."

I stand up, not being able to take another minute of it, and move next to my boys.

"Heather. You need to be honest. Tell the boys what you told me."

She opens her mouth and a squeak escapes her.

"Heather," I repeat, my voice stern.

I watch as she looks down at her lap and slowly stands up, swiping the tissue under her eyes before raising her gaze to the boys. She briefly looks to me then shifts her attention to them. "I'm so sorry." Her voice is quiet. "I'm so, so sorry. I wish I had better words for you. I wish I could be what you need. What you deserve. It's not you — you need to know that, okay? I do love you. That is not why I'm leaving. I'm just simply not good enough. I'm not cut out to be the mother you need. The mother *anyone* needs."

"Heather," I warn.

"Um. So. Your dad..."

"Heather," I warn again. "Do not put this on me."

"I'm-taking-the-cabin," she says fast, the words run together.

"What?" Reece asks, his voice low and angry.

"I don't understand," Aidan says, a moment of sadness escaping him.

"I know. I know you don't."

"Wait. Dad? Can she do that? Take the cabin?"

I sigh and drop my head, closing my eyes for a moment. "It's just a cabin. You're more important."

"Mom? Why would you do that?"

She glances at me then watches her — *my* — boys closely. Then she takes a deep breath and straightens her shoulders.

"Reece. Aidan. I lied to your father. I wanted to be what I thought he wanted me to be. I knew he wanted kids. I knew he wanted the life we had. And I loved him enough that I thought I could give that to him. But... and this is not on you. It's on me. Something inside me, it's... broken I guess. I figured that once I became a mom I would feel different. Happy."

"That still doesn't explain why you think you have to take away the cabin from us. From Dad's family. You're such a selfish bitch."

Heather gasps, and my eyes bug out of my head at Reece's quick use of the word, but now's not the time to be getting on him about using a cuss word. Besides. He's not wrong.

"Well, I hope you're happy now... taking away the cabin. Being away from us. What kind of person does that?" Aidan shouts. "You never even liked to go there!"

"Oh, kiddo... when you get older you'll understand."

I guarantee neither of them will *ever* understand her.

"Thanks," Aidan scoffs.

Reece apparently has had enough, though. He points at her, and she flinches at the anger in his eyes that's aimed directly at her. "You know what? We don't want you! We don't need you!" He's shouting loudly; his chest is rising and falling quickly. "Since you left? We've been so much better off without you in our lives. Dad is a hundred times better of a parent than you ever were." He takes a deep breath before he glares at her then says in a low voice full of hurt and *rage*,

"You're a crappy parent, and we hate you. Just leave. We're better off."

"Reece," I mumble and reach for him, but he yanks his hand away. Aidan seems slightly stunned by his brother's outburst but lifts his shoulders and puffs out his chest so he's at full height next to him.

"No. Dad. She wanted to tell us everything? Well, now she can hear everything we have to say, too." He turns to look directly at her. "We really, really don't need you around. What kind of awful person are you? You're taking the cabin? The cabin that's been in Dad's family for years? Our happy place? You hated it there! What do you even care!"

"I..."

Realizing that nothing Heather could say will make the boys, or me for that matter, understand, and if possible, she might be making things worse, I decide the conversation is done. "I think it's time for you to leave."

She looks at me, and I stare back, unfeeling. There was a point where seeing her cry would have brought me to my knees. Where seeing a hint of her sadness would have caused me to do about anything to change it. But those moments are gone. They've been gone for a while. Definitely since seeing her having sex with another man. But it was before that.

"I..."

"Bye," the boys say at the same time, not giving her any more emotion than she deserves.

She walks closer, and they both flinch when she opens her arms like she is going to give them a hug. Aidan turns away first, giving her his back. Reece simply shakes his head at her then walks away, back into the house.

Heather looks to me, tears flowing freely from her eyes. I shrug, not knowing what she wants me to say. She did this; I need to remind myself of that. This wasn't my choice.

Without another word, Heather turns on her heel and runs toward the house. Less than a minute later, I hear a car engine start up, and with that, she's gone.

Less than a minute after that I hear a loud crash and know the boys aren't as okay with it as they tried to play off. And I can't blame them. One bit.

THIRTEEN

CHRISTINE

I'm fumbling with grocery bags as I walk in the door. It's been a long day, trying to help at Balance while still managing everything at Dreamin' Beans. And, of course, the constant worry going on in my head since I woke up this morning, knowing that Heather was going to be meeting up with Andy today.

My phone rings, and the screen lights up with Andy's smiling face. It was a rare moment I caught him in, his worry for the boys being at the forefront of his mind, but he was laughing at something James said at his wedding to Carly, and I managed to capture the picture. James and Andy are even farther apart in age than he and I, but that hasn't stopped them from growing increasingly close. Their own little bromance. Which is nice because Carly and I are such good friends.

Andy has needed time to work out some of his frustrations, and he loves working with his hands. James definitely has plenty to do at Balance, so Andy's been helping at the restaurant as much as he can.

James and Carly had her son Jack and his daughter Lily

stand up for them in the wedding a few weeks ago. It was a quiet ceremony in Tess and Barrett's backyard.

Carly looked beautiful in her ivory lace fitted gown, and James looked amazing in his dark blue suit.

Andy and I didn't go together as each other's dates, but he didn't leave my side the entire night.

"Hello?"

"Hey."

By the sound of his voice, things didn't go incredibly well.

"I hate to ask, but how'd it go?"

"As expected."

"She left?"

"She did."

"How are they?"

"Not good. It's not like they weren't expecting it, but still."

My heart breaks for those sweet boys, and it makes me nervous, knowing what's to come. They already think it's their fault. I can't imagine what the finality of this will do to them.

"What can I do?"

"Come over?"

I pause, wondering if that's the best idea. Andy and the boys spent a few weeks at their home after Heather left, but it seemed like it messed with the boys' heads. And Andy didn't want any part of being there. Not with Heather having had sex with another man in their bed. He spent a little bit of time at Barrett and Tess's house until he found a temporary place to stay. Fortunately, what he found ended up being permanent, rather than temporary, and they were able to move their things just once. Helped give the boys some stability, which, in their world, was needed.

The friendship between Andy and me has grown naturally, and the boys don't seem at all bothered by my presence, but it's not lost on me that things between Andy and me seem to be progressing to more than just friendship. I don't know if Andy is ready for anything more, or if the boys are ready for that, or even I. But I can't say that I'm not interested in trying. In seeing if there really is something more between us.

"Are you sure that's a good idea?"

"Yes." His response is instant.

"Okay."

"You'll come?"

"Yes. As long as you're sure. And that it will be okay with the boys."

"I'm sure, and it is. I asked them before I called."

My heart does a little flip inside my chest, and my stomach tightens. "You did?"

"I did. They want you to come."

"They do?"

His voice softens. "They adore you, Christine."

"I adore them," I tell him, my voice soft also.

I want to tell him I adore him. That I could see myself more than just adoring him. But he just met with his wife, soon to be ex-wife, and now isn't the time to stake my claim.

He pauses also, and I wonder where his thoughts are heading. He clears his throat. "So, when can you be here?"

"Um, I just got home from the store, and I need to put away the groceries and..." I hesitate.

"And?"

"I haven't showered today. I look kinda gross."

He chuckles. "Not even possible."

"Oh, you have no idea."

"Christine, we want you here as you are, any way we can get ya."

A flock of hummingbirds must have just taken flight in my stomach.

"You want me to bring anything? Food?"

"Nah, just yourself. We're just going to grill some burgers since and relax here tonight. Maybe watch the new Avengers movie or something. I feel like we need a night to regroup."

"And you're positive I won't be in the way of that?"

"Absolutely positive. All of us would prefer you be here with us. Please, Christine? We need your happy tonight."

Well, how could I ever say no to that?

"I'll be over in just a bit. Let me get these put away. Maybe I can bring over the stuff for sundaes?"

"Do you have it or need to make an extra stop?"

"Umm—"

He interrupts, "Because if you have to make an extra stop, don't worry about it. We just want you here."

Sigh.

"I have it."

"Okay, yeah. They'd like that. I'll see you soon, yeah?"

"Yeah, Andy. I'll be there soon."

"Thank you."

"Of course."

Twenty minutes later, I pull up to Andy's house along the curb and get out. The boys are both in the front playing basketball in the driveway, obviously enjoying the unseasonably warm temperatures.

"Hey, boys! How's the game?"

"Hey, Christine," they both mumble, and if possible my heart breaks even more for them.

I round the car and open the passenger door. The second I get it open, Aidan is standing next to me, reaching around to grab the bag of groceries off my seat.

"Thank you, kiddo." I ruffle his hair, and he grins up at me but it doesn't quite reach his eyes.

"Dad said you were bringing ice cream?" Reece asks.

"Yup. And toppings so we can do sundaes. Where's your dad?"

"In the back starting the grill."

"Should we go put this inside then go join him?"

"Sure." Reece shrugs, and Aidan nods in agreement. I follow them both inside where we put the ice cream in the freezer. I love Andy's home. He had Tess, who's an interior designer, come over and help him decorate it. It's masculine but still feels homey and warm. They're watching me put things away, both quietly sitting on the bar stools by the counter. I wipe the crumbs off the countertop with a wet washcloth then lean over it on my elbows.

"Hey." At the sound of my voice, they both slowly shift their bodies so they're sitting up straighter. Without thinking, I reach out and grab each of their hands. I wait until I have their eyes on me and take a deep breath.

"You boys are absolutely incredible."

Aidan immediately looks away, and Reece's eyes become shiny with tears.

"Can you look at me?" My voice is soft and hopefully reassuring. As soon as they do, I squeeze their hands.

"This isn't about you, you hear me? You are amazing, sweet, smart, and lovable, and two of the best boys I've ever met. This isn't about you," I repeat.

"She doesn't want us." Reece sniffles.

"It doesn't matter," Aidan grumbles. "We don't want her, either."

"You matter."

Aidan scoffs, so I continue. "You matter so much. Your mom loves you. She just doesn't know how to be the mom you need her to be, you understand? I think she loves you enough..."

"She's a big stupid baby who only cares about herself, Christine."

"Aidan's right. She doesn't care."

I bite my lip to stop myself from crying, and I know they don't need words right now. I release their hands and round the counter. They turn to face me, so I pull them both up into a hug. Shockingly, Aidan breaks first, crumbling into tears as he leans on me. I lower us to the floor where the three of us sit, my arms wrapped as best as I can around both of them.

"Why aren't we good enough?" Reece cries.

"Oh, kiddo. You are. You *are* good enough. Both of you."

"She doesn't want us."

I try to think of what they need to hear and feel lost so I decide for as much honesty as I think they can handle.

I lean back, still holding both boys as much as I can.

"You hear what I'm about to say to both of you, understand?"

They both nod, so I continue.

"It is her loss. You are both fantastic boys. I told you already but it deserves to be told again, because it's truth. You're funny, kind, smart, sweet, easy to be around, and so many other things. Her leaving isn't anything that you could have changed. It is all on her. She's the one who will be missing out on all things as awesome as you two."

The boys don't respond; they continue to cry softly in my arms. I can taste the salt on my lips, my own tears making streaks down my face. After several minutes of crying and holding each other, I take in a shaky breath and, feeling eyes on me, look up. Standing in the doorway of the kitchen is Andy. I give him a small smile, which is returned with one of his own.

He slowly walks over to us and places his hand on top of my head then tugs playfully on my ponytail. I stare into his eyes, so full of sadness and worry. My heart breaks all over again, for the loss the boys will feel for the rest of their lives. For knowing that no matter what their father or I tell them, or even Heather, for that matter, they'll always think it was their fault for her leaving.

Andy slowly sits down, his right leg wrapping around me, his left around Aidan. He reaches through the middle of our circle and grips Reece's knee.

"I love you boys. Forever. *That* is something that will never change. I will never leave you."

"We know, Dad."

"And it's not your fault."

When they're both quiet, he repeats his words.

"Boys. It's. Not. Your. Fault. This is all her. You two could not be more amazing. She just..."

"What, Dad?"

"She's just not cut out to be a mom. But I'm grateful that she didn't realize that earlier because I have you. I can't imagine a life without you boys in it. I won't."

"Your dad is right. You two are the best boys I know."

I don't know what else we can say to make them understand, and quite honestly, I think words are not what they need. Actions always speak louder than words.

"Wanna toss around the Frisbee in the back yard while your dad gets those burgers grilled up for us?"

Reece and Aidan both look up at me then at each other before both gracing me with a slight smile. Reece has a dimple in his left cheek if he smiles a certain way, it's one of the ways to tell the two apart. When I first met the twins I had a hard time, but after spending quite a bit of time with them, it's pretty easy to see the differences.

I don't get the dimple smile yet, but that's okay. I know we've cracked through the surface, and right now that's all that matters.

FOURTEEN
CHRISTINE

When did I turn into a high school girl, doodling someone's name on my notebook?

Today, apparently, as I look down at my desk and notice Andy's name written all over my pad of paper that I had pulled out to make inventory notes on. It seems as though I wanted to order a whole lot of Andy.

The fact that I'm over forty and shouldn't be having these girly crush feelings doesn't escape me in the least. Nor does the fact that he's almost a decade my junior. Though, to be fair, he's not like most thirty-five year olds. And it's not really almost a decade. He's wise beyond his years and one of the gentlest souls I've ever known.

And strong. Don't get me started on the muscles that man seems to build more of daily. Once he figured out it wasn't safe for him to take out his anger on himself, or his boys, he took it out on the gym equipment he has in his basement. Bri's boyfriend, Grady, helped him get it set up, to figure out what he wanted, and what worked for him. If Grady didn't plan on going to school to become a vet, he would do well with personal training. It comes natural to him, and even though it's one of his passions, he says it's not what he wants to do for the rest of his life.

A knock on the door startles me out of my musings, my imagination conjuring up images of Andy working out in his basement, sweat dripping down his chest and incredible abs that I happened to get a glimpse of one night when he lifted his shirt to wipe his forehead. The same movement he made two weeks ago when he had been helping James work at Balance.

And that night I spent dreaming of Andy, and his boys, and Bri, and what it would look like to be a family of five. And in my dreams? It was beautiful.

"Christine? You okay?" Aidan's voice breaks into my thoughts.

"Huh?"

Reece laughs at me. "You were staring off into space. Didn't even acknowledge us when we came in!"

I look around my office to see all three of the Simpson men staring back at me, amused expressions covering the younger two and a heated look in the older, sexy one I was just daydreaming about.

I lick my lips and divert my gaze, clear my throat. "What are you guys doing here?"

"Boys wanted to ask you something," Andy says.

They both nod. Reece nudges Aidan in the side with his elbow.

"So, this might seem weird, but we're going to the cabin for spring break in a few weeks."

"The cabin?"

"Yeah, the one I told you about that's been in my family for years?" Andy reminds me.

"Oh! Yeah. Yeah, of course! That sounds like fun! You want me to get your mail or something?"

Reece looks at Andy who nods his head in encouragement. "Actually, we wanted you to come with us."

"You what?" I look to Andy, who simply smiles over at Aidan, who looks just as nervous as Reece.

"Yeah. We want you there with us. It's a lot of fun. We can fish and hike. The water by the pond will be too cold to swim, but there's a big hammock on the front porch so you can relax and read or whatever. And you can bring along Bri if it makes you feel better," Aidan rushes out the words.

My heart is racing. "Are you boys sure you want me to come along on your spring break vacation? Wouldn't I be in the way?"

"Are you kidding? No way! We want you there!"

I turn to Andy. "Is this okay with you?"

His smile drops a little bit but his eyes soften. "Give us a quick minute, boys?"

"But..."

"Why don't you go find Emma? She's trying a new triple chocolate muffin recipe I think you both need to taste test."

They both hesitate a moment before they agree and walk out the door.

As soon as they're gone, Andy takes three steps until he's behind the desk, spins my chair around so I'm facing him with his hands gripping my shoulders, and looks me in the eye.

"Christine. We want you with us whenever we can get you." He lowers to crouch in front of me and lowers his voice. "And, sweetheart, it would mean a lot to me. And the boys. They need this. They need *you*. She's... well, she's taking the cabin."

"What? Why?"

"Don't know. She just is. I get the boys." He shrugs as if he's not bothered, but I see it written all over his face. And it breaks my heart. "She's taking something that doesn't mean shit to her, but she knows how much it means to us. The boys want to show it to you before they lose the chance. After the divorce is final..." He trails off, not needing to finish his sentence.

Well crap. What's a girl supposed to say to that?

The boys and I got to Barrett's house about two hours ago. We ate dinner that we convinced James to make for us and are now currently sitting in the living room watching a basketball game on TV.

The girls are all over at Christine's, and I can't help but be a little jealous. I know she loves her time with her friends, and I would never take that away from her, but I've gotten used to spending time with her on the weekends.

"The boys and I asked Christine to come to the cabin with us over spring break," I announce with little pomp and circumstance. Just put it out there.

"I'm sorry. What was that?" Barrett asks as he's wiping his mouth with the back of his hand, just after spewing beer over the coffee table in front of him.

He reaches down and aims the remote at the TV to mute the game.

"So, you two are serious, huh?" Josh asks, eyes wide.

I shrug, not wanting to put too much stock in to the fact that Christine is coming with us to the cabin, yet... it's a pretty big deal that she agreed to come to the cabin with us over spring break. Especially if it's the first and last time we'll get to bring her there.

"What do you mean?"

"You don't play dumb well," James murmurs without looking at me as he tips his bottle of beer back and takes a long pull. He's the picture of relaxation, complete with the fresh tan from the honeymoon he recently returned from. He has one foot up on the coffee table.

"Fine," I concede after not putting up a fight what-so-ever. "Start asking. What do you want to know?"

"You're giving us free rein?" Josh asks, rubbing his hands together.

"Shh! Don't spook him. I get first question!" Barrett shouts, as if someone were challenging him. Just then, Grady walks into the living room.

"You're starting what?" he asks his dad as he plops down on the other end of the sectional, sweaty and heaving a sigh.

"What's wrong? Did the boys wear you out?"

When Barrett called to see if I wanted to come hang out with the guys tonight he made sure to let me know that the boys were welcome to join us. The minute we walked into the house, they immediately went to the basement to find Grady who, being the great kid he is, welcomed them both with open arms. They've been playing Xbox, had a Nerf war, and from the sounds of it earlier, had a little wrestling match when Grady's friend Blake came over.

"What did you feed them today? They have so much energy!"

I chuckle. He speaks truth.

They've exhausted me for fourteen years now, so this isn't news to me.

"You leave Blake down there alone?" Barrett raises his eyes

FEELS LIKE HOME   115

wide as he leans on the back of the cushion to look around the corner.

"Eh. He can handle it. He's hyper, too. I think he downed a Red Bull earlier. So, what are you starting?" he asks again.

"Oh, Andy's just about to tell us all about his and Christine's relationship."

"Uhhh..." Grady hesitates.

"Grady?" Barrett leans forward, his voice a warning. A warning that says, "boy you been holding out on me?"

"I know nothing."

"Starting out by saying that you know nothing when we never asked if you do only makes us more suspicious that you *do* know something. You know that, right?" James teases.

"Wait. Guys. This... just no. If he knows something because of Bri, then Bri trusted him with that and Christine trusted her with it. It's not right," I say, hoping they'll listen.

"But they won't know that you know," Josh says, leaning forward in his seat.

"Oh, they'll know that we know," Barrett jokes.

James groans, throwing his head back. "Stop! Holy shit y'all are so damn annoying. Between the Friends shit and talking in circles... just... stop! Grady. Kiddo. Sorry, but you're gonna have to throw Andy a bone here."

"I invited her to come with us to the cabin. Did I push it?" I blurt out the main question and concern that's been on my mind.

"Nah, man. You didn't. She's excited. Nervous, from what Bri tells me, but excited."

I blow out a breath.

"Good. Good. That's good. Anything else?"

"Just that she seems really happy. Bri said she's never seen her mom as happy as she is now."

We hear a grunt and some loud raucous laughter before Blake yells, "Grady! Get back down here! They're too much!"

Grady chuckles before standing up to head downstairs. "I'm glad you and Christine have each other, Andy. But as someone who's loved her like a second — or third — mom for a long time now, I gotta say... if you hurt her? I won't be happy. I mean that. She's a good woman, a great mom. She's one in a million, just like her daughter, and someone who means a lot to me and my family."

I press my lips together. A threat coming from an eighteen-year-old *should* be funny, but I know it's coming from his heart. Christine is everything he said and so much more.

I hold his eyes as I nod and reach up to shake his hand.

"Got it, and you don't need to worry."

"Good. I'm heading down to save Blake from your little heathens."

"Thanks for letting them hang out with you two. They really needed it. Been a bit of a rough week for them."

"It's no problem. They're fun to pick on," he says with a grin.

As soon as he's out of the room, the men turn to me, Barrett speaking up first.

"We wanna hear it from you, Andy. What's going on in your head? You gonna keep that promise to Grady?"

"I really like her," I admit. "I know that sounds like I'm back in high school but... I do. I feel like there's something bigger there. Stuff between Heather and me, it's been over for a long time. I just didn't want to admit it."

"The divorce with Heather? When's it final?"

"We meet with the lawyers the week after we get home from the cabin. Typically, it would take longer because of the kids. I'm not sure how my lawyer got it pushed through but I'm grateful. I don't know why she's dragging her feet."

"Probably to piss you off."

"It's working."

"She's really giving you the boys? No fighting?"

"Oh, she's fighting. Dirty. She's taking the cabin. She decided to top off her year of bitchiness by taking something the boys have loved since they were babies. She told us when she picked up her stuff. It was either the cabin or the boys, and I wasn't willing to continue to fight. I want the boys, and she knows it."

"Can't you just look for a different cabin?"

I glance over at James who's now leaning on his knees, his beer bottle dangling between his fingers.

"Could. But this one's been in my family for generations."

He whistles. "Exes, man. They're a real joy, yeah? There's a reason she's in your rearview mirror. Keep looking forward." He tips his beer in my direction, and I return the gesture.

"Right. Heather didn't even like it there. She's just doing it out of spite. And I think she caught wind that I was moving on — that I was hoping to keep things going with Christine and wanted to act like a supreme bitch one more time."

"How'd they take it?" Josh asks, motioning his head toward the basement.

"Not good. They both yelled. A lot. Which was good. They needed to get it out, and Heather heard firsthand what her actions did to them."

After Heather left and Christine came over, it was like the calm before the storm. Over the course of the next week, the boys went from sullen to pissed off to happy then back to sullen again. It was like living with a couple of hormonal teenage girls starting their periods. It made me feel for Barrett, having Maggie in the house and for Christine having to deal with that all on her own when Bri was going through it.

That's when the decision to go away to the cabin came to my mind.

A change of scenery had to be good for all of us.

Barrett grunts. "Good. Serves her right."

"That's what I figured. Called Christine after she left. She didn't hesitate. Jumped in the car, came over. I walked in from the back yard to see the boys practically sitting on her lap, all three of them huddled together on the floor as she held them while they cried. Man..."

"And that's when you knew," James says, eyes boring into me.

One single nod. "And that's when I knew."

"All right men, I think we've had enough girly chats for the evening. Wanna play some poker?" Josh asks the three of us.

We all agree, and for the next few hours, I lose my ass at some Texas Hold'em, my mind drifting to Christine, as usual. I know that as soon as I leave here, I'll end up going to Christine's house because I can't go a day without seeing her.

SIXTEEN

CHRISTINE

I love having the girls over. It's good for the soul and right now, with the way my head is spinning over my building feelings for Andy, and our trip to the cabin for spring break, I think it's needed.

Lauren is blending up another pitcher of margaritas, her face matching my own, white with the mask we just applied during our at-home spa day.

I glance over at Tess, her face black with the mud facial she applied earlier, her one hand in a nail light that she brought from home while the rest of us mess around with each other's nails to get them ready to be painted.

Carly just emerged from my bathroom, wet washcloth in hand as she continues to carefully pat off the black mud that was just on her face.

"What's up with you and Andy?" Tess asks, her expression expectant; clearly she's not going to let me get by with not disclosing what's on my mind today. Not that I would expect any different from her.

I shrug, feeling the mask on my face tighten and hoping that it hides the blush on my face. "I don't really know."

"Pinocchio."

I almost roll my eyes at how predictable Tess is.

Lauren crosses her arms and raises her eyebrows at me, the white mask cracking on her forehead.

"We're waiting."

"You guys are so damn nosey."

Carly scoffs. "You're just now figuring this out? Remember what happened the first time we had margaritas? It was like y'all were part of the CIA and I was on the receiving end of a training session for how to interrogate suspects."

"You're so dramatic," Lauren teases with a smile on her face.

"You got me drunk! For the first time in my life!"

"Ladies! Stop! We always do this! Task at hand. Task. At. Hand."

Six pairs of eyes stare at me, waiting.

"Ugh. Fine! *Fine!* Andy is... well... he's incredible. He's kind and sweet, and Heather is such an effing idiot because there is no one like him. He's helped me move forward in a way that I never saw coming, and his boys? They're just hilarious and so much like their father, thank the good Lord for that one."

"So, are you dating? Together? What? I'm so confused," Carly admits.

"Honestly? Right now, we're just hanging out. Getting to know each other. I'd be lying if I said I didn't want more. I mean, for one thing, look at the guy," I say on a sigh, to which all the girls follow.

"He is kind of dreamy." Tess giggles. "Even though I'm old enough to be his mother."

"Uh, if you could be, then I could be, and that's not something I'm okay with thinking about."

"Christine the Cougar," Lauren says, her body bending over in half as peals of laughter burst from her.

"Shut up!" I shout but laugh right along with her.

"He's not that young. And you're definitely not that old," Lauren shocks us all with a moment of sincerity.

Another sigh.

"I know. He's thirty-five so really, it's not even an issue. It's just... he's overwhelming."

"In a good way?" Carly guesses.

"*Very*," I admit and look out one of the living room windows.

"What is it?" Tess asks quietly, probably noticing my thoughts were beginning to run away from me. *Perceptive woman.*

"He asked me to join him and the boys at the cabin next weekend."

Lauren chokes on her margarita, and Tess erupts into a series of hand claps that makes her look more like a seal. I glance over at Carly only to see a wistful smile spreading across her face, her diamond ring glistening on her left hand as she reaches over and grips my fingers in hers.

She squeezes once and nods her head.

"This. This is a *good* thing."

"Is it?"

"It is. You've been through so much, Christine." And the way she says it, the look in her eyes, it makes me think she's not just talking about losing my husband to cancer. "I get it. Moving on is hard."

I narrow my eyes, trying to decide if she knows about the affair, too, and briefly wondering if Andy told her what happened.

As quickly as the thought enters my mind, it vanishes. Knowing that he would never do that to me.

Betrayal isn't in his bones.

More likely, she's remembering only a few months ago when she, herself, moved on. James pursued her with such patience.

"Carly's right. As usual. This is a good thing, Christine. You deserve the happy. You deserve the hot younger guy salivating over you — and believe me when I say he *so* does. It's almost sickening to be around you two, watching him track your every move like he's a lion on the prowl. Just... say yes to this weekend and enjoy yourselves. Let loose and allow him to be more."

"You make it sound so easy. He has little boys."

"Aidan and Reece are hardly little. They're fourteen now. And you know Andy. Would Andy bring *anyone* around his boys if he didn't think they were going to be a permanent part of their lives?"

"No. He wouldn't."

"Go to the cabin. Enjoy yourself. Is Bri going?"

"No. She wants to stay home and get some hours in to keep saving for college. I'll only be gone a few nights, so I'm not worried," I tell Tess, knowing she'll understand what I'm getting at.

"I'll keep Grady home as much as possible."

I laugh, knowing she will. Or she'll just make sure Bri is over there and under Harper supervision the entire time. Which is just as good as adult supervision.

"Maybe time away will be good." I shrug, hoping it to be true.

"See? You just need to get your mind on board because I can see already your heart is there. It's ready. For him. Take that leap into your happiness, Christine. Just rip it off like a Bioré strip."

"That's not the term. It's rip it off like a Band-Aid."

"I don't give a flying turkey what the saying is. Ripping off the Bioré strips hurt like a son of a bitch."

"It hurts?" Carly asks, a horrified expression covering her face.

"What do you mean, it hurts? Doesn't it hurt when you do it?"

"Ummm... I've never done it before." Carly... expression innocent and eyes wide after just shocking the crap out of each of us.

"You say what, now?" I shout.

Carly shakes her head and looks at the three of us.

She sniffs and finishes her margarita, because we've become bad influences and have taught the girl how to get her drink on. Safely, of course, and without needing to join AA.

"No way! You're lying!" Lauren accuses as she walks back into the living room, pitcher in hand, and tops off Carly's glass then proceeds to the rest of ours.

"I've never done it before! It's not my fault! I was a single mother to a boy! I didn't exactly have a lot of privacy."

How does her reasoning make a bit of sense? But far be it for me to question it because the focus is finally off me and Andy and our non-relationship for a few blessed moments.

"And that's your excuse? Girl, I've been doing it for years! Anyone who says they don't get satisfaction out of it is a liar, too. When it pulls just right... oh yeah. It's so awesome. Not only can you see the results, but you can feel it, too! I literally can't even with its awesomeness."

"She's right. You really haven't lived. You'll feel and look decades younger," Tess adds.

Lauren pats her arm. "Decades, Tess? Really?"

She pouts and shrugs her shoulders. "You don't know everything," she mumbles and throws back her margarita like a boss. Hmm, I wonder if her fine line has been reached yet. I'll let Barrett worry over that one.

"Trust us," Lauren says, but it sounds like the snake on the *Jungle Book.*

"Yeah, my hoo-hah trusted y'all once, too!" She points an accusing finger in their direction.

I raise my hand. "Do I or do I not want to know the when, where, and why to the *you* trusting them with your hoo-hah question?"

"Awww, Little James is rubbing off on you! Saying y'all all Southern like. So proud," Tess says, clutching her chest, ignoring me.

"Ladies! Focus! We need to settle this! Carly can't go through life without experiencing this at least once! And telling me the hoo-hah story."

"I'll do it at home! I promise!"

"No. We want to see!"

"For real? That's kinda gross, isn't it?"

"Not gross! It's so satisfying. You'll love it. Then you'll be addicted to it and want to do it all the time."

"Come on," I tell her, dragging her to my bathroom.

"Now? In here? In front of y'all?"

"Damn right. This is gonna be awesome. Don't take away our happiness, Carly. That's not what true friends do."

Lauren, folks. Master manipulator.

I reach into the closet in the bathroom and pull out the box.

"You have them on hand?" Carly shrieks.

"Keep up, Carly. We said it was addicting."

"Yeah, but..."

"Oh, stop being such a baby! Get yourself wet, ok? It won't work dry."

"How wet do I need to be?"

"Not like dripping — you don't want it to just slip away."

"Okay, hold still."

"Wait. Let me get ready."

What the heck does she need to get ready?

"How do you need to get ready?" Tess voices my question aloud.

"Just... let me take a breath. I've never done this before! I'm kind of nervous, and you guys are watching! You could turn around, you know."

Lauren scoffs and sticks her hand out to shake, "Hi, I'm Lauren. Nice to meet you for the very first time ever."

"Okay, fine. Just tell me if I'm doing it wrong. I mean... look what happened the last time I took your advice with my hoo-hah! I almost had to live the rest of my life on the bathtub! I'm not going through that again!"

Seriously, someone needs to tell me the story!

Tess brushes away her complaint.

"You need to get wet again since it dried up while you were delaying. It's not like you need to be dripping wet. Just enough to..."

"Fine! Okay, so I just need to get myself wet then..."

"Christine?" I hear Andy's amused voice come through the door.

"Yeah? We're in here, Come on in!"

"Uhh, not sure I'm supposed to come in there." I think his voice actually cracks at the end. He clears his throat. "Right?" His voice is full of fear.

The girls and I look at each other, trying not to laugh. The conversation he must have overheard coming to me, and oh yeah... we need to make this good.

"Yeah, maybe you're right. We're not exactly..."

"Decent," Tess says, trying not to laugh.

She fails.

Though, to her credit, it does come out low and husky, so we roll with it.

"Right. Wouldn't want you to see something you, uh, shouldn't," Lauren says.

"Umm, okay? Well, umm, can I? What I mean is... what is it you're... okay maybe I'll just... wait?"

"Maybe that would be best. It will only take us ten minutes."

"No!" Carly shouts. "We need more... time. Sometimes it takes me a... while."

Lauren shoves her face into a towel, and I bite my fist to keep from laughing. How she said it all with a straight face, I'll never know.

"Oh. Okay. Yeah. I'm just... I'm gonna get a beer, yeah? Yeah. That's where I'll be. In the kitchen. While you guys are in here. Getting Carly... wet," he says, his voice faltering.

"Sounds good!" I shout.

The second we hear his footsteps bound away, bumping into some piece of furniture in the bedroom, curses exploding from his lips, we all fall to the ground in a fit of laughter.

"Oh damn. That was so good!"

"If that were Barrett, the guys would have already been told."

"Right? Oh, my gosh. That's the best thing ever."

"That's what he's thinking right now," Lauren snickers.

When we finally regain composure, I straighten up. "Okay, Carly, here's the Bioré Strip."

SEVENTEEN
ANDY

"We're on our way. You ready for us?"

"Born ready," she jokes over the phone line.

When we first asked Christine to join us at the cabin for our trip, I could tell she had her reservations about it. I don't blame her.

For me? I guess having a cheat for a wife allows you to move on much quicker.

But after her night in with the girls, in which I was both horrified and turned on by what I overheard, things shifted with her. Whatever her squad, as the boys always say now, said to her seemed to work.

She called the next morning to let me know she was bringing the food, since I was supplying the place to stay. We argued over whether or not it was necessary, and she eventually won. I never stood a chance.

I don't think I'll *ever* stand a chance against her, if I'm being honest with myself.

"See you soon," I tell her and look to the boys who both have smiles on their faces.

"Can't wait," she says, excitement in her voice.

And that's all it takes for me to realize that bringing her along is probably the best decision I've ever made.

And after talking with the boys last night and settling on something, I'm even more anxious to get up there.

We've got plans.

Plans that feel like they've been a long time coming.

Plans that required me to bring a few groceries of our own.

When I pull up to Christine's house, Bri is standing on the front porch, phone to her ear. She sees me pull in and smiles, opening the door and leaning her head in before ending the call and sliding her phone into her back pocket.

"Whisking away my mom for a weekend without me, huh?"

"Hey, I told her you were welcome to come, but you seem to think earning money for college is more important," I tease her.

She descends a couple of the stairs, meeting me halfway. She leans down and gives me a hug, her affectionate side coming from her mother, no doubt.

"If you change your mind, call me, got it? I can give you directions to come up there and relax. Even if just for a day."

Her eyes light up, and she bites her lip. "Do you think it would be okay if Grady came with me?"

"I have absolutely no doubt in my mind it would be okay. Though I'm pretty sure the boys would monopolize his time," I chuckle.

Aidan and Reece look up to Grady like crazy. Even last fall when he had his little mishap, decking some punk kid who thought he could take advantage of Bri, they never wavered. They know what kind of man he is.

And if they are looking up to a high school kid, wanting to be like him? Grady is definitely who I would choose.

Bri beams in my direction before wiggling her fingers at the boys still seated in the pickup.

"I'll go get Mom. She has a ton of stuff." She chuckles.

Before she gets too far away, I snag her arm to ask her a question I was hoping I'd get the chance to ask her before we left.

"I need to ask you something first," I tell her, nodding my head to the pickup.

She looks at me curiously but follows anyway.

"Hey, boys, what's up?" she asks through the open window of the pickup door.

"Not much, Bri, how's it going? How's Grady?"

She smirks and reaches in to give each a fist bump. Reece leans clear over Aidan to get his turn, earning a scowl that he promptly ignores. "He's good. You ready for vacation?"

"So ready."

"Mind if Grady and I bust up the party one day?"

"Yeah! That would be awesome!"

"What'd I tell ya?" I chuckle.

"So, what is it you needed to ask me?"

"He's gonna ask your mom on a date! Isn't that awesome?"

She turns her gaze to me, smiling. She looks so much like her mother, it's almost shocking. Aside from her lack of diamond stud in her nose and red streak like her mom has, they could be sisters, especially considering Christine looks young.

"What?"

I look at the boys and wink before walking Bri away from the open window, not wanting them to overhear everything. "Well, that's what I wanted to ask you. While we're at the cabin, the boys and I have a plan for how to ask your mom out on a date. But you need to know, my divorce from Heather isn't finalized yet. We're supposed to meet with our lawyers at the end of the week so it will be, but I want to be up front about that. And I want your permission to date your mom. If she says yes, she's not just saying yes to me, but to my boys, too. And I want to know you're okay with us coming into your family that way.

Because I'm not just asking her, I'm asking you, as well. I'm not saying I'm asking her to marry me, but I like your mom. She means a lot to me, and I don't see things being short term with her. Before I go forward, I want to ask you. Are you okay with me dating your mom?"

"Are you serious right now?" Bri asks, her voice incredulous and her eyes wide. I can't tell if she's shocked or annoyed. Teenage girls are hard to read.

"Umm, yes?"

"This is so weird."

"That's not really the answer I was hoping for," I admit.

"Andy. I kind of thought you two were basically dating already."

Her statement doesn't really surprise me. Christine and I have been spending a lot of time together, usually the boys are present but not all the time. And I'm sure she knows how often we talk on the phone and text. But still... I need to be sure.

"You're okay with us dating? Officially?"

"Andy. Stop. You're crazy if you think I'd say no! Mom has always been happy. Everyone sees that, but there's something different about her happiness since she's been hanging out with you. And it's not just the boys. If you need to hear the words, *weirdo,* yes, you can go on a date with my mom," she teases right back, shaking her head and rolling her eyes.

I blow out a breath and sag a little bit in relief. I truly didn't know how this would go. I'm not used to having girls around, much less teenage girls. Boys are easy to read. They're simple. They say it like it is.

"Thank you, Bri. Even if you didn't think it was necessary, you need to know it was. Single parent dating is not the same as when we're just two single people. And even though you're eighteen, you're still her kid, you know? I don't want to get in the way."

"Never. I promise. You make her happy, Andy, and that's all I can ask for."

"Yeah, Grady kind of warned me to not mess it up," I admit, trying to hide my chuckle.

"He told me about his "talk" with you," she giggles. "What a dork." Her eyes roll, but the love is still shining in them. "He kind of goes all in when he cares for someone, doesn't he?"

"I would say that's an affirmative. Considering he went to jail for someone he loves."

This might not be the right reaction, but I feel a sense of pride knowing that Grady defended Bri when that punk Dawson assaulted her at a party during the football season.

He was stopped, by both Bri herself fighting back and Grady's friend stopping it before he got there.

She blushes, probably over me saying Grady's in love with her, but doesn't deny it.

"I'm glad he was there for you, Bri."

"Me, too."

The door to the house swings open, and I watch as Christine appears, flustered and sweaty.

I choke back a guffaw and shout, "What happened to you?"

"I am the worst packer in the history of packing!"

"It's true. She really is. One summer, she and I went on a road trip and she forgot underwear so now every time she packs like three times the amount she needs."

My eyebrows raise, and I press my lips together.

"You bring underwear?" I ask her when she gets closer.

"Ugh, Bri, you're such a brat!"

"You love me," Bri teases.

"Only because I have to."

She turns to me, beautiful as ever. "I think I need a little help with the bags," she admits sheepishly.

"Hi." I say and lean over to kiss her cheek, greeting her instead.

"Hi," she whispers when my lips linger on her cheek for a few extra beats.

"You needed help with the bags?"

"I may have over packed," she admits with a wince.

I chuckle and walk up the porch steps, thinking it can't be as bad as she's making it out to be.

Then I feel the need to stretch or run a few laps around the house to gain the ambition to carry the number of bags to the car that are sitting by the door.

EIGHTEEN

CHRISTINE

Two hours after we loaded up the pickup, we arrive at the cabin. I gasp when it comes into view. The simplistic beauty of the landscape that surrounds it is already relaxing me. If this place is in any way similar to where Barrett and Tess had their getaway last fall, I can see why they fell in love all over again.

"This is incredible."

I look behind me when no one responds and see the boys both staring out their windows, sullen expressions on their faces.

Andy reaches over and squeezes my thigh. He inhales deeply before letting it out with a loud puff.

"You guys ready to show me around?"

The sound of my voice brings the boys' eyes to me, and a faint smile appears on both their faces.

"Sure," Reece says sadly.

When Andy parks the pickup, the four of us open the doors and get out, the gravel under our feet crunching as we move. I stretch my arms above my head, bend over, and hear a sharp intake of breath. I stand straight and turn around to see Andy standing behind me, eyes wide and nostrils flaring.

His eyes make a lazy trail from my legs, slowing up to get their fill of my chest, covered by a fitted dark gray graphic tee shirt that says *Bless This Mess.*

"Damn."

I blush and raise my eyebrows at him, but he doesn't look apologetic in the least.

"Dad! Come onnnnn!" Reece yells from the door.

Andy digs the keys out of his front pocket and grabs my hand, threading his fingers through mine, as he walks us to the cabin.

As soon as we're inside, he releases my hand — because the boys take his place, tugging me through the open space to show me everything.

The square wooden beam that Aidan ran into the corner of, cracking open his forehead and needing stiches.

The slight slope in the hardwood floor that they dramatically slide down with their sock-covered feet, even though it's barely noticeable.

The giant washtub basin in the utility room that they once had to sit in to get a tomato juice bath when they were toddlers after they'd been sprayed by a skunk.

My heart sinks as they go through memory after memory in every room of the house. The three bedrooms both of them have stayed in on numerous occasions, never committing to preferring one room over another.

"This is your room this weekend, that work?" Andy says, sidling up next to me.

None of the rooms are fancy or decorated much. The room we're standing by is bright and decorated in a blue and yellow that reminds me of summertime.

"Yup. That works for me."

"And that's my room," he whispers, his hot breath tickling my neck as he points to the door right next to mine.

It doesn't escape my notice that there's a Jack-and-Jill bathroom that joins the two rooms.

I shiver when I feel his lips hit my temple and his hands squeeze my shoulders.

"Good to know," I whisper, my body falling back into his just slightly.

"Mm hmm. Come on, the boys want to show you their favorite part of this whole place."

He takes my hand, and we walk to the back yard, the pond a few hundred feet away from the porch on the backside of the cabin.

The four of us stand, side by side, as we stare at the small body of water that I'm sure held so many family moments. It's surrounded by trees and tall grasses, a long wooden — very old looking — dock that extends into the pond along with a bright blue windy slide that ends over the water, and two wooden benches.

The sun glistening off the water sparkles and shines.

The only sounds we hear are birds chirping and frogs croaking, leaves rustling in the light breeze.

Peaceful.

Serene.

"It's beautiful. I can see why this is your favorite."

"It's even better in the summer when you can swim and catch frogs. But one time Aidan caught a snapping turtle when we were fishing, and that was kind of freaky."

We all laugh. Them at the memory of it, and me at the image. "I bet." I smile, looking at Aidan. "It didn't snap you, did it?"

"No. Fortunately."

"You would have *died* laughing," Reece says, through his

own laughter. "Grandma's little white fluff ball of a dog just couldn't wait to dive into the water, but there was all this black gunk on the bank, and he just ran right through it after a frog. He came back, and you couldn't see a single bit of white on him. Then he jumped right into Grandma's lap. She screamed. And then she smelled him."

I giggle and wrinkle my nose. "That bad?" I ask.

"Worse," Andy chuckles, shifting to stand behind me, his hand resting on my hip. "It'll be too cold to swim this weekend, but we can fish, if you want."

"Really?"

"Of course! Christine, you have to. Dad fries fish the best."

I twist around to look at him. This close, he almost takes my breath away. Between his gorgeous eyes and radiant smile and smell, the mixture of cinnamon and man, ugh. He's just so *much* everything. "You do?"

"Well, to be fair, what we catch up here we fry right away, so it's fresh."

"Okay. I definitely can't wait for that."

"Let's go get our poles," Aidan suggests.

"Nope. You know the rules. Everyone unpacks first. Then you can go do what you want."

The boys groan but get to work without complaining.

We all make our way to the pickup, and I cringe when I see all the bags in the back.

"Are we staying longer than through the weekend?" Reece asks, a bit innocently, but the twinkle in his eye tells me he's teasing.

I roll my eyes.

"I'm a girl?" Like that explains everything.

"So, you pack enough for a month?"

"Yes."

"Girls are so weird."

"No. Girls aren't weird. We just prefer to change clothes every day."

Reece's face breaks out in a cheesy grin. "But, I'm on vacation and don't want to think. This way, I don't have to put any thought into what I'm going to wear every day. As long as it doesn't smell, I'm good."

"The boy has a point," Andy chuckles.

"I have no words," I joke.

Not only did I pack a lot of clothes, I felt like I was bringing enough food to last us a month rather than just a long weekend. Of course, no one complained about *those* extra bags. I've been around the boys (and Andy) long enough to know that you can't have enough food around, but Reece may be right. Not that I would admit it, but I know I over-packed just a bit for clothing. I'll just text Bri that if she decides to head up when she's done working, she doesn't need to pack clothes.

After unloading and getting everything put away, we make sandwiches, which they inhale quickly (see above about never having enough food) and decide to go for a walk so they can keep showing me around.

I use the bathroom off my room to freshen up a little bit.

"Come *on,* Christine!" Aidan hollers from downstairs.

"Yeah, yeah. I'm coming." I giggle and slide my arms into my jacket.

I walk into the kitchen just as the boys shove a grocery bag into a cupboard, Aidan whispering, "Hurry up before she comes!"

"I *know,* Aidan. I'm not an idiot."

"I didn't say you *were,* but Dad wants it to be a surprise."

"Duh. You don't think I know that? He only told us that like a million times."

"Then close the cupboard before she comes in!"

I hear a door slam and then, "I can't *believe* she didn't see the bag when we were unpacking."

Reece snickers, "That's because she was weighed down with all those bags of clothes."

I step back behind the wall, not having a clue on what they're hiding, but that's okay. I press my lips together to stop the giggle that's wanting out.

It's obviously something important to them, and so it's important to me.

So, I'll wait.

"I'M STARVING," both boys whine at the same time.

I giggle, feeling grateful that I packed as much food as I did.

Yesterday we hiked through the woods until we got to an open field where we plopped down on the ground on a blanket that Andy carried with him and ate sandwiches, laid back, and watched the clouds make shapes.

The last two days were glorious and relaxing, and last night ended with us munching on tortilla chips and Rotel cheese dip in front of the TV, watching a movie at the end of the night.

The boys both curled up in oversized chairs while Andy and I took the couch.

Andy had showered and changed into a pair of lounge pants but forgot his shirt.

Which under any other circumstances I would have enjoyed.

Immensely.

The fact that the shirt was forgotten when his sons were present and we were still officially-unofficially in the friend zone meant that I couldn't explore the shirtless chest the way I wanted to.

All it did was cause a distraction, and I'm pretty sure he knew it.

The smirk that didn't leave his face was one indication.

And the low chuckle when he heard me suck in a deep breath after he stretched his arm across the back of the couch was another.

"Payback could be brutal," I murmured to him.

"Oh, I'm counting on it," he whispered back.

So, this morning when I woke up, I decided Operation: What Goes Around Comes Around will commence after Bri and Grady arrive. I figure I've been wearing far too many clothes on this trip and my skin could use a little kiss from the sun. When we go outside a little later, I think I need to lie out by the pond. In my swimsuit.

It might not be the most unique of paybacks, but I'm using what's in my arsenal.

But until then, I have a couple of hungry boys on my hands.

"Help me make the marinara sauce for the lasagna tonight? Bri and Grady are coming up early, and I'm sure they'll be hungry. Then you guys can have a snack or something to tide you over until lunch. You know, since we ate breakfast a whole hour ago," I ask them both, noticing they smirked at my use of the word snack. So childish, I'm sure.

"Sure."

Shrug.

Smile.

Fourteen-year-old boys. Talking my ear off.

But nevertheless, we all get to work.

I give them each a job, and minutes later the three of us are working so well in the kitchen one would think we'd done it a million times. I show them how to chop the onions and garlic, and they laugh at the tears streaming down their faces before sautéing the vegetables.

They help me brown the hamburger and sausage, open the cans of tomatoes, measure out spices. They work hard and ask questions where necessary.

So often, when I'm with the boys, Andy is with us. For obvious reasons. This time alone with them is just what I needed. Especially with everything that's been happening lately. Between Bri getting closer to graduation and Heather being, well... Heather.

"Thank you for showing us this, Christine," Aidan says quietly.

"Yeah. It's actually kind of fun," Reece adds.

"Did you not expect it to be?"

"Not really. I mean, it's cooking."

"It's not just cooking, though. It's creating and providing and learning a skill you'll need for the rest of your lives. Trust me, one day you'll be thanking me that you have these recipes to fall back on. The girls love a guy who cooks."

"Is that right?" Andy's deep voice cuts in. I look toward the sound and see him leaning a shoulder against the wall, watching us.

I nod my head and narrow my eyes.

"You got back early."

He pushes off the wall and saunters across the tile floor in my direction.

"Doesn't take much time to grab bait. I see you guys found something to keep you busy?" he asks, his eyes blazing.

"Yeah," I croak out. "Boys helped me with the sauce for the lasagna tonight."

"I see."

"Lots of cooking," I say nervously when his eyes seem to be reading everything.

"So it seems," he murmurs.

"Wanna try the sauce, Dad?" Aidan asks, snapping the moment that was becoming electric between us.

"Do I wanna try the sauce?" he asks like it's the craziest question ever. "Of *course,* I wanna try it!"

He moves over to the pan on the stove and grabs a spoon from the drawer before dipping it into the pan.

He blows on the sauce a few times and I watch, mesmerized by the shape his lips make when they pucker a bit to cool off the sauce, by his tongue that snakes out to test the temperature.

I blow out a breath of my own, trying to calm the hormones raging inside me.

The spoon slips into his mouth, and I have an immediately irrational flare of jealousy over a piece of metal. It's ridiculous.

I assumed the more time I spent around Andy, the desire to basically lick him would start to go away. Or at the very least, lessen. But that's far from what's happening. The more I get to know him, the quicker, and harder, I'm falling.

I shift my gaze from his mouth to his eyes and find him watching me, his eyes practically dancing.

"Dad? How is it?"

I startle at the sound of Aidan's voice.

"It's incredible. I can't wait to have more," Andy says, never taking his eyes off me, the implication of his words weighing heavy in the air.

I clear my throat.

"All right, boys, we have to let the sauce simmer for a while then we'll make the lasagna later."

"Awesome," Reece mumbles around a spoonful of cereal, a little bit of milk dribbling out of his mouth as he speaks. Chews. Swallows. Shoves another bite in. "Can we go fishing now?"

I grin. I didn't even notice him getting something to eat. "Absolutely."

And that's what we do. We spend the rest of the day fishing

and relaxing by the water. We even get out the paddle boat and play around while trying to stay dry.

The boys even prove their claim that Andy makes some excellent fried fish when he makes us a shore lunch after the boys teach me how to properly catch a fish.

After we finish, the boys start tossing a football back and forth to each other while I try to execute my payback plan.

"So, you really love it when a guy cooks, huh?" he says in my ear.

"Mmm," I hum, hopefully letting him know that to me, a man who cooks is sexy as hell. But really, he could be slinging manure, and I'd somehow find it sexy.

"Good to know," he whispers.

My legs are stretched out in front of me, body resting on my hands stretched out behind me. His arm behind mine as we relax, hip to hip, my bare thigh resting against his swim trunks. I don't even fight the urge to make a cat-like stretch into him when he speaks so close to my ear.

I've lost all desire to fight this losing battle of resistance against him.

I may not be in a bikini, but I'm showing the least amount of skin he's ever seen on me. Add to the fact that the top pushes up my breasts, showing cleavage that I notice his eyes drifting to.

I thought I'd gain some sort of upper hand when I got into my swimsuit and lay out by the pond, but I was so, so wrong.

He takes one look at me, a slow perusal of my body. Then reaches behind his head, grips the collar of his shirt, and pulls it off.

When he notices me ogling him, his nostrils flare and he leans in close, his calloused fingers sliding across the minimal skin showing between my tankini top and my bottoms, causing me to shiver.

"You trying to kill me?" he murmurs in my ear, his voice

husky. His lips brush against the shell of my ear, and I tremble, causing my breath to come out in stutters.

"What?" I ask, not even remembering what my plan was in the first place.

"You're even more gorgeous than I imagined. And I have a big imagination."

And just like that, he is once again on top.

He chuckles, then kisses my cheek and runs off to play with his boys.

NINETEEN

ANDY

My control is dwindling. Fast.

Every moment I spend with Christine only proves what I want.

Every time I see her with my boys, spending time with them, giving the attention they so desperately need, deserve... I feel like my heart is about to explode from my chest.

Not to mention how much control I had to practice when she was lying next to me in her coral-colored swimsuit. It wasn't a tiny bikini, but it was almost sexier. That little sliver of skin between her top and bottoms seemed to call to my fingertips.

I've lost count how many times I've had to clench my fist to stop myself from taking her into my arms and just kissing the ever-loving shit out of her.

She's just... everything that I never knew I wanted. Needed.

Christine is happiness and sunshine and rainbows.

According to Carly, she's a unicorn.

Whatever the hell that means.

"Are you about to lock that down or what?" Carly asks me *while I'm trying to work with the stone that will be set around the new fireplace James installed at Balance.*

"Lock what down?" I play dumb.

I know exactly what — or who — she's referring to. I'm not an idiot. She's not as outwardly nosey as Lauren and Tess are, or hell, even as bad as Josh and Barrett, but she's still pushy. In her typical sweet way.

James snickers next to me and glances over at his wife, who's swinging her legs from her perch on the table near us.

"You gotta do better at your subtlety, beautiful."

To Carly's credit, she simply shrugs and smiles. Doesn't even try to deny a thing.

"May as well answer. If she's not the one asking, you know who's coming next in the interrogation."

"Why do you all have to know everything?"

"It's y'all, not you all, you Neanderthal," James chides.

"Not if you're from the upper half of the US, it's not. If you say y'all and you're not southern, it's just a charade."

"What?"

James looks at me like I've just grown a second head.

"Never mind," I murmur and continue to place stones in the pattern I'm creating on the floor before putting it up against the wall.

"So. Are you?" Carly asks again, not letting up on her line of questioning.

I sigh and sit back, figuring I might as well face this head on.

Apparently, my defeat is obvious, and she launches in.

"She's happy."

Single nod.

"She is," I agree.

Her head turns to the side.

"She was before but..."

"Now she's happier," I tell her, knowing it's fact.

She graces me with a small smile.

"Correct."

Her lips purse tightly and she points to me.

"You're the reason for that."

Now it's my turn to smile, only it's not small.

I shrug. "I'd like to think so."

"You're happy, too."

"I am."

"She's the reason for that."

I can't argue with that.

"She absolutely is."

She narrows her eyes and attempts to look threatening. It would probably work on someone who wasn't so inherently nice.

"You're not going to screw it up?" she asks, far more like a statement than a question, however.

"Man, I sure as hell hope not."

"She's a unicorn."

My eyebrows kiss my hairline.

I guffaw. "Pardon?"

"She's happy and sunshine and rainbows and she's just... unique. There's very few like her around. She's a unicorn."

"Um. Okay?"

"No. You're not understanding me."

"Carly, with all due respect. I do understand you. What you're saying are things I already knew about her. Do you think I'd be spending time with her if I didn't?"

"Well, I don't know you very well, so I can't really say."

"Babe," James interrupts.

Carly's eyes shift to James and then back to me.

"I trust you. But from someone who hid a major part of her past from everyone around her for a long time, I recognize the signs. She's happy. But at one time, she wasn't. And it's more than Todd's passing. But I won't pressure or push because like I said, I know about as much as anyone how important keeping

your past private is. That being said, I have a feeling you already knew that, too."

I don't confirm or deny that, but I also don't break eye contact with her, either.

"She's a unicorn," *she repeats.*

"I agree."

And I wasn't lying.

Last night, Bri and Grady got to the cabin, and I thought maybe the boys would quickly ditch the idea of finishing the lasagna with Christine in Grady's presence, but that was far from the case.

They were right there next to her while she showed them how to layer the noodles and cheese mixture and sauce they made with her that morning.

Their chests swelled with pride and they practically preened under the praise that Grady showed them for how good it tasted, watching him take a third helping, and for him letting them know how awesome it was for them to help.

Then we spent the last few hours of daylight walking off our pasta coma through the wooded area behind the cabin before sitting around the bon fire late into the night.

Christine laughed at their jokes and attempts at campfire stories. Showed them that using a peanut butter cup instead of chocolate bar when making S'mores takes it to a whole new level. Listened when they opened up about how they didn't really miss their mom, and the guilt that went along with those feelings. Gratefully accepted the sweatshirt that Aidan pulled right off his back when she shivered in the slowly dropping temperatures. Slipped it over her head and smiled her thanks, even commented on how fast he's growing, her being able to fit into his clothes *and* them being too big for her.

He's always been warm blooded, so it wasn't a surprise that he could handle the cooler temperature in just a t-shirt.

I gotta admit, a big part of me was jealous.

I love the relationship they're building, but I wouldn't have been sad about keeping her warm.

Especially when Grady and Bri were huddled next to each other, a blanket wrapped around their shoulders, heads dipped close together.

Ridiculous how jealous I was of teenagers in that moment.

I had briefly wondered if Christine's demeanor would change once Bri was with us.

Make her more comfortable.

But that wasn't the case.

She was exactly the same person around her family as... us.

The only downside of the time was when reality hit me that Bri would be sleeping with her mom.

Not that anything would have happened between us if she wasn't there.

It hadn't the other nights that she and I spent alone in our beds, me tossing and turning, knowing that she was just a bathroom door away from me.

But something about the possibility of more was enough to satisfy me.

Tomorrow we go back home.

Meaning that the rest of the day today is quite literally the last day that we will get to enjoy at the cabin before Heather...

I can't even finish the thought, so I shake my head and bound down the stairs to where I hear all the kids talking. Christine's in the shower — a million points to me for not barging in on her while she's in there, considering my current self-control issues — so now is the perfect time to make our plans.

"Okay. She's in the shower, so hurry."

"What? What's going on?" Grady asks from his place on the couch, stretched out and relaxed, Bri sitting between his legs as his long arms stretch in front of her. Xbox controller in his hand as he plays a game, Aidan watching while Reece plays, too.

"Dad has this plan," Aidan says rolling his eyes.

"Hey! She's going to love it!"

"What's the plan?"

"He's asking your mom on a date."

"Aren't they dating now?" Grady looks around the cabin confused.

Bri rolls her eyes. "They're like where we were" —she points to him then back at herself— "about six months ago."

"Ahh. Gotcha," Grady says, grinning and nodding his head.

"Can we please get back to the plan?"

"Oh, right. Of course."

The boys and I explain to Bri and Grady our plan and ask for their help. Tell them that they have to pretend to need me so I'm not around while the boys let Christine know they need help with something else.

The five of us are sitting in a circle, huddling close together, when Christine comes into the room. Then we fail miserably at trying not to look guilty.

We all stand up, busying ourselves, bumping into each other and mumbling nonsense.

She isn't convinced.

And why would she be?

We aren't doing a very good job *of* convincing her.

"What's going on?" she asks us, a teasing smile to her lips.

"Why would you think anything's going on?"

"Just a hunch."

"Not very trusting of us, huh?"

She raises an eyebrow.

"I'll let it go. This time." She winks and turns to go into the kitchen.

I motion to the boys and they quick snap to attention,

standing up abruptly. "Wait!" Reece shouts at the same time Aidan yells, "Don't go yet!"

She looks at them with a soft smile. "Yes?"

"Um, we need your help. You know how you taught us to cook yesterday?"

"Yes," she says, drawing out the word.

"Well, um, we want to know how to make dessert, too. Like, a cake or something? 'Cause, you know, I think it's important."

"To make a full meal, right?" Aidan adds to Reece's explanation.

"Yeah," he nods and swallows hard.

No Oscars will be won by these two any time soon.

But Christine isn't paying attention to their poor acting skills.

"You want me to help you bake a cake?" her voice is shaky and eyes glossy. She reaches for my hand and squeezes and it hits me then. That what we're building is more than just about Christine and me.

Christine

"WHEN THE TIMER goes off then we'll pull it out of the oven and put it on the cooling rack here. We need to let it cool before we put the frosting on, otherwise it will basically melt."

The boys look at each other, then down at their phones for the time.

"Oh. Will it take long?"

I look at the timer on the oven. "There's only six minutes

left of baking time, but then it usually takes a little while to cool."

"What if we put it in the fridge?"

"Um, well, we *can,* but it really only takes around fifteen minutes for it to cool. Are you in that big of a hurry to try it?"

"Something like that," Reece mumbles, and Aidan jabs him in the stomach.

"Not really. You made us put sour cream in the cake. It's probably gonna turn out gross."

"Yes. My goal is to spend time baking something disgusting with you guys."

They pace around the kitchen while constantly checking their phones for the time. When the oven timer goes off, they rush to the oven. Reece hands Aidan the oven mitts to remove the cake.

"First, you have to check to make sure it's done."

"It might not be done yet?" Reece cries out.

"Possibly. Stick a toothpick into the center, and if it comes out clean, it's ready."

They both pull a face that has me chuckling.

"Why wouldn't it be clean?"

"If it's not done, the center will be gooey, the batter still runny. It would stick to the toothpick."

"Oookaay."

"Just do it, already."

They both reach for a toothpick out of the plastic container I have in my hand and poke it into the center of the chocolate cake.

When they come out clean, the boys fist bump.

"Okay, so like fifteen more minutes before we can frost it?" Aidan says, way too loudly.

"I'm standing right here, kiddo. What's wrong you two?"

They've been acting shifty since we started mixing the batter for the cake. At first, I thought it was because they'd changed their minds, deciding it would have been more fun to be hanging out with Grady, who left with Andy and Bri shortly before we started making the cake. Grady said he needed Andy's help with something.

I never asked what that was, and he never explained further.

Aidan blushes, and Reece mumbles, "We'll be right back." Then he takes him by the arm and pulls him into the living room.

I hear loud whispering then, "Just try and act cool for once."

"Shut up!"

"Boys?"

"Yeah?" At the same time.

More shuffling and an "oomph," from one of them.

What in the heck is going on?

I round the corner, crossing my arms when I see them facing off.

"Everything all right in here?"

"Fine. Just... is the cake cooled yet? We really want to frost it."

"It's only been a few minutes, but I suppose you can try, if you want."

"Yeah. Can we do it alone?"

"Awesome idea, Reece! Yeah, can we, Christine?"

Now they're suddenly getting along again?

Reece shoots daggers at Aidan while trying to slyly shake his head.

But I'm on to them.

Something is up, and I have a feeling it involves the mysterious disappearance of the other three.

"You don't want my help?" I ask, hurt in my voice.

I can act, too.

"It's not that... we just want to maybe, um, surprise you?"

"I love surprises!"

"Well, that's good."

"Do you want me to help you make the frosting?"

"Nope! We got it all figured out!" Aidan says excitedly, showing me his phone, a recipe pulled up.

"Okay, then."

I make my way up the stairs but not before I hear Reece hit Aidan again then whisper shout, "You're *such* a horrible actor. You *know* she's totally on to us. You basically blew it."

"Shut up, Reece! I did not! She might *suspect* something but she has no clue..."

I plug my ears and keep walking.

If this group of clowns wanted whatever this cake business is to be a surprise, I'm not going to take that away from them.

I take the time to clean up a little bit and change my clothes.

When I make my way back down the stairs, I try to create as much noise as possible so they know I'm coming.

"Is it safe to come in now?"

"Just a second!"

I wait a few more minutes, then...

They appear in front of me.

Wide smiles and bouncing on their toes.

"We're ready."

"I see that," I laugh.

"Can you like... close your eyes or something?"

"For real?"

"Yeah." Aidan nods his head and licks his lips.

Reece smiles so wide his dimple pops.

I do as told then hold out my hands; they each take one and lead me into what I assume is the kitchen.

I feel a soft breeze as a hand moves up and down in front of me and swallow my laughter.

"Okay, open."

Standing in front of me are two *very* excited boys, holding the prettiest ugly cake I've ever seen in my life.

Chocolate frosting with yellow gel pen writing spells out, *"Will you date our dad?"*

I gasp after reading it over twice.

Then I look up to see Andy standing before me, a large bouquet of... wooden spoons tied together with a bright red bow.

A giggle bursts out of me.

"You mentioned a few weeks ago that all your wooden spoons were splitting and you needed new ones. So, I made Bri go with me to pick them out. There's three spatulas in here, too. All different colors. And" —he reaches behind Grady's back and produces a small bag from Grady's hands— "chocolate covered espresso beans!"

"Oh, my gosh."

"Surprise?"

"You're too much." I shake my head as I admire the wooden spoons. It might seem weird to most, but I'll take something from the heart over a bouquet of roses any day. It proves he listened to something I mentioned off-handedly.

"Mom! Pay attention!" Bri giggles.

"Christine. You have to answer the question!"

"Oh! Right."

"Will you? Date our dad?"

"Hmm. I might have to thi..." Before I can finish answering the question, Andy's standing in front of me, wooden spoons shoved into Bri's hands, as his fingers grip my hips.

"You have to what?"

Eyes smiling.

Bright white teeth biting his lower lip.

Oh, who am I kidding?

"Think about it?"

"And just how long do you need to... think about it?"

I tap my chin and pretend to mull it over.

He leans down, his face barely a breath away from mine.

The cinnamon scent of his gum tickles my nose as he exhales.

Inhale through my nose.

His teeth graze his bottom lip again.

It's one of the most erotic visions, and I wonder if he does it on purpose. If he knows how freakin' sexy it is.

I look up into his eyes then lick my lips. His eyes follow the movement.

My breath comes heavier...

"Take me fishing, boys?" I hear my daughter ask, her voice high, even for her.

It should snap us back to reality, but instead we stand still like we're doing that mannequin challenge thing that was popular for a little while.

The backdoor slams behind me, and within seconds his lips are on mine.

My arms wrap around his neck, fingers thread through his soft hair that's getting longer. I love it. I've never been a fan of long hair on men, but on Andy it's just so damn gorgeous that I know I'll never let him cut his hair again.

My lips part and his tongue slides in, not tentatively but not forcefully either. Just the right amount of pressure.

He tugs on my hair, causing my head to turn just the way he wants it, and I moan. Deep and guttural.

He responds with a groan of his own, pushing his body against mine, causing me to dip backwards slightly as he walks us to the counter, pressing me against it.

His hand snakes down my back to cup my butt.

Those white teeth that I've become obsessed with give his

own lip a break to nip at mine, and it sends a shock directly where I want *him*.

It's been so long since I've felt the touch of a man, and until I met Andy, I hadn't really missed it.

Sure, there were times I craved *something* because I'm a red-blooded human being, but I never really felt that desire. Then Andy and I grew closer, and suddenly my body felt alive, and fully awake after being stuck in idle.

There's been a stirring inside me for months now, but with his hands on my body, his mouth on my skin, and his strong frame crowding me against the corner of the countertop, that stirring quickly turns into a full-fledged riot, a battle of wills happening within me.

But there's not a single ounce of me that can find it in me to care whether it's right or wrong.

Whether it matters that he's technically still married to another woman.

Or the fact that our children are right outside and more than likely know exactly what's taking place right now.

All I can think of is how amazing he makes me feel.

How he makes me feel beautiful.

Wanted.

Loved.

His tongue.

It's possibly made of magic.

Tasting.

Tangling.

Giving.

Taking.

Loving.

I grip the back of his neck.

The hem of his shirt.

His hands trail up my side.

Underside of my breast.

Thumb grazes up the center of my neck.

Hand wraps around, long fingers threading into my hair.

Forearm tucks under my butt and effortlessly lifts me.

My leg wraps around his waist, my shoulders hunch as I press myself closer to him, if it were possible.

He leans back just slightly, mouth still touching mine.

"Fuck, Christine. Knew you'd feel good."

I should respond.

If I had the ability to speak.

He just kissed it out of me.

"Yes," I whisper.

Those damn white teeth drag across his bottom lip before a slow smile takes over his gorgeous face.

"Knew I'd talk you into it."

"Stop pacing, Dad. It's getting really annoying," Reece grumbles.

I glare at my *sweet* son.

"I can't help it. Shouldn't it be five o'clock by now?"

"It's only three." He isn't even nice enough to look up from his phone when he tells me.

I flop down on the couch, groaning and fidgeting. His head drops to the back of the chair he's sitting on. "Oh, my gosh, Dad!"

"You said to stop pacing and I did!"

"It's not any better!"

Aidan walks into the room with a giant bowl of ice cream, distracting Reece momentarily.

He licks his lips and nods to the bowl. "Give me a bite."

Aidan curls his lip and holds his ice cream close to his chest. "Gross. Get your own."

"I just want a bite."

"And I don't want your slobber all over my spoon."

"I don't slobber."

"Yeah. You do."

"No. I don't."

"That's not what Kelsey DeMarco said," he sing-songs.

"Shutup, Aidan!"

"Dad says we're not allowed to tell each other to shut up."

"I didn't! I said 'shutup' which is totally different."

"Whatever. It's the same but said fast, which is no different."

My eyes bounce back and forth between my sons. Teenagers may as well live on another planet for how strange they are.

"Besides, Kelsey so didn't say that, you liar."

"Whatever helps you sleep at night."

Aidan moves to sit closer to Reece, who's still laid back in the chair, one leg thrown over the arm of the chair, like he could care less.

It's a lie.

They both know it.

Aidan continues to taunt him. "Yeah. She said that you had no clue what you were doing. And she had to *wipe* all the spit off her face from where you practically attacked her like a lab."

"You're so full of it!"

Aidan laughs. Shakes his head. Now staring at his own phone while continuing to eat the ice cream. "Nope."

"Aidan. Enough," I put in.

"Yeah, Aidan. E-*nough*," Reece mocks.

Reece lowers his phone, and they narrow their eyes at each other, and I know they're about to try out some of those wrestling moves they learned this year. Only it'll likely become more like an MMA match instead.

"Boys," I warn, as Reece stands up.

"Take it back. I know you're lying."

"Oh yeah? And why's that, Reece? Why would someone ever lie about that?"

And then it clicks.

Why Aidan (or Reece) ever tries to lie to his twin brother is beyond me, but Aidan was clearly on to Reece when he told Aidan that he and Kelsey made out after the movies the night we got home from the cabin. Or... he just exaggerated. Either way.

Reece got home that night with a pretty big smile on his face. Similar to the one I've been sporting ever since we got back two days ago.

"Just let it go, Aidan, yeah?"

"Why should I? You *know* he wouldn't."

"Fine! I didn't make out with her, okay? But I did kiss her! Almost on the lips, too."

"Ha! I knew it."

"Almost?" I ask, hating to do so but curiosity winning out.

"Well, I sorta missed."

"Missed what?" I can't believe they're sucking me into their teenage antics.

"Her mouth! I went to kiss her and stumbled or something. I don't know! I was nervous, I can't help it!"

"So... where did you kiss her?" I ask slowly.

"Kind of like her chin?"

I glance at Aidan, whose eyes are as wide as saucers, and give a subtle headshake hoping that he understands not to dig at his brother right now.

"What did she do?"

"Just stood there. What was she supposed to do? She probably hates me now."

He plops down onto the couch and reaches over to pick up his brother's bowl of ice cream. The image is so perfectly cliché that I do let out a chuckle.

"Ice cream? Really?"

He scrunches his eyebrows at me and looks at the bowl. "Yeah? So?"

I shake my head and murmur, "Never mind."

"So, what do I do?"

"She doesn't hate you. I was just messing with you. She likes you."

"Really?"

"Yeah," Aidan rolls his eyes. "Just don't *stumble* next time," he jokes.

Between the two, even though Reece is far less outspoken and shyer in general, he's always been more comfortable talking to girls. Aidan has always become a bumbling goof, so I'm sure it threw Reece for a loop a little bit when he botched up things with Kelsey.

"Next time?"

Reece raises an eyebrow at me.

"Duh, Dad. Did you expect your first kiss with Christine to be your last?"

Stone.

That's how still I sit.

Young man laughter follows.

Punks.

Like the mature adult I am, I roll my eyes, stand up, and walk to the kitchen to text Christine to let her know her ass is going to be planted in my pickup a bit earlier than expected because I'm tired of waiting.

This first date can't wait any longer.

I STAND off to the side as I watch her throw a baseball at a metal target, trying to knock it over so she can win the giant stuffed panda bear.

I tried to do it, but she looked at me and said, "I got this."

Fourteen dollars later, and the panda isn't in her arms.

"Ready for some pointers?"

She huffs adorably. Plants her hands on her waist. She looks beautiful, as usual, in her dark jeans, skin tight and cuffed at the ankle, classic white Chucks on her feet and bright white tank under her army green jacket. Her head drops in defeat.

"Stupid game," she mumbles while handing me a baseball.

I make a big show of warming up before pitching the ball, hitting the target square in the center. It makes a loud *clank* before falling over.

"Well, of course it worked *now*. I've been tapping it loose for the last fifteen minutes."

"Of course."

"Your prize, sir," the game attendant says with as much enthusiasm as I have cleaning up vomit.

"The panda!" Christine says, perking up, bouncing on her toes.

He rolls his eyes but hands it over to her.

We wander through the carnival, eating fried food and sipping "real" lemonade, going down the giant slide together.

We take a picture of our feet dangling in the air from the ride that spins us around on a pendulum, almost causing a return of the fried dough we scarfed down earlier.

She shoves the panda on the other side of her after we step into the cage on the Ferris wheel, cuddling close together, I take a selfie then another when she kisses my cheek. Then another without her knowing when she curls into my chest, her head downturned and tucked under my arm stretched out behind her.

"You know, I wasn't even nervous for tonight."

I look down at her, and she lifts her face to me, and I see a flicker of vulnerability in those bright green eyes of hers.

"No?"

"No."

"And why do you suppose that is?" I ask, my voice taking on a husky undertone, even to my own ears.

"Probably because it's right," she whispers.

We stare at each other for several long moments, my eyes going back and forth between hers before I lower my mouth to hers, my tongue snaking out to taste her.

She responds immediately, her arm that was wrapped around my waist squeezing me closer.

Sugar from the hot doughnuts we had earlier lingers on her lips. My body responds to the feel of her, making me feel like a teenage kid getting hard in the middle of class.

Her jacket open, her breasts, covered only by the thin tank she's wearing, press against my t-shirt covered chest. I grip her thigh and bring her leg up to drape over my lap. She grinds against my leg, and I damn near combust.

Still kissing.

Still touching.

I'm positive I'll never get enough of her.

Round and round we go, coming to a stop every once-in-a-while and I'm sure there's so much beauty to be seen from the top of the Ferris wheel, but right now? I only see the beauty in us.

"You guys trying to give the kids a show, or what?" The sound of the Ferris wheel worker jars us.

I don't release Christine yet.

Instead, I trail the tip of my nose along her jawline and suck gently on the skin right below her ear.

"This is far from finished."

She shudders and nods.

We walk around a little while, her arm wrapped around my

waist and her fingers slide into the back pocket of my jeans while my arm is draped over her shoulder.

The possessive nature of her hold on me has my heart beating hard in my chest.

When I hear music filtering through the air, I stop, looking around for where it's coming from. There's a makeshift stage and bar set up toward the back of the carnival, a few high tables scattered around and a DJ booth placed off to the side.

"Just thinking out loud here," I tease and she giggles, her body shaking against my own. "But, I think we need to dance."

"Here?" she asks like she's horrified, but the bright smile on her face tells me that she's not the *least* bit horrified. "You gonna take me into your loving arms, are you?"

"Yup. Maybe even kiss you under the lights of a thousand stars."

I drop the panda on the empty chair closest to us and pull her back into my arms.

I twirl her out, arm extending, then spin her back to me. She throws her head back in laughter before shifting her body to align better with mine, fitting together like — corny as it may sound — two pieces of a puzzle. I keep hold of her hand on my chest, her other around my neck and fiddling with my hair. Something I'm learning she loves to do. Our bodies move side to side. "Mmm. I like the sound of that."

I lean in, kiss her on the lips and wrap a hand around her pony tail.

"Will you still be with me when my memory fades?" I whisper into her ear.

Christine

I GASP.

Not sure if he means what he just said in response to the words filtering through the speakers, but a large part of me hopes he did.

When I told him I wasn't nervous about tonight, I meant it.

I was jittery, yes. I was afraid Bri was going to slap me earlier. I was ready for our date hours early, anxious to get it started.

"Mom! Stop. You're driving me crazy."

"I can't help it! I just want it to be 5:00 already!"

"Well, calm down."

I glare at her.

"Need I remind you how whacky you were before your first date with Grady?"

"I'm good."

"Ha! Right. Don't throw stones, girl."

"Whatever. Still, you're acting like a crazy person."

"I can't help it!"

"It's Andy, Mom! You guys have practically been dating for months now."

"I know, but we don't spend a lot of time alone, you know? This is a big deal. You're sure you're okay with your mom dating?"

She rolls her eyes.

"Of course, I'm okay with it. I like Andy. A lot. Though, hearing my friends all talk about how hot he is, is rather disturbing."

I giggle.

"Sorry?"

"Yeah, right. You aren't sorry in the least."

I shrug. I'm really not.

And her friends are right.

He is literally the sexiest guy I've ever known. And he only gets sexier the more I get to know him.

My phone chimes with a text, and I jump.

Andy: *Any chance you're ready? LOL*

Me: *Now?*

Andy: *Yes? I'm...*

Me: *You're...*

Andy: *Excited. Does that make me sound like a creeper?*

Me: *I'm ready when you are.*

Andy: *Good. Be ready. Want you next to me.*

"By the smile on your face, I assume that was Andy?"

I bite my lip and nod, smiling at Bri. "He wondered if I was ready."

She throws her head back and laughs. "Not surprised. I don't know who's more obsessed with who, you or him. Have fun, Mom. You deserve this," she says, hugging me tightly.

"Do you think it was part of the plan?" I ask quietly.

"Absolutely."

Tears prick the back of my eyelids as I rest my head on his shoulder, feeling more content than I have in... well, ever. Being with Andy feels like home.

The song comes to an end, fading into another love song. This one about both knowing our own limitations and needing each other. He rests his forehead on mine.

"Thank you," he whispers.

"For?"

"Being mine."

I blow out a breath and glance away before looking at him again. "Am I? Yours?"

"You are," he says, voice firm. "Just as much as I'm yours."

"I like the sound of that."

"Me, too."

"Wanna go take pictures in the picture booth before we leave?"

"Alone with you in a tiny booth? Hell yes," he says, his eyes shining.

I'm so screwed with this guy.

He says I'm his. And he's mine.

And all I can think is I hope he means it because my heart? It's lost to him.

TWENTY-ONE

ANDY

"So once we leave here, we're done? Officially," I ask Heather's lawyer.

"Yes, as long as we can come to an agreement."

"Agreement? What's there to agree on now? You said it would be today. If this continues to drag on..."

We've been sitting in this small room for over an hour, and Heather keeps delaying, knowing that she has me by the balls. I want the boys. Full custody. She lost her right to my boys.

She already promised them to me in exchange for the cabin, so I don't know what could be holding her back.

"What's the hurry?" her slimy lawyer smirks.

"I want rid of her," I say, looking Heather dead in the eye.

Heather sits across from me looking like the whore she's become. Her top is so tight, her new boobs, which would rival the size of any seen in a titty magazine, are spilling out of it to the point I'm afraid she's going to have a serious wardrobe malfunction. "Why?" she asks innocently, tapping her fake finger nails on the tabletop. She knows damn good and well why. But Christine's not the only reason. Heather is toxic, and I don't want her around the boys. I want it in writing. Legal. No more contact.

Not that she really gives a shit. And now the bitch is just using them. Which makes her more than just a bitch. It makes her a despicable head case.

"Heather. Stop being such a bitch. I already gave you the cabin. Something that's been in my family for generations."

"Oh, yeah. I saw that you and your new happy family had a good little vacation at *my* cabin."

I wondered if she was still following the boys on Instagram. I almost told them to block her, and after today, I will.

I sit in silence. I dare her to bring up Christine.

She's none of Heather's business.

She smiles. A devilish smile that makes my blood curdle.

"Just spit it out," I growl.

"You're dating."

"Yes. My boys and I are spending time with another family."

She shrugs her shoulders, looks down at her nails and back up at me. "And?"

I scoff and shake my head. "You're such a horrible person."

My lawyer, Lynn, places her hand on my arm. I look down at her, and she shakes her head slightly at me.

"Did you know they've only asked about you twice?" I hold up two fingers, and she flinches. "And since you moved your shit out of the house? Not once. The entire time we were at the cabin they were happy, smiling. They don't miss you. Hard to miss someone who was hardly there in the first place."

Something comes over her face. Shame? Regret? Whatever it is makes me nervous.

"That's a terrible thing to say, Andy," she whispers but I can't tell if she's full of it or truly sad. I lost the ability to read her a long time ago.

I shrug, not bothered by hurting her feelings. Not anymore. "Truth hurts. Sign the papers. The house is sold, every bit of our money in it split between us already. The only thing we have left is this. I want this divorce settled now. I want my boys with me permanently. I'm not even asking you for child support."

Her shoulders drop, and I realize that until this point, she hadn't really given the entire situation much thought, mind blowing as that may be. She had thought of the boys as being a hindrance, not the blessing that they are. She looks at her lawyer, and he furrows his brow, clearly just as confused as the rest of us by her sudden change of attitude. Her chin wobbles, and she gazes out the window before turning tear-filled eyes to me. "I don't know... this is a big deal. I can't just walk away from Aidan and Reece."

"You already did," I growl impatiently, sick of the whip lash she's giving me.

"Not because I wanted to!"

"Right. You left because you were forced? Please. You told yourself, us, that it was because the boys deserved better than you. You left because you thought life would be better. That without the burden" —I use finger quotes— "of those two boys weighing you down, you'd be able to have everything you wanted. Guess what, Heather. Life isn't built on material things. On lonely experiences. It's built on *life.* On the lives in your own. On the relationships you build. On the love you show others and receive in return. Life isn't about having the best car or the most stylish clothes, or having your nails done and your hair blown out all the time. It's not about the house you live in, so yeah, go ahead. Take the cabin. Our family built memories that stand longer than the building itself." I pause and make sure she's looking me in the eye.

"One day, Heather, and listen to me and listen now because I'm not going to be gracious enough to say this again. You're going to look back on this and wonder what the hell you were thinking. You're going to miss seeing them play sports and graduate, build friendships and fall in love, go to college and become adults. You're going to miss their weddings, *their* children being born. You're going to miss all of it, and for what? For a few months in the sack with some dillhole who can't support the fact that you're a mom? But you know what? I'll be there for all of it. Because I will always know that they are more important to me than *anything* else. I don't need some cabin to understand what family is. I don't need it to make memories and feel whole."

By the time I'm finished speaking, Heather's cheeks are streaked with tears, and my chest is heaving. I pray that I didn't say enough to make her change her mind, but at the same time, I hope I did. The boys deserve to have their mom in their lives, just not the one they currently have.

"I'm sorry," she says quietly. "Keep the cabin. I don't know what I was thinking. I guess I just wanted..."

"To hurt me," I finish for her.

She nods. "I was upset."

"I would ask why, but I'm done trying to figure you out."

"It's just... when I heard..."

"You heard what?"

"You moved on, and I guess — I don't know."

"You thought I would pine for you forever?"

She shrugs her shoulders, and I roll my eyes. Not even going there.

Not worth any of our time, and I want this shit done.

"You got that change in writing?" I nod over to the mediator, making sure that she got it down that Heather's no longer taking the cabin.

"Yes, Mr. Simpson. I have it down. You will have full custody of Reece and Aidan. Heather also has given up any rights to visitation, and as per her recent change, the cabin is once again yours. Because the cabin change was something she was including late and hadn't been expressed to the courts, only told you, the original settlement drawn up is accurate."

I nod my head, feeling the weight of a million elephants lifted off my chest for the first time since I walked in on her with Preston. Also a little annoyed that I hadn't even realized she was trying to get the cabin without going through our lawyers.

"That's it?" I ask her.

She looks up from the papers and lifts her pen before signing, nodding her head but not looking directly at me.

"I can't be what they deserve," she admits sadly.

"Heather. You need to understand what you're doing," her lawyer interrupts in a strange moment of clarity. At least *he* listened to the words that came out of my mouth.

"He's right, Heather. Do you fully understand what you're doing? You'll never be able to have a relationship with your sons again. If you change your mind, and Andy sticks to this agreement, you have no rights." Even Lynn can't believe she's just signing her rights away. The boys are fourteen. They need their mother.

"I understand," she sniffles.

"I don't think you do, honey," Lynn says, reaching her hand across the table to cover hers, stopping her from signing. The way this meeting started, with Heather being such a conniver, I never anticipated it ending with my lawyer trying to make her see the light of day. But Lynn's a mother herself. She knows exactly what Heather is giving up.

"I do. I've thought about it a lot. Andy, you've always been the better parent."

My control is threatening to snap. I feel like I'm the ball in a terrible game of pinball, my thoughts going back and forth between wanting her to sign the papers and releasing me and not giving up on her boys, on being a mother. "It's not a competition, Heather!"

She looks at me with tears in her eyes. "I know that. But I also know that I've never been the mother they deserve." I open my mouth to object, even though it would be a lie, but she stops me by putting her hand up. "You know it's true. And everything you just said? As sick as it is to admit, the thing that made me sad is that none of it bothers me to miss. They deserve better than me."

I decide to say nothing and let her continue talking.

I can't argue with what she just said.

She has tears streaming down her face but still she reaches and picks up the pen, her hand hovering over the papers, poised and ready to sign. I've already signed so we're just waiting on her.

I sit with my mouth gaping, hardly being able to believe that she's actually signing away her rights.

"Aidan and Reece? They are *good* boys. They are worth so much more than having me for a mother. They deserve someone who is willing to give up everything for them. I have one request." She swallows and looks away, setting down the pen. My heart is pounding so hard in my chest I can feel my pulse pounding in my neck. She leans down and pulls two envelopes out of her purse and slides them across the table to me. Each one bears the name of one of the boys. I stare at them for a few beats before reaching out and pulling them to me.

"I want you to give these to the boys, whenever you're ready or whenever you think they're ready. I know you'll read them first, because that's what a good dad does. But I want you to promise me you'll give them these letters."

"I can do that." I promise this knowing, even though she's not a great mom, she still loves them. In some weird and twisted way. She would never do something that would hurt them, or say something in a letter that would mess them up any further. Her walking away at this point proves that. But she's right. I'll read them before I give them over. Because even though I believe her intentions are good, I still don't trust her.

"Thank you, Andy."

She looks down and takes a deep breath, signs the papers, and then stands up and walks out of the room without a backward glance.

"It's done." Andy's voice carries over the phone, and I wish I were next to him, being able to see his face, hold his hand.

"She signed?" I can hardly believe it.

"She did. I thought it was going to be ugly at first."

"What'd she do?"

"She gave back the cabin."

"What?"

"Yeah. She had a change of heart, I guess. But the boys are officially mine, and she has no legal ties to them, so..." The sound of his voice breaks my heart. I know he's sad that she couldn't see what she would be missing out on. Not for himself, for his boys.

"I'm sorry, honey."

"Me, too. I don't understand what she's thinking."

"Me either. I couldn't walk away from them," I admit quietly.

"Just them?"

"Well, you three," I amend.

"Happy to hear that," he mutters.

"Yeah?"

My heart is racing, my nerves kicking up at admitting it, even though I'm sure he knows, but he needs to hear those words at the moment, especially after what he just went through.

"Oh, yeah."

"Best thing that came out of this was you," his voice is rumbly in my ear and causes my body to tingle.

My smile could be seen from the moon.

I hum in response rather than say something embarrassing, and he chuckles.

It's low and makes my stomach flutter.

"What are you doing tomorrow?"

I smile into the receiver. "No plans, yet."

"Don't make any. The boys and I want to take you somewhere. I think they knew they would need a distraction after today."

"You guys want to take me somewhere?"

"Well, honest moment. It's not really something *I* want to do. But the boys want to go."

"What's that?"

"They want to take you to this ridiculously dumb haunted house that apparently is so awesome it can't be contained to just Halloween, so it's opening for two weeks at the end of spring for people willing to test it out, whatever that means. It's a new one, and they're using some new pyrotechnics. The boys found out about it online, of course. The goal is to get people talking about it until it actually opens, or something like that. Apparently, there are some complete freaks out there who actually like this sort of shit and want to be scared. Which is the stupidest thing I've ever heard of but..."

"They?" I interrupt, not caring about *when* the haunted

house is but latched onto hearing that the boys were wanting to include me.

"Are you going to just keep asking questions?"

"Well, you're not exactly giving me much information."

"I don't really like getting scared," he murmurs.

I can't help it — a bubble of laughter bursts out of me.

"Are you serious?"

"Oh, I'm dead serious."

"You do know the purpose of haunted houses is to be scared, right?"

"Oh, I know. Trust me. But the boys love it. They can't get enough. And they begged me to call you so you could come along."

My heart is so full with that one sentence.

"Really?"

"You mean the world to us, Christine."

Us.

"Ditto."

"Tomorrow. Be ready. You better wear flats because you could end up carrying me on your back out of there."

"You're really that scared?"

"I didn't say I *am* scared. I said I hate *being* scared," he says like that's any different.

"I have a feeling this is going to be fun."

"You like haunted houses?"

"Not like. Love. I love them."

"What is wrong with you?"

"Nothing! They're so much fun! The unexpected, the constant wondering when someone's going to jump out at you. The thrill of wondering if you're going to pee yourself?"

"You're not selling it," he chuckles.

"We're really going? Tomorrow night?"

"Yes." He sighs. "If we must."

"We must."

"I have a feeling you three are always going to gang up on me," he murmurs.

My entire body warms at his words.

"And then I get you to myself. You promised me another date, remember?"

"How could I forget? Prettiest ugly cake I've ever seen in my life got you unlimited date nights."

He chuckles, but it sounds distant.

"Are you okay?" I ask him, directing us back to his initial reason for calling me.

"I am. I hate it for the boys. She gave me letters for them. I haven't read them, yet. I'm not ready, and neither are they. I need to tell them."

"But..."

"How do you tell your boys that their own mother doesn't want them?"

I choose my words carefully and speak barely above a whisper. "Well, it's not like they don't know. They already heard it from her," I remind him.

"Yes, but this is final, you know?"

"I know. So, you do it like you've done everything the last several months. With gentleness, honesty, and love. You make sure they know it's her loss, that it has nothing to do with them. And at least you get to tell them that she changed her mind about the cabin."

"Silver lining, yeah?"

"Exactly."

"I would ask you to be there but..."

"No. You're right. You need to do this yourself."

"That doesn't bother you?"

"Why would it? It's not about me, Andy."

"I'm lucky to have you."

"Feeling's mutual."

"So, I'll see you tomorrow?"

"You will."

"Can't wait."

TWENTY-THREE

ANDY

I have a confession to make. When I said, I don't really like getting scared, what I meant was I'm *terrified* of being scared. It not only frightens the ever-loving shit out of me, but it pisses me off. But at the same time, I actually enjoy going to haunted houses, mainly because the boys have so much fun. Then again, I did stay with my cheating wife for several years after I suspected she was a cheater. So maybe I'm just a masochist.

Last night, I sat the boys down and told them that the divorce was final and let them know that she gave us back the cabin.

They were ecstatic about the cabin but weren't bothered by the fact that we were divorced. They simply asked if that meant everything was officially done and she couldn't take them away from me. When I assured them that we were together for good, they smiled and said that's all they cared about.

I had expected the worst.

And I got the best.

I zip up my black sweatshirt as I make my way up the steps to Christine's house. It might be the middle of spring, but

Michigan nights can still get chilly. And the cold snap we're going through right now feels more like early fall. Which is probably appropriate for going into the death trap the boys convinced me was a good idea. My nerves are already kicking in, and I wonder if it's from seeing her, or knowing that in about thirty minutes, I'll be screaming like a girl in front of her.

My hand is raised, about to knock on her door, when it suddenly opens. A *very* excited Christine stands on the other side, bouncing on her toes. Man, she's cute. My eyes have a mind of their own, and right now they desperately want to take in every inch of her. She's wearing another pair of skinny jeans, this time light-washed with holes in the knees and cuffed to show a little bit of her lower leg, same white Chucks she wore on our first date, and a maroon shirt under a thin gray zippered hoodie. Damn. Everything she wears makes her even more adorable.

Her dark hair is pulled into a high pony tail, and her bright green eyes meet mine when they finally make it up there from my completely shameless display of checking her out, shining with happiness. It almost makes me feel excited to go get the piss scared out of me. Almost.

"You ready?" she asks, smiling widely.

"As I'll ever be," I grumble honestly.

"You're this big strong man, but a total wuss. I kinda love it," she tells me, biting her bottom lip.

"You're such a brat."

"Watch it. While you're rocking in the corner tonight like a whiny little girl, I'll be the one saving your scared ass."

"One thing very wrong with that."

"What's that?"

"No way in hell will I sit down and rock in the corner. I'll be the one running so fast you'd think I could walk on water."

She bursts out laughing, and I find myself a relaxing a tiny bit. Only a teeny tiny bit.

"Gotta pee before we go?"

"Nope. Just did. Do you?"

"Peed before I came. This isn't my first rodeo, darling."

She grins. "So, no pants peeing tonight, huh?"

"Well, the night is young. I make no promises. House locked?"

She turns around and locks the door then puts her keys in her purse. "Sure is!"

"Well then... your chariot awaits." I throw a hand toward my pickup.

I open the door for her, and she climbs inside. As soon as she's settled, she immediately turns around to greet the boys. Aidan and Reece invited their friend, Nolan. The three of them have been amped up for hours, ready to get their scare on. My boys, of course, know how much I hate it, so that makes them love it even more.

"Who's this?" Christine asks as I climb in, obviously already greeting the boys.

"Our friend, Nolan."

"Hey, Nolan, I'm Christine," she says with a smile in her voice.

"Hey," Nolan says with a little low wave. Where my boys are typically pretty outgoing, Nolan can be fairly shy until he gets to know someone. When he's around just us, he's crazy, funny, and a goofball. Christine must be making him slightly nervous. "My mom told me to tell you that she loves your coffee shop and your pastries are the best."

"Aww, that's so sweet! Tell her thank you for me... and to come in next week for a coffee on the house so I can meet her, okay?"

"'Kay." He smiles, looking down at his hands.

Aidan stifles laughter and covers his smile with his fist, leaning against the side of the door. If I were in the mood, I would remind him that he was nervous around Christine at first, also. And still has quite the crush on Bri.

"How'd your day go, boys? Get all that yard work done?"

I'm a dad who requires my kids to do chores. I'm mean like that. And Nolan was over all day — they want to be big and strong, so I worked them today. Every time they complained about doing the work, I reminded them how Grady got big. He'll be playing college ball soon, and he got where he is now from working hard, and not in the gym.

I'm not an awful person, though. I pay them for doing chores, and even Nolan got cash, and of course, tonight I'm taking them to the haunted house then out for supper.

"We did!" they say together, proudly.

They grumbled about it to me most the day. To Christine? They act like they just got done with an afternoon at the trampoline park.

Little punks.

I barely hold back my eye roll, but I see Christine press her lips together to stop from laughing. One side of my mouth quirks into a smile, and I reach over the console and take her hand in mine.

She smiles at me and lays her head back against the seat. I take her hand and bring it to my lips, kissing the back of it softly before resting our joined hands on my thigh, contentment coursing through me as we drive.

Ed Sheeran's *Shape of You* comes on the radio. All three boys shout to turn it up and sing along.

I've apparently never *really* listened to the words of this song, but sitting in my pick up while three teenage boys belt out the lyrics and Christine's shoulders shaking from her laughter has me listening a little closer. And... yeah. Awkward.

That is, until I see we're already at the haunted house.

"We're here!" Christine shouts, pulling her hand away from mine and bouncing around in her seat like a kid heading into a candy store.

"Can't wait," I grumble, and she giggles.

"Oh, come on, you big wuss."

"Wuss? Second time you've called me a wuss now."

She grins and swings her door open. "Come on, boys! Let's go see if we can't get your dad to wet himself."

I groan, and the boys all burst out laughing.

"I kinda love her," Aidan says to Nolan quietly.

"She seems awesome."

"So awesome," Reece agrees.

I smile, despite the fact that I'm walking into hell.

We walk up to the front to pay for our tickets, and I take a moment, standing back to watch as my boys stand on either side of Christine. They're waiting in line to enter, looking way more excited than I am about what's about to go down. Not that it takes much.

She wraps her arm around Aidan's neck when he says something that I don't hear, but it must have been full of smart ass because she's rubbing the top of his head and he's trying to pull out of her grasp, but they're all laughing.

"And you—" Christine points to Reece who's still laughing. "You're just as bad, you little turd."

"Me?" Reece puts his hand to his chest and pulls his innocent face. The face that's gotten him out of many punishments.

"Yes, you. It's always the quiet ones to look out for."

He grins up at her, and I step forward, placing my hand on the small of Christine's back. The line moves forward slowly. I'm quiet as we watch the three boys chat and horse around while we wait.

"You're quiet."

I grunt in response.

"Excited?"

I look down at her, her eyes full of mischief. She winks, and I roll my eyes.

"Oh, come on, sourpuss. It'll be fun." She pokes me in the ribs then tickles my side. I jerk a little bit and I feel my lip quirk. "It won't be so bad," she says, laughter filling her voice.

I raise an eyebrow at her and she returns it. She redoes her pony tail and then slides her arms around my waist, looking up at me as her thumbs hook in my back pockets. I wrap mine around her and lean down, kissing her lightly on the nose.

We haven't been overly affectionate in front of the boys yet, a kiss here or there, but they know what's happening. They get that she's not just someone their dad's dating — but someone who's going to be around a while. And, from what they've told me when we discussed things progressing further with Christine, they approve. They like Christine and love having her around. I think they like her more than they like me most days.

"You'll protect me?" I half tease.

"I'll protect my man, scout's honor."

"I'm your man, huh?"

"Damn skippy."

"I'm on board with that." I nuzzle my nose in her neck, inhaling her incredible scent. She always smells a bit like vanilla and sugar. It's intoxicating, and I know I'll never be able to get enough of it. I groan, not being able to control myself, letting my tongue sneak out, getting a taste, too. I hear her breath catch, and I place my lips on her neck, kissing and sucking with just a small amount of pressure.

"Dad!" My head jerks up to see the boys smiling over at me. From their point of view, it probably (and hopefully) looked like I was just resting my head on her shoulder while I gave her a hug. I don't need the boys to know, or see, that I was just perving on my girlfriend.

"Yeah?"

"We're up." Reece nods his head toward the line, indicating that it's our turn.

Yaa-aa-yyy.

"STOP! NO! WHAT WAS IT?"

I twist around, hitting at the offending object.

"Andy! Relax. It was just the plastic curtain at the entrance." Christine is laughing at me already, not even trying to hide it.

"Okay, okay. Yeah. You're right. I'm just a little on edge."

"You think? Mr. Simpson, you need to chill man," Nolan tells me. The three boys walk ahead, and a surge of panic roars through me.

"No! Don't go in! Not without me!"

All three boys give me a look. "Dad. I think we can handle it. Probably better than you."

Okay. That hurt.

Might have been truth but...

"I can protect you!"

"Right," the boys say at the same time, shaking their heads at me and venturing farther into the haunted house while I'm still standing by the entrance.

"You ready?"

"Let's just get this crap over with. You owe me a lemon pound cake all my own after this."

"Whatever you say, honey." She pats me on the shoulder as I gently push her in front of me.

"So, I guess all Andys are scared of haunted houses?"

"What?"

"You know... that producer Andy. Watch the videos on YouTube sometime of him going through haunted houses. You'll pee yourself laughing."

"I don't pee myself laughing."

"Just when you get scared, huh?"

"Yeah. Wait. No! I don't pee myself! Can we just move forward? Who knows how far the boys are into this thing, and they're probably huddled up with some zombie right now, plotting something against me."

"Paranoid much?"

"No. I know my boys. They're not little angels."

"Wonder where they get it from?"

"Are you guys going to go through this thing or what?" I turn around and see a group of annoyed teenagers standing behind me.

"Whatever." I struggle to resist the urge to flip off the teenagers, not my proudest moment, and grab hold of the back of Christine's shirt as we move ahead.

I hear a noise to my left and jump almost a foot in the air, gasping and screaming but keep walking.

Everyone knows you don't stop moving through a haunted house.

That's when they get you.

When they smell your fear.

We make it about four steps when I feel something grab my ankles. "It's got me! Christine! It's got me!" My feet do a dance that would rival an Irish dancer's.

I dance my way out of Christine's arms and my back hits the chest of... something. I'm not sure what it is, but it's awfully handsy and the noises it's emitting are far from comforting. I bolt out of its grasp and run ahead to Christine a few feet. She's watching me with amusement on her face, but lets her guard down just enough for one of the horrific zombies to attack her, coming out from behind a curtain.

My eyes widen, and I grab her hand and take off. "Run! It's coming! Lord have mercy on us!" I'm screaming and yelling, fearful of this staged character getting to my girl.

We keep moving forward and every few steps, something either jumps out at us or grabs us from below.

"No!" I yell at one, pointing my finger at it as it tries walking toward me, blood and disgusting goo dripping from its face, but it doesn't stop grasping for us.

"No means no, dammit! Didn't you learn that when you were a kid?"

As I'm berating the haunted house employee for having bad manners, a small girl dressed to look like a ghost of some sort, emerges from behind a curtain. The small thing opens its mouth and starts turning its head.

All.

The.

Way.

Around.

"What the hell is that?" Christine yells, a tremor in her voice that does nothing for my own state of fear. That's a lie. It definitely heightens my fear.

"I'm not scared. I'm not scared. I'm not scared. I'm not scared."

"I'm frickin' scared! I'll admit it!" Christine shouts then screams as something comes at her with what I hope is a fake knife, then plunges at her feet and crawls toward her.

"I'm not gonna pee myself. I'm not gonna pee myself. I'm not gonna frickin' pee myself!" I shout.

"Where are the boys? Are they okay?"

"It's every man for himself, Christine. They lost the right to have us save them when they left us behind. Just keep going," I tell her, taking deep breaths and gingerly stepping around another corner, trying to keep my back against the wall.

I peek around once quickly, jerking back. I don't see anything, so I take a step, only to have a mummy of some sort try to attack me. "Ahhh! Stop! Stop! No. You're not real. You're not real."

"Andy? Where are you? Are you okay?"

"It's not real." I keep repeating it, my eyes squeezed shut. She grabs hold of my arm, making me scream loudly again and jump out of my skin. My heart is pounding so hard, it feels like it could explode from my chest. I place my hand over my heart then feel for a pulse.

She rolls her eyes at me. "Dramatic, much?"

I stop and look her in the eye. "I almost died, Christine."

She scoffs then we step around another corner, moving some hanging bodies out of the way because, you know, that's *normal*. As soon as I'm clear of the bodies, another one falls from the ceiling, right in front of us. I fall to the ground, taking Christine with me, and start army crawling away.

"Hurry! Hurry! Just keep going! We got this. I promise. We can do this. Just keep going."

We step into a room that looks oddly normal, which of course makes me on edge. I have my arms around her, making it darn near impossible to walk, my legs on either side of hers, but I won't let go.

"It's okay. It's okay. We're fine! Did you hear that?" I shout. "We're not scared! We know you're not real!"

And even though I knew something was going to happen in the completely normal bedroom, I didn't expect a herd of zombie clowns to come tearing through the walls.

"Ahhh! Lord help us! No! Mother of shiiiiiit! Help!"

"Andy! Run!"

I take off sprinting, pulling Christine along with me.

"My heart! I can't!" Christine's panting, and it gives me an oddly satisfied feeling to know that she's as terrified as I am, given the fact that she was so sure of herself just moments ago.

"I thought you just *love* haunted houses? Not so tough now, are you?"

"I do love them! The getting scared part is the best! I never said I didn't get scared while going through them!"

She barely gets the words out when another bloody zombie (never watching The Walking Dead again, thank you very much) comes at us, jumping into our path before lunging in our direction.

We both screech and jump away, her back slams into my front, and I wrap my arms around her. I would like to say it's because I'm trying to protect her, but really, it's just to keep it away from me.

"We're fine. We're okay. We're almost there." She's trying to assure both of us. "Did you pee? I haven't peed. I didn't pee my pants."

We *are* almost there. Which means something scary as hell is about to happen.

We come to an opening that looks like we're at the end...

"Baaahhhh!!!!"

Something hits us both from behind, and Christine and I crouch down and swing with our arms at whatever is screaming at us and about to attack us, eat our brains and leave us for dead.

Clearly, we haven't been watching too much TWD or something.

Then we hear the telltale signs of three little shits laughing at us.

We stumble into the house after a heavy make out session on her front porch. I shove her against the door, kissing her hard and soft.

Officially, we've been dating for four months.

Four months of getting to know each other better, of spending time as a family. When Bri graduated from high school, the boys and I were sitting right next to her.

Four months of blue balls and cold showers.

Bri and her girlfriends went on a weekend trip with one of her friends' parents, and my boys are spending the night at Nolan's.

"About damn time," she rasps as my mouth caresses her neck.

She's absolutely right about that.

Her eyes are teasing.

Her smile is enrapturing.

Her voice light and sweet and sexy and everything that makes my body, my heart, come alive.

"What?" I ask, incredulously, a bit of laughter in my own voice.

"I said—" She takes two steps closer and places her hands on my chest, her bright green eyes looking up at me from under her long thick lashes. "About." She kisses my chest, and my heart feels like it could explode straight from my chest. "Damn." She kisses my neck, and it's a direct shot to somewhere much further south than my heart, but the feeling is the same. "Time," she whispers into my ear, her tongue sneaking out to graze just below my ear.

"You're..." I start saying but my voice cracks like my boys' going through puberty when her hand travels lower, confirming that I didn't need to ask her if she's sure but damn if I won't anyway.

"Yes?"

I clear my throat and lean back slightly, reaching down to grab her hand in mine to slow her movements. We've come too far to not be sure.

"Are you sure?"

"Andy, honey, are *you*?" She bites her lower lip then lifts on her tiptoes, kissing me lightly on the mouth.

"Am I?"

Hell, yes, I'm sure.

I'm so keyed up, I may explode at first contact.

She giggles, the sound so sugary I can almost taste it. "That seems to be the question, doesn't it?"

"Sweetheart, I'm always ready."

"Always?"

I fight the urge to growl when I feel her fingertips graze over the front of my pants. She hooks a finger in my belt loop and pulls me even closer, so our bodies are flush against each other. "With you? Yes."

"Good to know."

"It is." I swallow. Hard. Her hands are distracting me from just about everything. Every thought? Gone. It takes one touch from her and I forget my name. She's intoxicating and alluring and the most gorgeous woman I've ever met. The fact that she wants me is blowing my mind.

"No more waiting, Andy. You and me."

"Just you and me." I nod in confirmation.

So much of our time is spent with our kids, especially since Bri will be leaving for college soon. It's been Christine and Bri alone together for a lot of years now. Until we came along, that is.

But we're alone now.

I've never been a hesitant person before. If I'm being honest, I've always been the leap before you look type of guy, so this feeling is a little out of my element.

I'm looking, and she's leaping.

But there's so much more at stake here.

Bri.

Aidan and Reece.

Let's not forget... our hearts.

And apparently, the fact that I grew a vagina recently.

She's staring up at me, both hands lightly gripping my waist, and she's practically begging for me to take her. To make her mine. And I'm sitting here wondering if it's the right time like a scared little bitch.

I think on this for approximately point six more seconds before...

"Fuck it," I growl and slam my lips onto hers with such force it causes her to stumble backward.

But I'm there to catch her.

Always.

I grip her ass and lift, and God bless her, she wraps her strong legs around me with the strength of a python.

I start moving, our lips never parting.

It's not smooth.

It's messy and a tad awkward, and anyone who tells you they can kiss while holding the woman they love while trying to maneuver through a house and not bump into anything is a liar. Because it's hard — pun intended — but so worth it.

Once we eventually stumble our way into her bedroom, we fall in a heap onto the bed. The plush down comforter is soft under my back.

I grip the hem of her shirt and lift, pulling it off her body.

"Holy shit, you're gorgeous," I breathe out, taking in my fill of her.

Her shiny, dark hair falls over her shoulders, kissing the swell of her breasts still covered by her simple white bra. A few freckles cover her chest, something I'll take my time counting when I'm not straining to be inside her.

I love that she's playful and fun and is always up for an adventure.

I love even more that she wants that with me.

I reach around her back to unhook her bra and I feel her hand softly caress my cheek. I look up, ready to bawl like a baby and beg for mercy if she's telling me to stop.

The look on her face has me pulling away just an inch. "What's wrong?"

She slides the straps down each arm before unhooking her bra and removing it slowly.

"Umm, I need to tell you something before you... you know, lick or suck or whatever you were planning on doing there." She points to her breasts, and my eyebrows shoot to my hairline at her nervousness.

"Okay?"

"This is embarrassing, and you're gonna think I'm the vainest person on the planet but..." She looks down at her breasts and shrugs her shoulders.

I resist the urge to look down at her bare chest for what I

think is a pretty damn commendable span of a few seconds before jack knifing up, spinning us around so she's pressed to the mattress, and I kiss her hard.

"Just tell me. I swear I won't. I couldn't ever think that about you."

"I have implants." That is *not* what I was expecting at all.

"That's it? That's what you have to tell me?" She nods while still avoiding my eyes. "Christine, look at me. I'm not here to judge you. I don't care. I love every inch of your body, whether it's been touched up or natural. You're still you."

"You don't, like, think I'm a slut or an egomaniac or anything? I just did it because I was tired of being even less than an A cup. No other reason than that."

"A slut?" I guffaw. I fall over laughing, pressing my head into the pillow beside her head.

"It's not funny, Andy! I'm serious!" She's giggling to herself and pushing lightly on me.

When I finally have my laughter under control, I sit up, straddling her. I take her hands in mine and move them so they're above her head, giving her a look that I hope she reads as "Don't you dare move those hands or I'll spank your sweet ass."

My fingers make a trail from her wrists to her biceps, leaving goose bumps in their wake. I cover both breasts with the palms of my hands, my eyes never leaving hers.

"Beautiful," I murmur before leaning down and pressing a kiss at the center of her chest and showering the rest of her with feather-light kisses.

"Perfect."

Kiss.

"Mine."

Kiss.

Suck.

Lick.

Bite.

I alternate between sucking and licking, giving both fair attention. Her nails are digging into my scalp. A muffled curse explodes from her lips, and I have to fight back the urge to laugh at the unexpectedness of it.

I knew being with Christine would be amazing, but I hadn't taken into account how much fun it would be to learn all the things that make her tick. And I plan to take my time doing just that.

I lick and then bite softly, causing her to writhe beneath me, crying my name from her lips, her voice husky and sexy and addicting.

Making her come didn't scratch the itch. Not a single bit. It's like I rolled in a field of poison ivy, flaming the appetite my body had for hers. It tingles in awareness, wanting its turn, but I have other plans.

So does she, it seems.

Before I can comment anymore on how I could give two turkeys less if she has fake boobs, I'm naked. Not sure how it happened, but she's right there with me and we're both breathing heavy and she's grabbing at anything she can of mine, and I'm touching anything I can reach of hers.

We've had months of foreplay.

Barely touching until I was divorced.

And now that I've had my first touch. My first taste. I'm glad we waited.

The anticipation only made this night that much greater.

Not to mention, the number of times I went home and had to take care of myself just from being in her presence. With any luck, my stamina will help us go on for hours.

My fingers make their way to her center, and I groan at the slickness I find. My earlier moments of hesitation are completely gone, and now I'm in the mood to take. I plunge two fingers into her and watch in fascination as her green eyes flash and her back arches, the back of her head digging into the pillow beneath her. I make quick movements, not letting up on my rhythm or strength. I can feel her pulse against the ends of my fingers, and I know she's getting close again. I add my thumb of my other hand, pressing against the most sensitive part of her. She frantically grips the sheets above her as she twists and turns, alternating between gasping for air and screaming out curses that would make a sailor blush and calling my name.

When her body quakes and her hand comes to rest on my wrist, I let up, slowly pulling my fingers out.

I bring them up to my lips, sucking them into my mouth. Her eyes never leave my lips. There's something incredibly sexy about a woman who's completely comfortable with herself. She's not lying in front of me trying to position herself to look like a model. She's not hiding the fact that at one time she had someone put silicone into her body to make her feel a little better about the way she looked.

"So, I take it you don't care that I have fake breasts?"

Her eyes are so bright they look like emeralds, her skin flushed a beautiful shade of pink.

I chuckle. "That would be a no."

"Because you like 'em big?"

To that, I do laugh. "That would also be a no. I don't care, Christine, because I love you. Every part of you. They aren't fake. They're still you."

Her eyes widen at my words that so effortlessly slipped out, as if I've been saying them to her my entire life.

"What did you just say?"

Smiling, my teeth drag across my bottom lip. I can't think of a better time to let her know how I feel than right now. I look into her eyes and hope she can see in them what I said is true.

"Did you..."

"Mean it? Hell yes. I love you," I say again because now that the words came out, they're pretty easy to say.

"I love you right back."

I kiss her. Hard. Bruising. Because there's no other response worthy.

When I move my head back, her eyes are twinkling. "You make me happier than I've ever been."

The pride in hearing that swells inside my chest. "Damn glad to hear that. I don't plan on that changing, either."

"Never. Now. Are we gonna do something about that?" she asks teasingly, pointing at my straining erection.

"What did you have planned?"

"Do I get to run the show now?"

I twist, landing on the bed beside her and move my hands above me like I had positioned her earlier.

Rather than trying to look seductive or feigning innocence, she latches onto me like she does with anything in life.

Vigor.

Enthusiasm.

And a whole lot of...

"Holy shit!" I yell out, my hips bucking up into her mouth when I feel myself hit the back of her throat.

"Sorry, but damn. Couldn't help myself."

My pushiness doesn't seem to affect her, though. She simply hums in response. Her head is bobbing up and down, her soft hair creating a curtain around her face.

I reach down and fist it, pulling it away so I can see her better.

Her hand is wrapped around me, twisting as her mouth continues to move, sucking at the tip.

I feel myself tighten, but no way am I ending our first time together this way.

"Woman, you need to let up. Now," I growl.

She moves quickly, straddling me, using her hand to center me while sliding down ever so slowly.

We both groan. Neither of us moves for a few beats. I'm enjoying the feel of her wrapped around me, of me filling her up.

She wiggles around, causing me to push in deeper. Her head falls forward as her hands scrape along my chest.

"It's so... oh my... it's just so good," she breathes out.

"Yeah," I grunt.

If my brain felt connected to my body at the moment, I would probably be able to say something a hell of a lot more eloquent than just mono-symbolic grunts.

"I think... I need to move."

"Yeah."

O-for-two in the response category of the evening.

Since my mouth is currently not working with me, I decide to rely on showing her physically.

I grip her hips and twist, wanting to be able to look down at her. Needing to see her splayed out beneath me.

Her dark hair is a stark contrast to the white pillowcases, her emerald eyes sparkling with emotion. Her breasts bounce wildly. Her skin shiny with a sheen of sweat.

There's nothing in this world that I could ever find more beautiful than her.

I lift one of her legs and place it on my shoulder as I continue to thrust into her, giving me a different angle. I can feel myself hit the spot so deep inside her it, almost brings stars to *my* eyes. I pull out slowly, pushing back in harder each time. With each thrust, I can feel us both getting closer.

"Oh! Oh, my gosh! Yessss!"

"Right there?"

"Mmm hmm. Yeah," she rasps.

"You almost there, baby? I can feel you pushing against me."

"So... oh yes. Now! I'm..."

And that's all it takes.

I follow her right over the edge, resisting the urge to collapse right on top of her.

I land half on the bed next to her, half on top, twisting us slightly so I don't slide out of her completely. I'm still pulsing through the last of my release when I feel her squeeze me twice.

Christine's eyes are closed, a soft smile covering her face. She lifts her hand then unceremoniously drops it, like it's simply too much work to keep it raised for any amount of time.

I know the feeling. Everything in me is used up. Spent.

And yet, I know if she were ready right now, I would start back up again in a heartbeat.

We both chuckle. When she cracks an eye open and she sees that I'm staring at her, she scrunches her face up adorably and covers it with her hands.

"Stop staring at me!"

"Why?"

"Because!"

"Your response is worthy of a second grader's."

She shakes her head and shrugs her shoulders. "I don't take offense to that in the least. Have you heard some of Harper's comebacks?"

"Touché. Want to get cleaned up?" I don't know why I ask. Of course she wants to clean up. It can't feel good to have that dripping out of you, but selfishly I have no desire to let her go.

"I do."

"Your wish is my command."

A laugh bursts out of her.

"That sounded as cheesy as I think it did, didn't it?"

"Totally. But that's okay. I love you anyway."

I'll never tire of hearing that.

I watch as she makes her way to the bathroom, doing a funny little waddle that cracks me up.

"What are you doing?"

"You're leaking from me!" she squeals.

Well, crap. Now I'm just turned on again.

Or still.

TWENTY-FIVE

CHRISTINE

"**W**hyyyyyyy?" I whine.

"Stop being lazy!" Andy teases, poking me in the side.

I grin. "No thanks."

"That's it? That's all you're saying? No? No response to me calling you lazy? No explanation? Nothing?"

"Nope. I *am* being lazy, and you know what? I *want* to be. I'm enjoying myself."

"Such a bad influence. What am I supposed to tell the boys?"

"That you're dating a brilliant woman who realizes that, contrary to what the population would like us to believe, it's perfectly okay to be lazy once in a while. God gave himself a day. Why can't we? We aren't meant to run constantly."

"So, you're doing nothing today?"

"Day of rest," I say by way of explanation.

"For real?"

"For real." I sit up from my place on the couch where I've been relaxing, reach over to grab my iced tea off the coffee table in front of me. After taking a sip, I sigh contently and sit back.

He nudges my leg, jostling it around. "Come on! Let's do something. I'm boorrrred."

"You're bored," I deadpan.

"Yes."

"You're thirty-five years old."

He nods then shrugs. "And I'm a thirty-five-year-old man who's bored."

"You're worse than the boys."

"Well, the boys are playing football with their buds, and I wasn't invited."

I giggle and roll my eyes. It's been three weeks since we were first together, and there's been only a few days we haven't found time alone.

The slow burn of our relationship seemed to go up like wildfire, and there's no way of putting it out.

"Fine." I sigh like it's a huge burden to spend time with him. It isn't. Not in the least. And if I know Andy, I have a very good idea how he wants to fix his so-called boredom. "What do you want to do?"

He waggles his eyebrows at me, smiling wolfishly before taking my kindle out of my hand and placing it on the table. He crawls up my body, situating himself firmly between my legs, forcing me to lie back on the couch.

"So, when you said you were bored..."

"It's hard being bored," he says pushing himself against me.

A giggle bursts out of me. "Oh, my goodness did you really just say that?"

"You bored?" His lips are on my neck, causing a delicious shiver to pebble my skin.

"No. I'm a grown up."

"I distinctly remember you telling me that you were in the mood for exercise and needed a cure for your boredom."

"I don't..."

I'm cut off by the feel of his hands working their way up my shirt, lifting it away from my body, as his fingers blaze a trail across my stomach.

He leans back, looking down at me before swiftly removing my shirt over my head, my hair tie that was haphazardly wound around my hair flying across the room in the process.

He smirks at my lack of bra, and I shrug.

I told him it was a day of rest, so I was giving the girls a day off from the confines of a bra, too.

Before I can say a word, his mouth is on me once again, his tongue making no pit stop to ask for entrance or to see if I'm ready by taking its sweet time.

There's no grace.

He's forceful and strong.

He tastes like the cinnamon gum that he's always chewing and smells delicious. A combination of his body wash and outdoors and just a tiny hint of sweat from his run over here.

His muscles are firm under my fingertips while I let them move over his hot skin. They flex under my touch, and when I feel for the hem of his shirt, he wastes no time in pulling back, helping me to remove it.

Our bodies come together in a sweat-slicked collision, my breasts pressed against his bare chest. The small amount of hair that speckles his chest causes a friction against my smooth skin that makes my stomach tighten. I wrap my legs around his waist, needing some sort of pressure to help relieve the sudden ache.

That's the thing with Andy that I've never had with anyone else.

I can be feeling my ugliest, wearing no makeup, pajama pants, and a T-shirt that I've had for decades, glasses covering my eyes rather than my contacts, and he'll make me feel more beautiful than a Victoria's Secret model. The way his eyes devour every inch of me, his heart beating wildly beneath my hand, and his body's reaction to me that I can *feel* so fully pressed against me makes me feel like I'm Wonder Woman.

Ten minutes ago, I was in the mood to do absolutely nothing. I was all settled in for a full day of being lazy and honestly was looking forward to it.

Doing nothing just got run over by a steamroller, and now all I can think about doing is... Andy.

"Andy," I moan, stretching my neck to the side as his mouth makes its way from my mouth down my jaw, continuing its jaunt until he's found my overly sensitive breasts. Getting older isn't entirely for the birds. I'm hornier than I've ever been — though that could be only because of Andy — and my breasts have become so tender, so sensitive, that I can go from zero to holy-moly-I'm-going-to-come-from-one-swipe-of-the-tongue   in seconds.

"Whatcha need, baby?" he mumbles, still taking his time to kiss, suck, lick. He bites down gently, causing sparks to shoot from my fingertips, and I arch my back in response.

"You," I gasp.

"Oh, you've got me."

"Now, Andy!" I scream, but I'm still soaring. Flying through an orgasm so rapidly I should feel in danger of having a heart attack.

He lifts his head as I'm coming back down, my nails digging into the back of his head, and he smiles.

"Still lazy?" he jokes.

"For the love, Andy. How do you do that?"

"Do what?"

I don't answer him. I stare into his eyes, so happy and full of life. Of love. I pull him down to me, taking his mouth with mine as I tug on the waistband of his shorts. He helps me push them down, allowing my hands to immediately go to his ass. The tightness of his cheeks spurring me on.

"So damn sexy," I whisper.

A slow smile spreads across his beautiful face.

I lift a hand and trace one of his cheekbones.

He captures my hand and kisses the tip of each of my fingers; a jolt of electricity shoots through my body with each graze of his lips.

"Hang on, baby," he commands, wrapping my arms around his neck and motioning to my legs to grip tightly around his waist.

In one swift motion, he lifts, bringing me with him, clinging to him like a spider monkey.

With a grunt he stands, pushing his shorts the rest of the way down and steps out of them as he walks us in the direction of my bedroom.

He lays me down gently on my bed, spreading my tangled mess of hair out all around me.

"You deserve more than a quickie on your couch when I'm in the middle of my run." His eyes are assessing me, taking in every inch of my face.

"What?"

"You're worth so much more than that. You're worth... dammit, Christine. You're worth all of it. I know we haven't been together that long, and you might think that I'm just rebounding from her, but that's not it. You. You're it for me. I can't believe I spent so many years without knowing that, without you in my life and taking over my thoughts. But I want you to know, this isn't just some passing thing for me. This is everything."

I bite my lip, but the sting of tears comes anyway. I can't stop them. The floodgates are opened, and it's all his fault.

"I love you, Andy."

His thumb swipes away a tear from my cheek with his thumb. "Well that's good because I sure as hell love you."

TWENTY-SIX

ANDY

Life is good.

Aside from the fact that Bri leaves for college in two days and Christine is a basket case almost every single moment.

Yesterday she came over straight from the coffee shop, and it looked like she had gotten into a fight with a bag of flour.

I even saw it in her ear.

She's still beautiful, but she has bags under her eyes from lack of sleep and her skin has been breaking out from stress.

Between trying to get Balance up and running and sending Bri off, she's wearing herself thin, and I don't like it.

So, the kids and I planned a fun night.

We're getting back to the basics and having a family night in.

Playing games, watching a movie, vegging out, eating all the food.

Bri and the boys are at the store together grabbing a few snacks then they'll order pizza and I'm on my way to pick up Christine. I don't even want her worrying about driving at this point.

I pull into her driveway and climb out, heading up the porch steps. After we got more serious, we gave each other an open-door policy, exchanged keys. Hopefully, eventually we won't need separate keys. But that's for another day.

"Christine?" I yell out when I don't see her immediately but I don't get a response. I make my way to her bedroom and find her sitting at the foot of her bed, hunched over a little bit as she slides her feet into a pair of sandals.

"Babe?"

She looks up at me, tears flooding her eyes.

Ah, shit.

"Oh, sweetheart," I say, my voice softening as I move closer to her, sitting on the bed and wrapping her up in my arms.

Her head falls to my shoulder, and she sniffles before breaking down completely.

"I d-don't want her to l-leave. We didn't get enough t-t-time," she cries. At least, I think that's what she says.

"She's not leaving for good," I *try* to remind her.

"Yes, she is. She's leaving and never coming back."

I chuckle then quickly stop when her eyes dart to me, glaring.

I can't help it, though. She's so irrational right now.

Not that I would *ever* say *that* out loud. I'm a quick learner, and she's obviously not in the joking mood.

"You really think that Bri is going to go to college and never come back home? Never check in with you?"

"Well, I don't know. It sure seems like she's just itching to get out of here. She doesn't leave for three days. Three days, Andy! And she already has her bags all packed! Who does that?"

Normal people?

I don't dare explain that she's probably ready to leave because her mom has lost her damn mind the last few days. Or the fact that she and Grady are going to the same school, and she's more than likely *very* ready to have that newfound freedom that comes with college.

Or the simple fact that Bri is a healthy, active eighteen-year-old young woman, who is ready for the next stage of her life.

Instead...

"She loves you, and she's going to miss you so bad that she's probably going to want to come home right away."

"Why would you say that?" she cries and hits me on the shoulder.

Did I mention she's irrational lately?

"Umm. How about..." I hug her tightly, look to the ceiling for answers that obviously aren't there, and mentally whisper a prayer for the right words.

"I love you?"

"Andy! You're not a help at all."

"Gotta be honest here, babe. I have no idea what you want me to say."

She sniffles and stands up, points at me. "Just wait. One day the boys are going to leave us, and you'll be crying, and I won't have an ounce of sympathy for you."

I scoff. Roll my eyes. "Oh. Okay."

They won't leave me. They're Daddy's boys. Even at fourteen years old they still want to spend time with me. I'll home-school college if I have to. I'll figure that shit out.

"Okay? Okay! Andy! They're going to *go away* for college! Away from us! Soon, they're all going to be gone."

She bursts out laughing when I stand and pace around the room. "They're not going to leave us." I shrug like it's settled. No big deal. "I'll lock their bedroom doors. From the outside."

"No, you won't. They'll be like Bri. Just itching to get away from us, too. And they'll never come back."

"Hey! No need to be so mean!"

"Oh, I'm the mean one?"

I realize that we've gone from her wearing the crazy pants to both of us hopping on that train and I need to derail us quickly.

"Come on," I tell her and reach my hand out to her. She takes it and squeezes

I walk us down the hall into Bri's bedroom. The door is open, so I figure it's safe to go in. I point to her bedside table at the picture sitting there. The framed photo is a collage that Bri made of her and Christine for Mother's Day but wanted one for herself so made a second copy.

"Who does she keep next to her bed? The first person she sees every morning?"

Christine nods, smiling as her fingertip trails over their faces.

Then I walk over to the mirror above her dresser, where she has several pictures hung up around the outside edge. Pictures of her and Grady, more of her and Christine, some of her friends, a few of Todd. Then...

"When did she take these?"

In several frames on top of her dresser are selfies of Bri with the boys, one of me standing behind Christine with my arms wrapped around her middle. One of Grady with the boys. And one of the five of us sitting around the fire at the cabin, Christine on my lap, the boys sitting on the ground in front of us with sticks over the fire roasting marshmallows, and Bri standing behind the chair we're sitting in, her elbows resting on the back, my face upturned to her, a smile on all our faces.

"At the cabin. Grady took them, I guess. Bri didn't even know he did it until they were on their way home the next day and he handed her his phone."

"These are..." I can't even finish the sentence. They're great seems inadequate. They're everything sounds cheesy.

"I know," she says. "Now you see? She's not allowed to leave."

I glance around her room at the boxes and suitcases she has stacked and ready.

"Think she'll be pissed if we unpack these quick?"

A laugh bubbles out of her, and she leans in, hugging me tightly.

I kiss the top of her head and sigh.

I didn't realize how quickly I'd grown attached to Bri. It started out slowly, and now I feel like we haven't had enough time. When she visited us at the cabin, it was kind of a turning point. A vision of what our family could be.

And over the summer, we've made a lot of memories. Fishing with the boys, a few more trips to the cabin, bonfires in our back yard.

In general, we just had a great summer.

But now she's leaving.

Which is why we're supposed to be at my place right now, enjoying one of the last nights at home with her.

"Let's go make a few more memories," I tell her, squeezing her close to me.

She nods once, lifts up on her tiptoes, and kisses me on the chin then on the mouth. I take it and deepen the kiss. We don't make it to family movie night at home like we planned.

But we do make a few memories of our own.

"AIDAN! Stop. You're putting too much on!"

"There's never too much, Bri. Do you know *anything*?"

"I know a heck of a lot more than you do, obviously. And I'm saying it's too much."

"Reece. Tell her she's wrong."

"I'm staying out of it. Just minding my own business over here."

"You're such a suck up!"

"How is that sucking up? I'm saying I'm neutral. Not getting involved in whatever weird crap you two have going on."

I look at Christine and shrug my shoulders. Her wide smile proving that our extra time spent alone before joining the kids was definitely worth it.

In more ways than one.

I wasn't kidding when I said that she's been a little out of it lately. Way more emotional than normal, but considering she's sending Bri off to college soon, I get it.

"What are they talking about?" Christine whispers.

"I have no idea."

"Enough already! It will just be soggy and gross. Ugh. Move over and let me do it."

"You don't know everything, Bri. Just let us help."

"Guys! Dad is going to be here any minute with Christine, and we want this done, right? Just..." We both hear Reece sigh like he's irritated. "Stop arguing and work it out. It's like one of our last nights together before Bri ditches us, and I don't want to spend it fighting. Can't we do one with extra and regular?"

I glance down at Christine as we stand on the other side of the wall that separates the kitchen and the living room while we eavesdrop on our kids. How they didn't hear us walk in the house, I'll never know.

"Regular? See! I knew you were taking her side."

"Holy crap. Why are you acting like a girl?"

"Hey! I feel like I should be offended."

"Why?"

"Duh. 'Cause I'm a *girl*."

"But you're not like a *girl* girl. You're just Bri."

"Umm, thanks?"

I press my lips together. My how their image of her has changed. No longer are they harboring any crush-like feelings for her.

"They're full on siblings now, huh?" Christine whispers, but her voice quivers.

I nod then look down at her. "You're going to cry again, aren't you?"

"Shut up! I can't help it," she says through giggling tears as she wipes under her eyes.

I shake my head then pull her into the kitchen but stop short when I see what they were arguing over.

The kitchen counter is littered with ingredients. Pizza sauce, a half-empty package of pepperoni, chopped green peppers and onions, crumbled sausage, a can of mushrooms, and lots (and lots) of cheese. It looks like they even tried making their own pizza crust.

How long was I gone?

Doesn't it take a while for the dough to rise or whatever it has to do?

I look at the watch on my wrist and scrunch my eyebrows.

Huh.

Turns out, the kids decided to forgo ordering pizza in and decided to make homemade.

Knowing my son, Aidan was trying to put too much cheese on the pizza.

I clear my throat, and three heads pop up from their tasks.

"Go away!" Reece yells.

"Uhh."

"You weren't supposed to be back yet. We were going to surprise you."

Christine. Bless her heart. Starts crying. Again.

I sigh.

Reece and Aidan both get a deer in the headlights look on their faces, and Bri barely contains an eye roll.

"She's fine. Just a bit emotional," I say, leaning down to kiss her on the side of her head.

"I love y-you guys so m-much."

"Mom," Bri murmurs consolingly.

"I'm sorry," she sniffles. "I'm happy. I promise."

My eyebrows reach my hairline.

"I am!" she says, nudging me with her shoulder. "Sad. But happy. Good steps, right, baby?"

"Good steps," Bri agrees.

"Okay. So, what do we have here?"

That gets Aidan and Reece snapped out of their emotional-lady trance.

"We're making homemade pizza!"

"With extra cheese," Aidan adds proudly.

Bri groans, and the five of us set to working together as best we can in my small kitchen.

Three hours later, pizzas devoured, two games of Yahtzee, one round of Watch Yo Mouth, and a heated game of Farkle, during which the boys both kept asking us "Who Farkled" and found themselves hi-lar-ious, we settle in for a movie.

Reece starts popping popcorn, and as soon as the smells wafts into the living room, I notice Christine stiffen up.

"Hey," I say, trying to get her attention. "You okay?"

She noticeably swallows, and nods her head a couple times.

"Fine," she mumbles.

"You sure? You're kind of pale."

"Just... excuse me for a minute."

She gets up and runs to the bathroom.

I exchange a glance with Bri, noticing her furrowed brow.

I follow her, worried.

"Christine?" I ask through the closed door, knuckles knocking against the door a few times.

"Yeah?"

"You okay?"

"I'm..." I hear the sounds of vomiting, and we know from Margarita Madness night how well I do with that. "I'm okay. I'll be out in a second."

"You sure? Do you... uh... want me to..."

Even though it sounds like her head is in a toilet bowl, she still manages a giggle. "No, Andy. I'm good. I think the day is just catching up with me. You know, Bri leaving and all that."

"You sure? I can get you some 7-Up or send Bri in or something."

"I promise. I'll be right out."

Toilet flush.

Gag.

Me.

Not her.

"Oh okay. Was it the food?"

She's been feeling a little off for a few days now, but she's also exhausted. She works way too hard, and Bri leaving is taking a bigger toll on her than she expected. Until the boys and I came along, it was basically just the two of them.

I hear the sink turn on then off after a while.

"Um, maybe? I don't know. I think so."

"Okay, well. I'm here if you need something."

She opens the door, a smile bright on her face.

"See? I'm fine."

I look at her closely and see nothing but truth, so I decide on giving her a hug and holding her tight, hoping that she truly is.

TWENTY-SEVEN

CHRISTINE

Five minutes ago, Andy picked me up from the coffee shop. I'm obviously capable of driving myself to and from work, and sometimes it's a pain in the butt to not have a vehicle there, but it's something that we've started doing so we get a few moments of quiet and alone time together each day. He'll bring me to work in the morning then pick me up at the end of the day.

We started it the week after I brought Bri to college. He knew I was feeling the effects of her leaving and, in true Andy fashion, recognized exactly what I needed.

Him.

Today, though, he picked me up from work early. He noticed this morning that I wasn't feeling great and asked if I wanted to try to leave earlier than usual. I wasn't in a place to fight it this morning.

For a few weeks now, something has just felt off. Not bad. Not good. Just... different, and I can't put my finger on it. I'm not willing to let it ruin our evening, though.

"What's wrong?"

I huff at how annoying it is that he's so in tune with me. "Nothing!"

He narrows his eyes at me.

"Something's wrong. What is it? Missing Bri?"

Always.

She's been gone for six weeks.

But that's not it.

"I said nothing's wrong with me! What's wrong with you?"

He chuckles, obviously on to my deflection.

"You gotta poop?"

"No I do not have to... poop." I whisper the last word.

"Hey, it's okay if you do. I have some spray if you need it. Tess gave it to all the guys for Christmas. She came to the office one day and said she was sick of it smelling like shit, literally, in here so bought us each a bottle of this spray to use when we poo."

I scrunch up my nose and can't help but ask, "Like to help you poop?"

"No." He busts out laughing, leaning over the steering wheel as he does it. When he finally regains composure, he looks at me then cracks up again. "Not to help you poop." He wipes a tear from his eye. "I'm not like an eighty-year-old man who needs prunes in his diet. It's to make it smell better when we do."

I shake my head. "I don't understand."

He pulls the bottle out of the console of his pickup and hands it to me.

"You carry it with you?"

He gives me a look. "Yeah. What if I have to poop in public?"

"Then you go poop! What do you need spray for?"

"To make it smell better! I thought we covered this already."

Oh, my goodness. I can't believe we're even having this conversation. "And you said your shit doesn't stink..."

"It doesn't! Now." He laughs to himself. "So, is that it? You need to poop when we get to your house? I promise I won't judge. And I won't smell a thing — you just spray that" —he points to the bottle that's still resting in my hands— "in the toilet first, and I swear it's like poop magic! No smell. Trust me — it's necessary in our house of boys. You'll be grateful forever to Tess for introducing me to it. You'll never have to smell my poop."

"You do realize we've been talking about poop for fifteen minutes now, right?"

He shrugs. "Yeah? What else do you want to talk about?"

The sneaky little shit! "Oh, you're good."

"I know." He grins wide then looks at my panicked face and sighs. "Christine, baby, what's wrong?"

"You won't let it go, will you?"

"Not a chance."

He pulls into a Walgreens and shoots me a grin.

He stares at me for a few beats, squeezing my hand a couple of times. "Wait here, alright?"

I look around us. "Why? What are you doing?"

"I'll be right back, then I'll explain."

"You're really confusing me right now."

He smiles softly and leans over to kiss me. It's short and sweet. He rubs his nose against mine before leaning back and grabbing the door handle. "It'll be perfectly clear in just a few minutes. I promise."

I nod my head, sitting quietly in the cab of the pickup while he strides into the store. I watch as the clerk in the front watches him enter. She stands up straighter and smooths her ponytail. *Bitch.*

These stupid hormones of mine are all over the place right now. Getting older sucks sometimes. And lately, I can't seem to get a hold of my emotions. I have had the fleeting thought that I'm going through menopause early, but that can't be it. I'm barely over the age of forty!

I lose sight of Andy when he turns down an aisle. I worry my lip, wondering what he's doing in the store, what he's buying. I'm also getting increasingly concerned over the fact that I feel so crappy lately.

As soon as Andy makes his way to the front of the store again and places his basket on the counter, the clerk's shoulders fall. His grin is wide as he pays then knocks his knuckles twice on the counter, grabbing the plastic handles of the bag and makes his way back to the pickup.

He jumps into the cab and winks at me, placing the bag in the backseat. He stares at me for a moment, the grin covering his face making my hackles rise.

"What?"

"I could feel you watching me the entire time."

"I was not!"

He's so irritatingly confident. But, he has reason to be. He turns heads everywhere he goes.

"You were."

"You're such a brat!"

"Men aren't brats, Christine." He's smirking while he shakes his head in mock disappointment.

I cross my arms over my chest and try my best to glare at him. "Well looky there, you're defying the odds because you absolutely are a brat. A cocky brat, too."

"Cranky," he teases.

"Well, maybe I wouldn't be *cranky* if you weren't so secretive."

"Fine. I see you're not going to snap out of it until I prove to you why I'm so happy and you have no reason to be cranky."

He reaches into the back seat and hands me the bag. Before

I can look inside, he pulls me over to him, meeting my lips with his in a kiss that makes my toes curl. He turns his head to the side, and I lean closer, damning the center console for being in the way.

His tongue slides against mine. I nibble on his bottom lip, and he groans, igniting a fire deep in my belly. We're sitting in the middle of a Walgreen's parking lot, making out like a couple of teenagers, and I have no cares to give. I hope that clerk is watching us, turning green with jealousy.

And apparently, I'm a sixteen-year-old.

We separate when we need to break for air, and he smiles, biting his lower lip. I love when he does that. It's endearing and sexy and everything Andy.

"I only have eyes for you, Christine. Not the Walgreens check out girl. Not some mom from the boys' school. Not the lady from the mall who was helping me when we were getting jeans for the boys. Only you. You have no reason to worry. No reason to be jealous. Never forget that, yeah?"

I'm a puddle of mush when I reply a watery, "Yeah."

Once I'm settled back in my seat, I look down at the bag still resting in my lap.

"You got something for me in there?"

"I did. Well, it's kind of for both of us. And the kids. Look inside."

I spread apart the handles and peek inside the bag, feeling an instant rush of heat flood my system.

I stare without blinking. Definitely without touching the contents of the bag.

Andy's hand gently grips my thigh and squeezes once. My eyes slowly lift from the bag to his face. I expect to see anything but the smile that's spread widely.

"You didn't know?" His voice is soft and so reassuring.

"I think the better question is, how did *you* know?"

"Christine. I'm a man, not an idiot. I do understand a little about a woman's body."

"But... what if I'm just off? Or what if..."

"What if you really are?"

"Holy shit, Andy! What if I am?"

"Then we'll have to have a discussion about your language," he teases.

"Stop it! I can't be... I'm just off. Premenopausal. Something..."

"Say the word, Christine. I've been rolling it around in my head for the last month and I gotta say, the first few times I damn near pissed myself, but now?"

"Now?"

"Now it feels pretty amazing to think about."

"Shit. I'm *such* a moron. *This* is why we have sex ed! Because women live in this state of confusion! My period is never normal. Never. It's just all over the place so I just... craaaaap. When I stress too much, I never get my period. And ever since I turned forty, it's just been weird. I can't believe I'm such an idiot."

"We weren't exactly careful, either. My fault. I should have asked. I mean, we had discussed that we had both been tested, but we were pretty irresponsible about the birth control part."

"I suppose we won't be asked to be teaching those sex ed classes anytime soon, huh?"

"Yeah. Probably not." His eyes twinkle. "I'm not some scared teenager, though. This might be unexpected, but I can't say that it's not an incredible gift."

I watch him for a little while, realizing that he's being completely honest. I shake my head, closing my eyes. "Andy, we can't... I can't."

He places his hand on mine, and I lift my lids to look at him again. "We can. We will."

I don't know how he's so calm. I suppose because he's smarter than I am and figured out that I could be pregnant. And don't think I didn't stumble over even *thinking* that word. "What's Bri gonna think? The boys?"

"They're gonna know that we're in love and the proof of it will be her."

I gasp at the surety in his voice. "Her?"

"Of course."

"You're really sure about this?"

"Nothing would make me happier than to see you carrying my baby."

The tears that I was miraculously holding back start falling down my cheeks. His eyes soften before he presses a kiss to each cheek, then to my lips. I can taste the lingering salt of my tears on his kiss. When he pulls back, he doesn't move far. He rests his forehead on mine, wrapping one hand behind my neck.

Every time I exhale he inhales, taking in my breaths as his own.

His hand comes up, caressing my cheek with his thumb.

"Is this really happening?" My voice wavering.

He lifts his head and winks. "Well, I have a pretty good guess, but we'll need to use what's in that bag to find out."

I look in the bag again and let out a giggle.

"Andy, you bought over a dozen pregnancy tests."

He gasps. "You said the word! I'm so proud of you." He lifts his hand for a high five and I hit it away, rolling my eyes.

"Why did you buy so many?"

He shrugs. "I just figured you would want to make sure."

"And the Cheetos and Wheat Thins?"

He scratches the back of his neck and looks away before admitting. "I've noticed you're eating the Wheat Thins a lot more lately." He chuckles. "I assumed it's something you're craving."

My heart could explode from the sweetness.

"And the Cheetos?"

He grins, making his dimple pop, just like Reece. "They sounded good."

"You're like a teenager sometimes."

He gasps, pressing his hand against his chest. "Are you mocking the age of your baby daddy?"

"Eww! Nope. Don't ever say *baby daddy* again."

"Is it as bad as moist?"

I nod my head and shudder. "It is."

He laughs and leans over, kissing me once again.

He places his hand on my stomach, and we both look down as his thumb makes a circle against the fabric of my shirt. "Ready to find out if I'm right?"

"You'll never let me live it down if you realized I was pregnant before me, will you?"

"Probably not."

I flop back against the seat. "Ugh. Fine. Let's go see if I'm carrying your child."

"That was quite literally the sexiest thing you've ever said to me."

"I don't think I can pee, honey."

I smile from the other side of the bathroom door, she sounds so nervous and adorable and... I am so freakin' lost to this woman.

I knock my knuckles twice against the door.

"I'm coming in, okay?"

"In here?" she screeches.

"Babe. You've peed with the door open after we've had sex. And I have boys who whip it out and pee basically wherever they please, so yes. I'm coming in. Nothing I haven't seen before."

"Okay. Just... I'm really embarrassed."

I creek the door open and poke my head in.

"Hi."

Her shoulders sag, and she bites her lower lip, letting out a pitiful laugh before she drops her head.

"Watching to see if anything will come out?"

A burst of laughter leaves her. "No, you jerk! This. It's all... I don't know. It's too much."

"Why?"

"Are you kidding me right now? Why do you think?"

"Honestly. I don't know. I'm a little ecstatic."

"You're mental," she grumbles.

"No. I just love you and I know this is pretty perfect. We didn't get a normal start, and our family is blended, and we haven't done this baby thing in a really, really long time —"

"Don't remind me."

"— and we're walking blind here, but there's no one else I'd rather do that with than you."

"How do you always know the exact right thing to say?"

"I don't. Not always. Remember when I asked if you could fold my towels differently when you were helping out with laundry at my house? Or when I asked who taught you to drive? Or what about when I told you that I was going to take away your tools when the curtain fell on my forehead after you hung them? Or what about..."

She holds up a hand to stop me from literally digging myself into a hole. "Or now? Seriously. I don't need a reminder." She rolls her eyes playfully.

"See? I'm not perfect. We're just perfect together."

"Daaaaaw! You say the sweetest things."

"Only for you, baby, only for you." I kiss her on the forehead. "Now take a piss on that stick and prove to me that I'm right and that you're carrying my little girl."

"Fine," she grumbles. "But I seriously can't pee!"

I reach down and grab one of the bottles of Vitamin Water I picked up at the store and the curly straw, because it's more fun to drink out of that way. I twist the top off and drop the straw in, lifting it to her lips, encouraging her to drink.

"Good girl," I coo when she drinks down several ounces. "Want me to tell you a story while we wait?"

"What kind of story?"

"Hmmm, how about a love story?"

"Oooh — will I like it?"

"Pretty sure you will, yes. Once upon a time..." Her giggles interrupt me so I repeat, "As I was saying, before you so rudely interrupted, once upon a time, there lived three bachelors. They weren't the best at living. That is to say, they weren't the happiest members of society. Too often, they would find themselves eating dinner in front of the TV, barely speaking to each other. They were angry and cynical and frustrated with life. Until, this raven-haired beauty and her daughter walked into their lives one day and reminded them that there's an entire world out there of lightness and it's dumb to let the darkness ruin everything. The two younger bachelors *may* have had a little crush on the daughter before they realized that they loved her for so much more than her looks. But the older of the three bachelors? Well he just fell. And fell pretty damn hard and fast for the beauty. He soon learned that it wasn't just her outside that was so gorgeous. But her inside was, too. And it made him want to be... better. And it made the younger bachelors want to be better, too. So, after talking to the youngsters" —she giggles again— "he decided that she needed to be in his life more. And possibly, probably, absolutely, forever. And then she let him get a look at her rocking bod, and he was a goner. The end."

"Oh, my gosh! You were doing so good!" She laughs so hard and then... pees.

"You're peeing though, aren't you?"

"Well you don't have to *comment* on it! Yeesh. It will scare the pee back up!"

"I'm not a doctor, but I don't think that's medically possible. Did you get it?" I ask, nodding toward the stick dangling between her legs.

She nods then swallows. "I think so."

She places it on the counter, stands up, pulls up her pants

and washes up. I take her face in my hands and lean in to kiss her. "No matter what that says, you're still mine."

"Promise?"

"Forever."

"That's a big promise."

I shrug and kiss her again.

"Easiest promise I've ever made."

I kiss her hard and long enough that we barely hear the timer I set go off. But, considering that we're waiting to find out whether or not our entire lives are about to change, we break apart and together look down at the stick.

"Holy shit," she breathes out.

"Yup."

"But..."

"Wow," I say in awe.

"I mean..."

"Yup."

"Is that all you're going to say?" she cries.

"Well... I could start with I was right, but..."

"That would go against me saying that you always know the perfect thing to say, though."

"Yup. Pretty much."

"You realize I need to pee on the rest of these, right?"

"Yup."

"Stop saying yup!"

"If I say what I want to say I'll get in trouble!"

She rolls her eyes.

For the next hour, we go through the same process of me forcing more fluids down her throat while she tries to pee in front of me. Every pregnancy test she uses comes up positive.

"They can't *all* be positive, right?"

She's still sitting on the toilet, so I crouch in front of her, rubbing a hand up her calf.

"Well, considering that you're pregnant, yes. I'm pretty sure they can."

"I'm sure sometimes a bad batch is made."

I scoff. "Oh. Okay. Yes. That's exactly what happened."

"Andy!"

"Christine!" I mock with wide eyes.

"You're not being helpful!"

"How am I not being helpful? I bought you the tests, gave you something to drink, told you a story to help you pee."

"But..."

"Sweetheart. It's going to be great. Why are you worried?"

She gives me a *duh* look. "I'm not young, Andy."

"That doesn't matter. I'm basically like a fifteen-year-old, so it youngs you down."

"That's not even a word, and hey! Rude!" She backhands me playfully.

I chuckle and pretend like she knocks me over. "We got this, yeah?"

She sniffs, and I wipe her tears.

"Yeah," she agrees, nodding her head.

"Want me to pee on one, too?"

She snorts and quickly covers her nose. "You would do that?"

"To expel your bad batch theory? Yes."

"Do you need some water?"

"Nope. I've been watching you pee for over an hour now, I've actually had to go for a while," I admit, causing her to laugh.

We swap places, though I stand up, and she peeks around, watching me.

"It's so unfair that you can just stand and go anywhere you want."

"And we don't get periods. Don't forget that."

"You're supposed to say something to make me feel better! Like, "well at least you don't grow hair on your chest.""

"Why would I say that? It's pretty awesome. And sexy. Especially when I trim it and keep that shit tamed. And don't deny that you love it — you play with it allllll the time."

"Whatever" she grumbles.

"Done." I place the test on the counter and zip up my pants then wash my hands. Because I'm a grown ass man and don't need reminded to do so, unlike my boys.

After three minutes, the timer goes off again and we both look down.

"Damn."

"Yeah, baby!" I yell, spinning her around her small bathroom. I place her on her feet and take her face in my palms, kissing over every inch of her face.

"I love you so much," I tell her before dropping to my knees and lifting up her shirt. I kiss her now-bare stomach, not yet rounded with *my* baby. "And you, munchkin, trouble causer. I love you, too."

When I get back to my feet, Christine has tears in her eyes and a watery smile.

"Andy..."

"Hey. No tears. It's going to be great. I promise."

"But the kids..."

"Will love having a little brother or sister to help take care of. Just saying, the boys always wanted a little sister, so why don't you work on that?" I tease her.

She rolls her eyes and threads her fingers through my hair. "Ha ha ha. I'll see what I can do. You know... since it hasn't *already* been decided or anything."

"I'm happy." I smile before dropping my forehead to hers.

"Really?"

"Really. This is a good thing, Christine. A blessing."

"I'm nervous."

I nod my head. "Of course, you are. I am, too. But that doesn't mean we can't be happy about it. Besides, the best things in life don't come easy. I think God just wanted to shake things up for us."

"You ready for this?" Christine asks as she places the pan of oatmeal fudge caramel bars on the table. Our way of buttering up the kids.

"No!" I scoff. "The boys might be aware their dad is dating, but now they know all that it entails."

She laughs. "You think I want Bri knowing? How am I going to convince her that she and Grady shouldn't be having dorm room sleepovers?"

I wince. "We're screwed."

"Why are you guys screwed?" Bri asks, walking into the room. I didn't even hear her come in, but it makes me happy that she's comfortable enough in my house that she doesn't knock anymore.

"My baby's home!" Christine shouts and hugs Bri tightly before she releases her and I give her a small side hug.

"How was your drive?"

"Good. Easy, since Grady drove. I got your text to come here first, though, so my stuff is still all crammed in Grady's car."

"He didn't want to come in?"

"Nah. I think Tess would flip if he didn't get home as soon as possible."

"Ready for a break?"

"So ready! I know it's only a long weekend, but it will be nice to not think much for a few days."

"Want a bar?" Christine holds up the pan right in her face, and I wince again.

It's obvious she's sucking up.

"What happened?" Bri asks, lifting a bar and biting off a chunk. She rolls her eyes and groans. "So good," she mumbles. "You have to make these for me every time you give me a care package at school, okay?"

"Stop talking about leaving again! You just got home!" Christine cries.

I chuckle and pull her into my side, kissing her on the head.

Bri watches us and smiles softly. "Relax, Mom. At least you have Andy and the boys here for you."

"I'm outnumbered by boys! Don't you feel the least bit sorry for me?"

I roll my eyes and turn to the fridge, grabbing a few bottles of Gatorade and a water when I notice the time on the clock. The boys should be getting home from football practice any minute now. Since we live close to the school, they're able to walk home.

Bri settles in at the table, tucking her legs underneath her.

"Head's up," I shout before I toss her a water, which she catches quickly with a smile.

"When do the boys get home?"

"Soon."

And before she can respond, Reece and Aidan come storming in the house. Stinky and hungry.

They don't even notice Bri sitting at the table. They have one thing on their minds. Raiding the fridge and pantry.

"Boys."

"Yeah, Dad?" Reece asks, head shoved into the fridge. He turns around with some lunchmeat and cheese in his hands before he notices Bri.

"Bri!" he shouts, setting down the food, causing Aidan to stumble out of the pantry.

They both run over and give her sweaty hugs. "Holy crap!" she says, pinching her nose.

"Yup," I say, nodding my head.

They both sheepishly apologize but grin while doing it.

"How was practice, boys?" Christine asks, setting a bar on a plate for each of them.

"Good. Kicked our butts tonight. So many up downs."

"Coach Mac is tough."

"Freshmen football a little different?" Bri teases.

They both just smile around a mouth full of food before it hits them. "Wait. Why are you here?" Aidan asks.

"Fall break."

"You suck! I wish we got fall break!"

"So, why was it so important to come here rather than the house?" Bri asks.

"Andy and I have some news, but we wanted you three to be here together."

"Okay?"

I clear my throat before launching in and gesture so the five of us are sitting in the living room. Once settled, Christine in the chair and me sitting on the armrest beside her, I take a deep breath. "You kids know that we're close." I pause and look around to see the kids' faces masked in confusion. "What I mean is, when a man loves a woman..." The kids groan. "I guess what I'm trying to say..."

"Dad. Just spit it out."

"Right. Well it seems that we're going to be a family of six."

"I'm sorry, what?" Bri asks.

"I, um. Yeah. So, I thought this would be easier to explain, but it turns out not so much. Christine hasn't been feeling the best lately, and after taking about a dozen tests and going to the doctor, we discovered that she's pregnant. In about seven months, we'll be welcoming a little boy or girl into our family."

"You guys are going to have a baby?" Reece asks, eyes wide.

"Indeed, we are."

"Mom?"

Christine nods her head.

"Wow. I'm sorry, but... how?"

"Can you have a girl?" Aidan requests.

"Yes," I say as Christine, so knowledgeable, points out, "I can't really control that, kiddo, and it's already been decided."

"Well, I want a baby sister."

"Me, too."

"Bri? You okay there?"

"I'm just in shock. I mean — are you happy? I know that sounds mean, but are you okay? Will the baby be okay? You're not..."

"Young. I know. And we'll go to plenty of checkups, and so far, everything is good."

Bri blows out a breath. "Wow. I so didn't see that coming. I thought maybe you were moving in together and getting married."

I know Christine wants that, and so do I. I just haven't found the right ring or the right way to ask her yet.

"I'm happy, Bri," Christine says, reaching out to hold her daughter's hand.

"I'm happy for you guys."

"Boys?"

"Yeah?"

"How you feeling about all this?"

Aidan, ever the smart ass. "It seems like maybe you two didn't pay enough attention in health class. You know what leads to babies..."

"Aidan," I growl, but he just smiles that cheeky smile.

"We're cool. This is actually exciting. We've never had a little brother or sister."

"So, you guys are all on board with this?"

"Well, obviously it wouldn't change anything if we weren't, but yeah. This is kind of amazing. I'm finally gonna be a big sister!"

"Hey!" the boys shout in unison. I notice how Christine gets tears in her eyes immediately. In technical terms, we aren't a family of five or known each other too long. But the kids have embraced our relationship as if they were siblings.

She rolls her eyes and looks at them. "You know what I mean."

"Still..." Aidan grumbles.

My heart feels like in the Grinch movie when it just keeps expanding and growing. I didn't know that I could be so full of love until now.

"And then there were six," Christine says wistfully, placing her hand on her stomach. I cover hers with mine and lean down to kiss her on the lips.

"Gross! That's what got you two into this in the first place!" Reece laughs.

THIRTY

CHRISTINE

"Hey lady! What's happening?" I ask, bringing Carly in for a hug. We haven't seen a lot of each other lately with Balance getting ready to open, school back in session, and me not feeling the best. Not to mention the amount of time I spend with Andy and the boys, and visiting Bri when we can. When I pull back, I take a look at Carly and notice that her normal smile is missing.

"What's wrong?"

She looks away then back to me.

"Can we go to your office?"

"Um, okay? Yeah. But you're making me nervous."

"I'm sorry. I just think we need some privacy."

I wring my hands together as we make our way to the office, and I take a seat on the couch next to her.

"What's going on?"

"First, I need you to know that I don't like gossip, and this seems like gossip to me, but..."

"Just say it already," I tell her, trying to keep the growing nervousness and fear from my voice.

"I know what happened with Todd."

"What?"

"I said..."

"I know what you said. But I want you to *clarify* what you meant. From the beginning, Carly. What the hell are you talking about?"

"Heather. She's been talking. And maybe she's just feeding everyone a line of bull crap because, let's be honest, she's not really known for *her* honesty but... I don't know. I think, maybe... is it true?"

"What's she saying?"

"That she and Todd had an affair," she whispers sadly.

I feel the blood drain from my face and sweat start beading on the back of my neck. I lean over, not knowing if I'm going to throw up or pass out or possibly both.

"I don't... what did she say exactly? Where did you hear this?"

She licks her lips and reaches over to grab my hand in hers. "First, you need to understand something. Heather is crazy. Everyone knows this."

I nod my head, hoping she'll just get on with it.

"Tess is the one who told me. She said she wanted you to hear it from me. Heather came into her shop the other day, saying she was looking for an interior decorator."

My breathing goes shallow at the thought of Heather being back in town. Of messing with the boys' lives. With their hearts. "What? She's back? Like living here?"

Carly shakes her head. "No. Thank goodness. Tess said she wouldn't work with her and didn't travel that sort of distance anyway. I guess she's living in Illinois or something. Anyway. I don't think that's why she was here anyway. The vindictive slut."

I purse my lips together because hearing Carly use any sort of swear word always cracks me up.

"So yeah. She wasn't here searching for a business relationship. She was here to spread craziness. She said that the day Todd found out he had cancer, you found out he was sleeping with her."

I gasp. It's true — well, partly — but it stings. Hearing the words from someone else's mouth. Even after all these years.

"Christine. It's worse."

"How can it be worse?" I part groan part screech.

"She said that the only reason you're with her husband, is because she was with yours."

Everywhere I look, eyes are on me. At the grocery store. Filling up my pickup with gas. When I pulled up to the school to get the boys from practice.

My phone rings, and I look down and see Barrett's name lit up. I swipe to answer immediately.

"Hey, Barrett! What's up?" I say by way of answering, scrunching my eyebrows at two moms standing next to their car, glancing at me every so often.

Would I get in trouble if I flipped them the bird sitting in the school parking lot?

"Uh, man. We got troubles."

"Shit. What'd Gavin do now?"

Gavin has been screwing up left and right lately. Well, no, that's not true. He's been screwing up since we hired him. Lazy shit.

"It wasn't Gavin."

"Okay, then what?" I ask irritably. All the looks I'm getting starting to piss me off.

"It's Heather."

I groan and throw my head back against the head rest and pull my beanie off my head, tossing it in the passenger seat.

I scrub my hand through my hair and down my face.

"What's she doing now?"

"Flapping her tongue. In a big way. It's bad, Andy. Catastrophic."

"What could she be flapping her tongue about? Divorce is done. Final. Has been for months."

"Christine."

"No. We were never together until the divorce was finalized. Why the hell do you think I waited so long to get with her? Wasted months not being with her."

"That's not what I mean. She's flapping her tongue about Christine," he explains, then continues on after a beat of silence, "and Todd."

I sit up straighter in my seat and lean over my steering wheel, looking to see if the boys are coming out of the building yet.

I don't see them, so I figure I've got a few minutes to clear this shit up before they get here.

"Spit it out, Barrett. What the hell are you talking about?"

"Man. You know I joke around a lot about hating secrets and loving to know everything and spreading it around, but I'm not really that way. I mean, I am with the fun shit, but this... dammit. I would never. This isn't me gossiping. You need to talk to Christine." I hear him blow out a breath. "Apparently Todd cheated on her. Did you know that?"

I sit for a few seconds wondering what I'm supposed to say to that. I don't want to betray Christine by spilling her secret, but it sounds like he already knows. Still, I say nothing.

"I take it by your silence this isn't new news to you. Did you also know that when he cheated it was... shit, man, it was with Heather?"

"What?"

I touch my chest to make sure it's still beating because his words feel like it stopped my heart.

He continues on as if he hasn't just rocked the ever loving shit out of the already rocking boat I was sitting in. "And she's saying the only reason Christine is with you is revenge against her. Christine's with her husband because she was with Todd."

And just like that, my world falls out from beneath me all at once.

Memories of Christine's words describing her husband's affair rush back to me but never once do I remember her mentioning anything about it being with Heather.

Is it possible?

Did I misread her this entire time?

Was she holding on to that much anger over Todd cheating that she'd actually get pregnant on purpose?

I can't believe I'm in this situation all over again.

With a liar.

Except this time?

I got the girl pregnant before I discovered her betrayal.

Christine's known this entire time that Heather has been a cheater for years.

And not only that, it was with her husband.

She... what? Thought the ultimate way to get back at Heather was to make me fall in love with her?

Prove to Heather that she's the better woman?

Did she really plan to get pregnant?

We were stupid and never discussed birth control, but still...

The questions that are rolling through my head are endless, as is the anger boiling up inside.

"Dad! Hey, you okay?"

The sound of Reece's voice and the door closing jars me back to reality.

I didn't even realize that I'd hung up on Barrett. My phone is resting on my thigh as I look blankly out the windshield.

"Dad?" Reece's hand is on my forearm, and I look over at him, then to Aidan in the backseat. Both have confused looks on their faces.

I clear my throat and try to give my best, most reassuring smile. "Yeah. Bud. I'm good. How was practice?" I reach over and clap Reece on the shoulder and squeeze once.

They both give me weird looks. "Good, Dad. Practice was good. So was school. Are you sure you're okay?" Aidan asks, leaning forward in his seat.

"Just a bit off today, boys. I'll be fine. Ready to head home?"

"I'm starved!"

"Is Christine coming over?"

Shit.

Christine

I GET in my car and drive as quickly as I can to Andy's house, wanting to be there when he gets home.

I don't want him to hear it from anyone else but me. And if Heather is running her mouth, he's bound to hear it.

I open the garage door using the opener he gave me and notice he's already here. I park on the opposite side of his pickup and shake out my hands, trying to calm my nerves.

The second I step out of my car, Andy is pushing through the door to the house, marching toward me.

"Is it true?" he growls.

All I can do is nod.

"You... this is all revenge on Heather?" he asks, genuine shock covering his face. His gaze drops to my stomach, that's now rounded slightly, and points. "You did *this* all to get back at some bitch who means nothing?" This time his voice isn't holding back the venom.

I stumble back a few steps, shaking my head wildly. "Andy, no. Let me explain."

"Oh, I know enough. Trust me. I get it. I can't believe I fell for another liar," he scoffs, scrubbing a hand down his face.

"No, you don't get it. Please," I plead with him. "Where are the boys? Are they inside?"

"They're next door at Nolan's house. I was getting ready to come over to you when you pulled up."

I nod my head. "Let's go inside. You have to let me explain this."

"Explain what? That you found Heather — my ex-wife — having sex with your husband and didn't think you should tell me? And then, by some random stroke of fate, I came into Dreamin' Beans, and you latched onto your one chance to get back at the bitch your husband cheated on you with all those years ago?"

"That is *not* how it happened. You know this, Andy. You *know* my heart. It wasn't like that at all. Yes. Heather is the person who Todd had an affair with. That part is true. Yes, I admit I hid it from you. Not just from you, though. From *everyone*. You know I didn't want to tell anyone about it. It wasn't important."

"Not important?" he screams. "How can me not knowing *years* ago that my wife was cheating on me be *not important*?"

I stay silent, not knowing how to get through to him.

He already knew. He admitted that time and time again.

So, the fact that I knew Heather cheated is not what's got him so angry.

The misguided idea that I got pregnant on purpose — all for some crazy revenge against Heather years later — is what has him ready to end everything.

"Please. Just listen to me," I whisper.

"I'm done listening."

"What?"

"I said, I'm done. I'll be there for the baby. She's a part of me, and whether you planned to get pregnant as some sort of twisted revenge plot or not, I would never take that out on our precious baby girl. But you and I? We're done."

"We are *not* done, Andy. You won't even listen to me!"

I cover my mouth when my sobs begin to come out uncontrollably. I rest my hand on my belly, praying for the baby to calm my ever-growing nerves.

He stalks over to me and leans down to get in my face. Not in a menacing way, but in a way that is sure to keep my attention. "Oh, we so are, Christine. I was screwed over by one woman before. Duped into thinking that I had to stay with her for the sake of my children, but I know better now."

Well now I'm just angry. To be put in the same bucket as Heather, of all people? "You can't be serious. You haven't even let me tell you my side of things! You think I got pregnant on purpose? Fell in love with you on purpose? Did all this to what? Show Heather that you would love me instead of her? Are you even listening to yourself?"

He stays silent, staring daggers into me.

"You are wrong, Andy. Whatever is going through your head. Whatever you're thinking right now is wrong. I knew Heather cheated on you with Todd. You're forgetting that I found out my husband cheated on me and that he had cancer *in the same day*. My top priority was not running off to tell on Heather. I'm sorry if I made the wrong choice."

"You had *years* to tell me, Christine. *Years*."

"You're right. I'll give you that. But you know what? It wasn't my place. And after Todd passed away, everything else just kind of faded. I'm sorry if I made the wrong choice in not telling you, but do *not* throw me into the same *anything* with Heather. You know better than that, and if you'd just get out of your head for one second, you'd figure it out."

I get in my car and slam the door shut, backing out of the driveway and praying that I'm able to make it home safely before breaking down entirely.

And when I get there, I see the cars of Carly, Tess, and Lauren waiting in my driveway.

"We have ice cream," Lauren says when she makes her way to my car. She hugs me tightly. "Are you okay?" she whispers in my ear, giving me a tight hug.

I nod even though I feel nothing close to okay.

Wondering if I'll ever feel close to okay again.

"Tess, just wait until we're all here," Barrett's voice yells down the hallway, and I scrunch my eyebrows together and throw the pen I had been spinning on my finger onto my desk.

"Oh, you're gonna stop me? Seriously?"

"Fine. Your funeral, pretty girl."

"What the—?" I mumble as I stand up from my desk and slowly take a few steps to the open doorway of my office, only to be shoved back inside by my boss's irate wife.

"Just where in the hell do you think you're going?"

"Uhh..."

"Did you warn him?" Josh's voice comes out in a rush as he starts charging into my office. The second he sees Tess staring me down, he quickly begins backing away only to stumble into his wife and Carly. "Abort mission! Abort mission! Andy, it's every man for himself! You're on your own!"

"Idiots," Lauren mumbles.

"Complete morons," Tess agrees.

"Ladies," Carly says with a raise of her eyebrows and nod in my direction.

"Oh, right. No. They're not the moronic idiots. It seems you're the current owner and the reigning champion of that particular title." Tess glares at me.

"What did I do?"

"Are you kidding me?" Carly screeches.

Lauren places a hand on Carly's arm and motions to all of us to have a seat. Josh, suddenly super helpful dimwit that he is, pushes another one in from the office he shares with Barrett so all the women can have their own.

"Aww, thanks, babe. You're the best," Lauren says in a voice so sickeningly sweet it makes me want to vomit.

"Anything for you, baby," Josh croons.

"Gag me," I mutter, which, apparently, I didn't do quiet enough, and six pair of eyes turn to me, glaring.

"Shut up. It's not your turn to talk. We'll tell you when it is," Carly says, slamming her fist down on the desk, causing all of us to jump. Carly's normally sweet and gentle nature is clearly missing.

"You. Are a jackass. Supreme Grade A assholic jackass."

"Wow, Tess. Tell me how you really feel," I grumble.

"I would, but I'm a lady and don't use unkind words."

"But you just..."

"Right. That was me being kind." She pauses for dramatic effect then adds with a hard voice, "Jackass."

"Is there a point to this meeting, aside from you guys calling me names?"

Carly pipes in, "Of course, there is. You're being stupid, and we're either going to slap the stupid out of you or you're going to have to sit and listen to us. Which is it gonna be?"

"I gotta be honest. Neither sounds appealing at the moment."

"That means he's all for the slapping!" James's voice bellows from somewhere in the office.

"I thought you were on my side!"

"Not when you're behaving like a total tool, I'm not!"

"Fuck me. Is anyone not in on it?"

"Christine," Lauren, who's been oddly quiet, tells me.

"Okay, we're getting nowhere," Tess, always the voice of reason, well, unless she's calling me mean names, cuts in. "Andy. This is an intervention. Because you're being a jackass of epic proportions."

"Oh, so her dating me to get back at Heather isn't her being a jackass of epic proportions?"

"Are you literally insane? Certifiable?"

I glare at Barrett, who has just poked his head in the doorway.

"Get your ugly mugs in here rather than shouting down the entire office," I shout back. "Wusses!" Chairs scrape, and suddenly the three stooges are pushing chairs into my already small office, only made much smaller by the fact that I have six extra people staring me down.

All the husbands kiss their wives gently then turn cheeky smiles my way.

"Who's the jackass now?"

"Still you," Carly says with a smile.

James smirks at his wife then leans forward on his elbows, looking straight at me. "Andy. You're one of my best friends. You know this. This past year with you helping me? Man, I couldn't have done it without you. And I got a first row seat to the weird courting ritual that you two had going on. I watched as every time she came into a room your entire demeanor changed. Your face lit up and it was like you inhaled a deep breath, finally being at peace or something." I open my mouth to interrupt him, but Tess throws a hand in front of my face, effectively telling me to shut up. He chuckles at her. They're so much alike it's freaky — and they're not even twins.

"As I was saying. I watched as every time you were around her you became calm. Relaxed. The same way that all of us" —he gestures around the room— "are when our husband or wife is around. And she was the same. When you were around her? Her entire face would light up just like yours would. And no, jackass, it wasn't because of some weird plan to make you fall in love with her. That happened on its own. Just like her falling in love with you happened on its own. Do you really, truly believe that it's in Christine to act that way?"

I think for a moment before blowing out a heavy breath. "It's just... you have no idea what it's like. To walk in and see your wife like that? That shit doesn't just go away. And to find out that Christine knew all along?"

"Andy," Lauren says gently, "Is that really what you're upset about? That she knew? You've said time and again that you already knew Heather had cheated long before you caught her."

"I did but..."

"But nothing, Andy," Tess interrupts.

"Stop being such a moron, open your damn eyes, and see what's right in front of you! Do you really want to be the dumbass who loses everything because of your stubborn pride? What are you thinking?" Carly ends on a shout.

Everyone's eyes widen at her yelling and she blushes lightly, biting her lip. James leans over, pulls her lip out of her teeth's grasp with his thumb and murmurs something to her that causes her to blush even deeper.

"Sorry. Got a little carried away there. But you've gotta know, she's not that way."

"And how do I know that, huh? Heather once promised in front of three hundred of our closest friends and family and God that she'd be faithful to me for the rest of our lives. I believed her. Why wouldn't I? What if Christine is just a really good actress? I mean — she fooled all of you all these years into believing that Todd was a stand-up guy."

Josh leans forward, his elbows resting on his knees. "I know you're pissed. I get it. Really, I do. Clearly, even after that bitch is gone, she's still managing to mess with your mind. Think about it. Do you honestly think Christine is a liar? Or is that Heather. She's pissed that you and the boys moved on and knew she could fuck with you by spreading shit around town. But if you want to believe Heather... then maybe you don't deserve Christine after all."

And on that, the six of them stand up and walk out the door.

Before Lauren is out the door, though, she walks over and gently lays her hand on my cheek then hauls back and slaps me. "Make smarter choices," she says before storming out of my office, while I sit holding my stinging cheek and thinking on the words that are stinging my heart.

THIRTY-THREE
ANDY

The boys are at their friend Simon's house for the night. Something I've learned about having twins is that when and where one goes, often does the other. Well, at least with my boys. They have mutual friends, and in a lot of ways they're identical. Obviously in looks, but in the things they like to do; their interests. But in a lot of ways they're different. Opposites. And I think that's part of the appeal when their friends invite them over. They both bring something different to the table.

I've cleaned the kitchen, vacuumed, basically power washed their bathroom, and now understand why moms consistently complain about the fact that boys have shit for aim.

I shower, make myself something to eat, turn on Netflix, get bored, turn it off. Or rather, struggle to avoid thinking of Christine. Something I *really* had to do while showering.

I tug on my hair, glad my hair has grown out and is now longer to pull on as I pace in my living room. I feel like a bull, waiting its turn in the chute to rip into some cowboy who thinks he can overcome the beast.

The carpet under my feet getting more and more worn as I continue to walk the same path. Back and forth. Back and forth.

Storming into the kitchen, I rip open the fridge door and pull out a beer. Twisting the cap off, I throw it onto the counter, watching as it bounces a few times then spins on its top until it comes to a stop. Once again, the house is quiet and I can't stand it. My thoughts threaten to take over, reminding me of the ass chewing I received from my friends a few days ago. Reminding me of what I lost.

Christine.

Son of a bitch.

My *baby*.

Our baby.

Fuck.

They're right.

Of course, they're right.

I know Christine.

Our love isn't made up or misconstrued or created out of some wild revenge plot. It isn't fake. In fact, aside from the boys, it's the most real thing in my life.

I chug down half the bottle in one pull, slamming it back onto the counter with a loud thud.

I know I should let it go.

Actually, I know that I was wrong to even accuse her in the first place.

I know it's not her fault that Heather cheated eons ago.

I know she had no obligation to tell me. We didn't even know each other very well then. And, she was not only dealing with learning of Todd's dumb ass cheating, but also with the fact that he had cancer. Telling some guy she barely knew that his wife was a cheater was, I'm sure, the last thing on her mind. Sure, she could have said something to me after we started seeing each other but I also understand why she didn't.

But the bigger realization? I also know that she didn't start anything with me to get revenge on Heather. It's just one more of Heather's stupid lies that I got trapped into believing.

Part of her venom.

I think back over the time Christine and I spent together.

From the time I walked into Dreamin' Beans right after I caught Heather with her boy toy, every single moment we spent together has brought me nothing but happiness.

I went to her.

Not the other way around.

Why am I letting Heather's vindictive lies still get to me? Still change the course of my life?

Even divorced, with no legal ties to my boys, she's still a cunning bitch, trying to control me.

And I let her.

Like an stupid mother fucker.

With an animalistic roar, I grip the edge of the counter, jerking my body back and forth, trying to steady myself and my raging emotions.

Out of the corner of my eye, I glance at my keys in the bowl then look away quickly, not wanting to be tempted. Christine deserves more than me showing up on a whim.

"Dammit," I growl.

I storm over, pissed at myself that I couldn't resist temptation for even two seconds and rip my keys out of the bowl, shoving them into the pocket of my jeans. I open the garage door and stand in place with my hands on my hips, wondering if I'm really going to leave. That lasts just a few seconds also. Once in my pickup, I push the button to start it up, throw it in reverse, and peel out of my driveway.

Driving around town, I'm feeling pretty proud of myself. I just needed out of the house. The quiet is what was making me go insane.

There's this song that has a line about being tangled up in barbed wire. Damn it all if that's not the truth. I feel like the time when I was a kid and went to a buddy's house who lived in the country. He had four-wheelers and, like a typical city kid who had no clue what I was doing, somehow lost control of the four-wheeler his family let me drive and ended up in the barbed wire fence. I had no idea how it had happened, or what to do to remove it. But his mom came out, calm as you please, and pulled up on the top half of the wires, pushing down with her feet on the rest, and my buddy got it pushed out of the tangled mess I had created like it was no big deal.

That's exactly how I feel. My heart is so tangled up in Christine and won't let her go, and I'm starting to wonder if this is my life now or if I even need to keep fighting this. Get over myself, recognize *I* was the one who fucked up. Not her.

I need to just pull myself out of the mess and apologize. Grovel like the moron that I am.

And move on.

With Christine.

Because I'm not entirely sure I can really move on without her by my side.

I know all those things I'm feeling are totally illogical. And I also know that if I don't pull my head out of my ass soon, I'll not only lose her forever, but I'll lose a little bit of my children, too. Not just the baby she's growing in her beautiful stomach. But my boys, too, who have taken to her like she's an angel who was dropped right into our path.

My heart knows I need to move on. Accept it, apologize, and crawl on my knees for her to forgive my jackassery.

But my head?

That's in my way.

I didn't think it possible to have more hatred for Heather, but in this moment, I do.

She didn't only screw me and the boys over.

She screwed over Christine, too.

How many men did she try to seduce?

How many times was she successful?

Why wasn't I enough for her?

Why weren't the boys enough for her to realize that she was being selfish?

Why am I going through all these stupid questions again?

Before I know it, I'm sitting in front of Christine's house.

I knew I would end up here, my hands itching to pull on the handle, letting me out of the confines of my safe space. The light in her living room is on, and I can see the shadow of her walking around before she disappears. I crane my head, hoping to get another glimpse of her. Needing it more than I need the air in my lungs.

The desire to storm up to her house, throw open the door and take her into my arms, begging her to give me another chance is heavy. Desperate for some feeling, I give in and rush across the street, bounding up the stairs.

Memories assault me the second I'm on her porch. The time the boys and I picked her up to go to the haunted house. When I picked her up to go to the cabin for a long weekend. When she stood in the kitchen and taught them not only how to cook, but how to bake a cake, only for them to sneakily help me ask her on our first date. Of the evening I picked her up at her house for the first time we would go out to dinner, ending up at the lake where we sat on a blanket on the beach under the stars.

The feeling of her pinky finger always linking with mine whenever we were near.

Of the first time my lips touched hers in this very spot I'm standing right now. It wasn't our first kiss, but it is still burned into my memory.

I knew the flame between us would burn bright. Our first

kiss only confirmed that. My lips touched hers, and I could feel the fire ignite. The longevity of what we were starting.

When I walked through this door, holding a bag from Walgreens full of pregnancy tests and bottles of vitamin water, dragging her behind me. I knew she was pregnant. There wasn't a doubt in my mind. And I couldn't even bring myself to be upset about it. I was, and still am, damn near giddy at the thought of her carrying my child.

So why can't I get over it?

Because it hurt my pride. Wounded my heart.

Scared the shit out of me.

I bend over at the waist, feeling overwhelmed by the emotions clawing at my heart.

My love.

My baby.

My future is sitting inside this house.

Not being with her, my heart is torn to pieces.

She doesn't deserve the words I spewed at her.

She doesn't deserve the doubt I showed.

I don't deserve to still be torn apart by Heather's vicious lies.

It's not fair to either of us. Or the boys.

Gaining the courage, I raise my hand to knock.

Planning to beg until she forgives me.

Needing her to understand my head is screwed up and I'm blindly walking through this.

Just as my fist readies, the lights go out. Of the house and my heart.

I lower my hand, wondering if I should knock anyway, or if I should let it go.

Pissed at myself for losing courage so quickly. For doubting myself.

Punking out, I hang my head and sit down on the top step of the porch.

"Dammit," I whisper into the wind.

Resting my elbows on my knees, I scrub my hands through my hair and link my fingers on the back of my head.

My throat closes up as I anxiously try to take in a breath.

Once.

Twice.

Three times.

What am I going to do? Life shouldn't be this complicated. Right now, it feels like an episode of Jerry Springer.

So, tell me, Andy, what brings you here today?

Well, gee, Jerry. See, my wife cheated on me, left me and our boys without a glance backward, which didn't piss me off nearly as much as when I found out my pregnant-with-my-child girl-friend's dead husband had an affair with my ex-wife years ago but had known for years that it had happened and never told me.

Why was I so hung up on the fact that she kept that from me?

Why did it feel like a betrayal?

Why did I have to be such an asshole to her when she did tell me? Rather than just listen to her and try to figure out how to move forward.

Do I really want to live this way? To find a way to live without Christine in my bed, in my life as nothing more than just the mother to my child? I decided I didn't want to yester-day, but why am I still dragging my feet?

The answer to every single one of those questions?

Hell no.

The decision I made when I discovered she knew about Heather's indiscretions years ago as well as the accusations I placed on her that she could have possibly planned this entire relationship and pregnancy snakes its way through my veins, turning them hot then ice cold. Recognition of my mistake takes over, and I know I messed up royally.

But I also know she deserves more than me just coming by in the middle of the night, begging for her forgiveness.

I messed up and need to own up to it.

The grand gesture.

She's worth it.

And I know exactly what to do to prove that I'm all in.

I just hope I'm not too late.

I remember pretty clearly after Grady got in trouble for beating up Dawson who was getting a little too aggressive with Bri. It felt like the world stopped for a few minutes and nothing seemed right. And he isn't even my kid. Though now, after getting to know Bri, I'm pretty damn grateful to Grady for doing what he did. But, what I remember most is that Barrett said to me then that it was one of the worst phone calls they ever imagined getting. That their son had been brought in to the police station. Because he'd been in a fight.

Even though Aidan isn't in jail, thank goodness, considering he's only fourteen, a call letting me know my son was in a fight and I needed to come to the school isn't fun either.

I walk up to the office and the secretary simply points to the principal's office. The door is partially closed, and I can see Aidan sitting in a chair, his head leaned back against the wall behind him. The secretary gives me a sympathetic smile, and I nod once before trudging toward the door.

This is not at all how I expected today to go. I planned on begging Christine for forgiveness, hoping that she'd understand my temporary bout of insanity, accept my apology, and after at least twenty-four hours of make-up sex, we'd all live happily ever after.

Instead...

I knock twice, even though the door's slightly open.

"Come in," Principal Moore states gruffly. "Hey there, Mr. Simpson. Thanks for coming in."

I nod my head again and swallow. I wasn't a bad kid growing up, but I did find myself in the principal's office a few times, and even though I'm not the one in trouble now, it still makes my body break out into a sweat. I swallow hard, glancing over at Aidan, who rather than looking scared like I admittedly am, looks furious. His beat-up gaze focused on the person sitting across the room. He has dried blood by his nose and what looks like a pretty good shiner developing on his left eye.

The other boy, who I'm assuming is the one responsible for the way Aidan looks, is holding an ice pack to his cheek but also looks just as roughed up as Aidan. His expression is one of fear, though. His, what I assume are his parents, are already sitting next to him.

I clear my throat and take a seat next to Aidan, resting my elbows on my knees while I glance over at him before focusing my attention back on the principal.

"What's going on, Mr. Moore?"

I realize I can call him Patrick, considering we're both adults, but like I said, being in the principal's office makes me nervous and twitchy. Plus, there's a level of respect I want my boys to witness.

"It seems we have two boys who aren't ready to fess up."

"Care to explain what happened?" I raise my eyebrows at Aidan then look over at the boy and his parents, trying to gauge their mood, however they're not giving too many clues away.

"We're waiting on one more person to arrive, but let's go ahead and get started, shall we?" I wonder who else could be coming, but he continues before I can voice my question. "Boys, let me tell your parents what happened, what we heard from the other students. No interruptions, okay? I want to hear a response from both of you, but not until I've finished and it's your turn."

"Yes, Mr. Moore." Their response is instant and at the same time, reminding me of the no-nonsense leadership of Mr. Moore.

"Good. Andy, Ben, Amanda. Obviously, your boys were in a bit of a fight today." Amanda looks ready to start sticking up for her boy, but Mr. Moore raises a hand, and she relaxes back into her seat. "Let me finish, please. Neither of your boys have been in here for fighting until now. Before any of you start pointing fingers or blaming anyone, you need to know, it's not as if either of them are in the habit of throwing a punch for no reason."

Before he can continue, there's a subtle knock on the door, and the secretary pops her head in.

"Mr. Moore. Christine Jameson is here."

"Send her in."

I scrunch my eyebrows and look at Aidan, who doesn't look me in the eye. When the door opens all the way, I can't help but swing my eyes to meet hers. I suck in a breath when our eyes meet, not having been this close to her in what feels like centuries. She quickly shifts her attention to Aidan, her eyes softening. Mr. Moore pulls another chair around, placing it on the other side of Aidan.

She breezes past me, the scent of coffee and something sweet wafting over me.

Before I can stop myself, I inhale deeply, hating that I've missed her scent almost as much as I've missed her. And I have. So much more than I expected to.

"Hey, Patrick. How's it going, old man?" she teases, earning a bright smile in return.

"Could be better, Christine. What? No coffee?"

"You have my boy in lockup and you expect me to bring you coffee? No way. You come in and pay for it."

I want to laugh at her natural banter with him, though he has been in our school system a long time and was Bri's principal, too, but I'm a little stuck on the 'my boy' statement she made.

A term that slid out her lips so easily that I know it wasn't forced or fake.

That came direct from her heart, and dang if it doesn't make my heartbeat pound in my ears.

She leans down and hugs Aidan, who returns it, and then looks at him closely, inspecting his injuries.

Her dark hair is pulled up in a messy bun; she's wearing a pair of black leggings, sneakers and one of my work hoodies that's so big on her it covers her butt. And damn if she doesn't look more beautiful than I've ever seen her.

After she settles into the chair, she reaches over and grabs Aidan's hand.

"Sorry I was late. Did you explain what happened?"

"I was just getting to that," Patrick tells her; a look of fondness and adoration crosses his face as he watches her. It has my fists clenching. She might not be mine anymore, but that doesn't mean I'm okay with her being someone else's either. Though I highly doubt that's the look he's giving her.

And I'm going to get her back.

There's no other option for me.

I knew it after the six amigos hijacked my office with an impromptu intervention.

I knew it the night I drove over to her house.

But really, I knew it the second I walked away from her.

"Get on with it, then."

He chuckles at her then stands to move around the front of his desk, leaning back against it.

"Here's what we've gathered from what the other students have told us, who witnessed the fight before Mrs. Lyons intervened."

"Dana pulled them apart?" Christine laughs, and Amanda starts giggling.

"Oh, I bet she loved that," Amanda agrees.

"She's probably been waiting all year for her chance to get in the middle of some catfight."

"Hey! It wasn't a catfight! That's what girls do! And... it should be known that she pulled my ear! And called me a punk!" Aidan says incredulously.

Christine pats him on the arm.

"Be lucky that's all she did. She does Crossfit. She's strong."

"She pulled *me* by the hair. I probably have a bald spot." Amanda scrunches her eyebrows and stretches her neck, looking at her son's head.

"That would be a blessing to have that mop of hair cut off," Ben grumbles to his son, and I have to choke back my laughter.

"From the sounds of it, you were both acting like punks, so the term seems appropriate." At the sound of my voice, Christine's head jerks up, and she stares at me.

"Actually, she calls me punk all the time. I think it's her way of saying she loves me best," Aidan says proudly with a cheeky grin, gaining our attention again.

"Aidan," I snap, and this time his smile dies, and he shifts in his seat. "We need to get back to the reason why we're here."

"Right. Boys, from my understanding, one boy made some comments and the other boy didn't stand for it. The ending result was they used their fists. Preston? Aidan? Would you like to expand on this?"

Oh, this is rich. *Of course,* his name is Preston.

I bite back the snort that's threatening to escape.

"Nope," Aidan says, full of smartass.

"Aidan," Christine says quietly.

He shakes his head at her, pleading with his eyes before mumbling, "Not worth it, Christine."

"I think it is. Care to explain to us?" I ask him, this time my tone is softer, less angry.

He looks over to me and sighs then looks over at Preston, who narrows his eyes at him, glaring the best he can. Aidan rolls his eyes.

"He said some bad stuff. I didn't like what he was saying."

"What do you mean, he said some bad stuff?" Amanda asks, disbelief that her boy could do something wrong lacing her words.

"It was nothing, Mom. Nothing that he didn't know already. Everybody—"

"What's that supposed to mean?" Ben interrupts.

Aidan's knee is bouncing up and down until he drops his head and groans. When he gains the courage to speak again he looks at me, the dejected look in his eyes breaking my heart. "He called Heather a whore, and that she'd probably love him better because his name was Preston, and he called Dad a loser who couldn't keep his wife, and Christine..." He closes his eyes and balls his fist. He stands up, pacing the small room as best he can.

"Christine what?" I roar, not being able to hide my anger. I hear Ben grumble, scrubbing a hand down his face, and Christine's gasp, but I want to know exactly what's been said about Christine. He's right about Heather. Not that it's right to call a boy's mother that.

"A what?" I ask again when neither boy respond. I look to Preston, who's shaking his head and glaring at Aidan. I stand up, bracing my hands on Aidan's shoulders to get him to look at me.

Sad eyes meet mine, and I know whatever I'm about to hear

is gonna piss me the hell off. "What was said, son?"

He swallows then looks right at Preston when he answers me. "That Christine was just some replacement whore." He swallows hard and my heart breaks when I see his eyes glisten. Then he continues. "And she wouldn't stick around either because she couldn't love us, just like our own mom couldn't."

"Preston Michael!" Ben roars.

"Oh please, like he said that," Amanda scoffs.

"Are you calling my son a liar?" Christine asks, standing from her place and making her way in front of Amanda at a shocking rate of speed.

I move to stand slightly in front of her so she doesn't do something she'll regret. And by the looks of things, she's about ready to rip Amanda's hair out.

I *know* I shouldn't be turned on right now.

Doesn't mean I'm not.

Pissed off Christine is hot.

"He's not even your son!" Amanda says, voice a little scared but also full of snobbery.

Uh oh.

Wrong thing to say.

Ben shifts in his seat so he's leaning away from his wife.

"Are you saying I can't love him like he's my own?" Christine's voice is low and scary even to my own ears.

She takes a step toward Amanda.

Amanda shakes her head. "I-I didn't say that."

"So, parents who've adopted their children aren't real parents?"

Amanda moves to step closer to her husband, who shakes his head lightly at her.

Smart man.

"Stop putting words in my mouth, Christine! You know what I mean!"

"I certainly do not know what you mean. *My son* is a good kid. If he punched your kid, it sounds like it was well warranted. Where does a fourteen-year-old learn that type of behavior? Where did he hear those words about Heather? Huh? About his dad and me? It certainly wasn't from Aidan himself. Because yeah, Heather left. It wasn't because this boy isn't lovable. I fell in love with him just as quickly as I did his father and his brother. Heather left because she knew *she* wasn't worthy. To me, that makes her a hell of a lot better mom than someone who's raising a son to spout off nasty things like that to another kid. Especially about something they know absolutely nothing about."

Oh damn. My eyes widen, and Ben coughs, seemingly uncomfortable not knowing if he should step in and stand up for his wife or just stay silent, since we all know in this case what Christine speaks is nothing but truth.

But Christine isn't done. She's in full mama bear mode and isn't about to back down. "Patrick. I trust you'll do something about this? Aidan. You can go back to class, right, Mr. Moore?" She's confident and in charge in the small room, no one daring to look away from her.

"Dad?"

"You heard Christine, son. You want to defy her?"

He shakes his head quickly, wide eyes turned my way. "No, sir."

"Mr. Moore?" Christine asks impatiently. She crosses her arms over her chest and taps her toe.

He chuckles, probably not knowing what else to say at this point. "Nope. Me either."

"Amanda. I sincerely hope you learned from this experience. Ben? Always good to see you. Preston. Make smarter choices. Listen to your father." I cough to cover up the laugh that's trying to escape.

And with that, she leans down and kisses Aidan on the cheek.

"Christine..." I whisper, but she hears it. She shakes her head angrily at me, and I'm pretty sure those green eyes just shot fire in my direction.

"Not now," she whispers back.

We all watch as she walks out the door, Reece standing on the other side of the office windows. Probably worried for his brother. As soon as he sees Christine, he runs to her, hugging her tightly. I wish I could hear what she's telling him as she has her hands around his face. He nods, and she gives him a kiss on the cheek and he smiles up at her, like the sun rises and sets on her, and she makes her way back out to her car.

"Well, she was rude." Amanda truly doesn't know how to keep her mouth shut.

I raise my eyebrows at her, and Mr. Moore leans up and shakes my hand.

"That'll be all, Andy. Aidan. Get a pass and head back to class. Unless you need to head home with your dad."

"Nah. I'm good."

"What? Why do they get to leave?" Amanda's whiny voice carries through the room.

Before the door closes behind us, we hear the authoritative voice of Patrick Moore. "Amanda. Ben. Preston. Stay in your seats."

"I JUST DON'T UNDERSTAND. Why was she there?"

"Because I called her, Dad!" Aidan yells in defense, his face turning red and chest heaving up and down.

I didn't go back to work after I left the school, rather came straight home. The boys got home from school an hour ago, but

Aidan stormed into his bedroom the minute he walked in. About five minutes ago, I'd had enough and made him come out to the living room.

Shockingly, he obeyed.

We sat staring at each other for about fifteen minutes until I cracked. Not being able to hold in my frustration.

"But explain to me why you would call Christine. Why not call me? You called her, but the school called me?"

"Why does it matter? She was there for me. Just like I knew she would be."

"What do you mean?"

"Forget it," Aidan mumbles, beginning to walk away.

I grab his arm and bring him back to me, making him sit down with me on the couch. "I won't forget it, Aidan."

"Dad, I called her. She came. Because I wanted her there." He shifts uncomfortably in his place, and I reach out a hand, touching his knee and shaking lightly to get his attention.

"But not me?"

"It wasn't that," he grumbles.

"Kiddo. It's me. You know you can talk to me."

He crosses his arms and glares in my direction. "It doesn't matter. You left her. Like you care."

Ouch.

I wish so badly I could explain to them why Christine and I aren't together. Why I felt betrayed all over again when I found out that she knew for years that Heather had a one-time affair with her husband. What bothered me the most was that betrayal hit me in the gut harder than when I walked in on Heather having sex with another man.

I guess if I were getting wishes granted, it would be that none of this ever happened in the first place. I'd wish that I wouldn't be dealing with the knowledge that Christine is pregnant and I have no idea how I'm going to handle having a baby with a woman I'm no longer with. But wish I were. And still loved so deep down it's rooted in my bones. A woman who, it seems, they still very much want in their lives.

"I do care. But I care about you more. What's going on with you? Why would you pick a fight?"

"I already told you the story, Dad. It doesn't matter! If you didn't listen when we were in the principal's office then it's not like you're going to listen now."

I take a deep breath and blow it out slowly, trying to think of the words that will make the boys understand best.

"I'm listening," I promise.

"You're not going to get mad?"

"I won't. I just want the truth. Explain to me what happened today and why you called Christine to come to the school."

"I already told you what happened today!"

"I know you did, but I want to hear it again. Outside of the school walls."

"It wasn't his fault," Reece says as he steps forward. "Preston... he... he was egging him on. And I know we aren't supposed to allow that to happen, but you don't understand. He's been picking at both of us since mom left. Always saying how our mom was a..."

"A what?"

The boys glance at each other and do that annoying twin thing where they talk to each other without actually talking. "It's not my word — it's his, okay? So, don't get mad."

I clench my jaw and nod my head once.

"Slut. He called her a slut. And a whore. And he said that we weren't good enough. That even our slutty mom couldn't love us or want us."

"You know..."

"We know! We know it's not true. You tell us all the time

that we're enough and wanted. Whatever, Dad. You can say it all you want, but yeah, we heard. We heard how mom did that stuff with other guys. And last with... Preston. Nice name, right?" Reece's voice comes out shaky.

Holy shit. They know everything.

And if they aren't my kids, putting the two names together like that.

I scrub a hand down my face and tug on my hair, something I'm doing way too often lately.

"I... shit, boys. I didn't want you to find out like that."

Aidan gives me a look that basically screams he thinks I'm stupid. "You think we didn't already know? We're not idiots, Dad, so stop treating us like we are! We can't go anywhere in this stupid town without someone whispering about us. But you know what? Finally, it stopped. When we were with Christine? It wasn't happening. No more whispering. No more people making fun. Well, except for Preston," he scoffs and shakes his head. I glance over at Reece just as his eyes roll back down. "Christine has always stood by our sides. She was always there for us. And I knew she would be there for me today. Not mom. I *wanted* her there. You know what? Screw that. I *needed* her there, and guess what. I still do! Reece still does! *You do!*"

Shocked, I sit back in my seat and rub between my eyes before pinching the bridge of my nose. I didn't realize they knew so much. I should have known. No. I should have told them myself. I shouldn't have let them find out anything from someone else.

"Boys..." I sigh.

"No. Enough already. It doesn't matter what you think is such a big deal. She loves us, Dad. And if you don't want her anymore then you're stupid, too. But we aren't going to give her up. And not just because she's pregnant, Dad. Because we love her. *You* love her."

Reece stands up and storms away, leaving me staring after him, wondering how they knew *that*, too.

Aidan clears his throat, and I look over at him. His left is eye starting to swell just slightly. "Dad, he's right. We love her, and I don't know what she did or what you did, but please fix it." His voice starts to waver right along with my conviction. "We need her, Dad. And you've been miserable without her. *We're* miserable without her."

"I'm not miserable."

"Yes, you are, Dad. You're cranky, and I hear you up in the night. You don't sleep. I know you want her back. Fix it."

"So, I just go over there?"

"Dad. I'm fourteen. How the heck should I know? I assume you should probably start by saying you're sorry because I saw the look on her face today when she left the school, and she was super pissed. And not just at Preston. At you. But we already built that thing, so it's not like you weren't planning on winning her back. You just need the courage to do it."

"You caught that look at me, huh?"

"Uh, yeah."

"How'd you get so smart?"

"You just got lucky, I guess." He smiles and shrugs his shoulders.

"I'm sorry."

"For what?"

"Screwing up. It seems that's all I do."

"Dad. You didn't screw up with us. Yes, we're mad because we want Christine back and we want her here with us so we can help with the baby, but we're not mad at you. Just fix it. Or maybe we will be."

"Love you, kid."

"Love you, too, Dad."

He gives me a little boy grin and pushes on my shoulder

lightly. I pretend he hit me harder than he did, causing me to fall back down onto the couch. He shakes his head, laughing at my antics, then trudges up to his bedroom. I shift my gaze to the window. It's a cloudy day, gray clouds covering the skies. The threat of rain in the forecast. My knee bobs up and down, a nervous habit. I stand up, anxious, and move to the window.

I wanted to give her the grand gesture, but I don't think I can wait. I just want to be with her again. These last several days without her in my arms, in our home, it's been too much. She deserves my admittance to my ignorance and stupidity sooner rather than later.

Decision made, I whistle loudly. "Boys! I gotta go see about a girl!"

"Did you just use a line from Good Will Hunting on us?"

That stops me in my tracks. "How have you seen that movie?"

Their footsteps come bounding through the house. Aidan skids around the corner on the wooden floor in his socks, and Reece bounces into him. "Netflix, Dad. Chill." They both grin.

"Punks!" I point my finger at them but can't hide the grin of my own. "No Netflix and chilling for you!" They both give me an odd look, and I hope to God they have no clue what that means. Chances are not good on that.

"Go get her!"

"Yeah?"

"Yeah, Dad! Go!"

The word *go* is barely out of their mouths before I'm sliding my arms into my jacket and running out the door.

It doesn't take me long to get to her place from ours, but one thing that keeps rolling through my mind during the trip is her declaration of her love for me while we were in Mr. Moore's office.

I'm pulling into Christine's driveway, honking the horn like a lunatic. But the thing is? When you finally figure something out, like how you love someone and can't live without her, you don't want to waste another minute.

Great.

I jumped from Good Will Hunting to When Harry Met Sally in a ten-minute span. That's gotta be a record. Clearly, I've had too much extra time on my hands lately.

I kick the car door open, falling halfway out the car before getting hung up on the seat belt I forgot to take off. I quickly hit the button and fall the rest of the way onto my back. I stand up, brush the dust off, throw my leather jacket back into the car, and start walking.

The front door swings open, and an angry Christine appears in the doorway, her arms crossed over her chest. Still wearing my sweatshirt, and stupid or not, I take that as a good sign.

She's fired up, pissed off, and beautiful.

Breathtakingly beautiful.

But the look in her eyes stops me where I'm standing.

I quite like my balls, and I have a feeling if I follow my instincts and take her in my arms and kiss the hell out of her right now, I'll no longer be in possession of them.

"Hi."

She raises one eyebrow at me, and I shift on my feet. She remains silent, her bright green eyes never leaving mine. She's scary. In the hottest way.

I clear my throat and take a step toward her.

When she doesn't move away, I take that as another positive.

"Thank you for being there for Aidan today."

"Of course. Just because his dad is an asshole doesn't mean I'm going to take that out on him."

Okay. Ouch. So her gloves are coming off, and she's standing firm in her anger.

"It meant a lot to him. And..." I pause, struggling more than ever not to rush up the stairs and wrap her in my arms.

"And?"

"Me." I point to myself like that will help drive the point home. I then spread my arms out to my sides, hoping she sees the transparency in my presence here. "It meant a lot to me. To see you standing in there, going mama bear on Preston's mom when she tried dismissing everything he did."

"Well, someone had to do it." She sniffs and rolls her eyes at me.

"I agree."

"What are you doing here, Andy? I think you've already said what you needed to say."

I shake my head adamantly, my heart beating wildly in my chest. "No. I didn't. I said a bunch of bullshit that I didn't mean. I was angry. Hurt. Scared."

"Scared?" She scrunches her eyebrows adorably.

I take another step toward her when I see her body relax just slightly. She's still on her porch; I'm on the walkway below.

"Shitless, to be honest."

"Of?"

"You. Us. All of it, my feelings for you. They didn't come on slowly, building over time. I think that day that I came into Dreamin' Beans after walking in on Heather, I started falling. Whether it was because I found this person that understood what I was going through or if it was something deeper than that... I like to believe it was deeper."

She nods like she understands, which makes me feel like I could climb the Himalayas.

"Mostly, I was afraid of how badly it hurt to think I had been betrayed by you, even though you weren't the one who betrayed me. What scared me the most? When I saw Heather having sex with that guy? I felt nothing. Well no. I felt disgust, but my heart? It didn't hurt." I watch as her eyes soften, but not with pity. "I wasn't bothered. But the tiny thought that you had kept this information from me and you could have possibly been fooling me all the while I was falling head over heels in love with you? It felt like I was being crushed."

"But..."

"Let me finish. Please?" My voice is quiet, pleading.

She nods her head and takes a single step down.

"I love you. I love you more than I ever loved Heather. But that's not the point. The point is that you brought something out of me I thought was gone. No. That's not right. I didn't even know it existed in me. I think I knew I loved you when you came with us to the cabin, then again when you saved me in the haunted house. Again, when you peed on a stick right in front of me to prove that I was right. But I fell in love all over again when you stood up for Aidan. When you said he was *yours*. When you didn't back down. When you completely ignored me in that room because I wasn't the reason you were there. Please say I didn't screw up too badly. Please tell me that I still have you. That *we* still have you. That we'll be able to raise her together. When we met, I was in a dark place. I admit that. But you brought me back to the light. You made everything in my world shine brighter."

I take another step closer, and she moves down the stairs so she's on the second to bottom stair, but she's still taller than me. Which is just fine. I like it that I get to look up to her in this moment.

"Christine. Don't let me go. Please. I know I have work to do. I know I don't deserve you, but I'm begging you to give me that chance to prove to you that I can be worthy. I know I'm asking you for blind faith here. And honestly, I can't guarantee anything. But, I can promise you one thing. I won't treat your heart that way ever again. I'll never make you doubt me or my love. I'll never let you feel like you aren't the best thing that ever happened to me."

She presses her lips together tightly and places her hand on her stomach. I tentatively reach out and do the same. Her stomach is still small, not much of a bump there yet. We haven't told a single person aside from our kids that she's pregnant. I know our friends are curious. She hasn't exactly been feeling the best.

"Okay, so maybe one of the best things."

"Yeah?" Her voice is full of the tears that are falling down her cheeks, and her smile is watery.

"Yeah, baby. I love you so damn much."

"I'm still pissed at you, you know."

"It's the red streak in the hair. It makes you fiery." I smile, and she bites her lip.

"That's it, huh?"

I nod my head. "Pretty sure."

"Andy, I mean it when I say I'm still a little pissed."

"Actually, you said you were pissed. In ten seconds, you went from full on to just a little. I'm taking that as a score."

She rolls her eyes at me while I smile up at her.

I feel a raindrop and look up at the skies that are darkening, but it's not affecting my mood. Because she's not pushing me away, and I feel like I'm about to win the girl all over again. That doesn't mean I'm not willing to pull out all the stops, though.

"Baby, please forgive me. I'm so sorry for saying that you betrayed me. I'm so sorry for making you feel like less. For making you feel like I thought of you the same way as I think of Heather. For all of it. I can't live without you. I'm not saying I won't fall again, but I won't stay down. I'll always rise up to you."

"Andy..."

"Please," I plead, placing my forehead on her belly. I kiss the tiny bump and wrap my hands around her legs. "Please. Please. Please. Please."

It's full on raining now, and I don't know if she can hear me because my voice is barely a whisper, but I'll continue to beg and apologize until she tells me she forgives me. Until she says that she's still mine.

She lifts my head, her fingers cold from the rain, hair dripping wet, mascara streaking down her face.

"I always will, Andy. I will always forgive you. We hit a bump. You acted like an ass. I knew you'd come around." She shrugs her shoulders like it's nothing to her. "I learned a long time ago that time is precious. Not forgiving someone is a hell of a lot harder in the long run. Holding on to that hurt and anger just blackens the soul. You will always be forgiven. You will always be my heart."

I stand, taking her face in my hands, and waste no time pressing my lips to hers. My heart feels like it could burst straight out of my rain-soaked t-shirt. The feel of her lips, her tongue tangling with mine, her fingers gripping my waist.

"Don't let me leave again."

My lips don't part from hers while I murmur the words, still begging her to let me stay. "Never."

I pick her up, my arms under her butt, her left leg around my waist. I move us up the stairs, reaching a hand out to the rail to steady us so I don't trip and fall on top of her. She kicks the door shut after we get inside and slowly slides down my body. We make our way inside, shedding our wet clothes, struggling like hell when my jeans stick to every single inch of skin on my legs. Desperately, she shoves me to the floor, laughing and yanking at them from my ankles. When I stand, she drops them dramatically onto the floor and bites her bottom lip. I shake my head and smile then continue to walk with her while tugging off her clothes, leaving a trail to her bedroom.

Standing before me in just her bra and panties, me in my black boxer briefs, both of us breathing heavy and still wet from the rain, I look at her and drop to my knees, kissing all over her stomach. "I'm sorry," I whisper, but this time it's not to Christine. She pulls on the band securing my hair, letting it fall, and threads her fingers through the wet strands.

I close my eyes and rest my forehead against her stomach, my hands wrapped around her waist. "I'm so sorry, baby girl. I'll never leave you. You or your mommy. You're everything to me and the boys. I promise we'll always be here for you."

A sob erupts from Christine, and I lean back to look at her.

Her smile widens as a tear slides down her cheek, getting caught on her lip.

I stand slowly, kissing her stomach one more time, and take her hand that's now covering her mouth. I thread my fingers through hers and lead her to the bed, but she spins around, shoving me so I land on the mattress on my back.

She climbs over me, kissing over my stomach, my chest, my neck.

I groan, welcoming the feeling of her lips on my skin.

"I missed you. Missed this." My hands make a trail up the back of her thighs, to the dip in her back and down, sliding between the material of her panties and her ass. I squeeze lightly and she bites my neck.

"Missed you, too, honey."

She rolls her hips and I push up to meet her, causing us both to moan. We're still in our underwear, providing a barrier between us. A barrier that is both annoying and necessary so this isn't over before it starts.

"I want you." Her voice is husky, breath hot on my skin. "If you ever leave me horny and pregnant again, I'll take your balls and shove them down your throat."

I laugh. Hard.

"So really, you just want my body?"

"Duh," she says with a smile in her voice.

She kisses over my chest, my shoulders, teasing me by kissing me over my boxers before making her way back up to my face, mouth, everywhere she can reach.

After she's had her fun, it's my turn. Loving how she feels sitting on top of me, I run my hands over her stomach, swelling with the baby we made together. Then I trail a path up her arms, over her chest, and cup the back of her neck, bringing her closer so I can kiss her. I can't get enough of her, and I'm pretty sure I'll never be able to. Her legs are straddling me, her hot center over right where I want her most. Five minutes ago, I would have had sex with her right on the front lawn, but now that I'm here with her? I want to take my time. We haven't been together for two weeks. She leans down, kissing me on my neck, pressing my hands into the mattress. She loves when I give her control, and I love giving it to her.

I nudge her, wanting her mouth and roll us over, settling between her legs. I have to stop from embarrassing myself by dry humping her like a damn teenager.

I stare down at her, the mother of my unborn baby, the woman who stood up for my son like he was her own, and held both my sons when they felt the weight of their mother leaving them. She became a part of our world so seamlessly, effort-lessly... it was as if she'd been there the entire time.

"I love you so fucking much. You're mine forever, baby. You know this, yeah?"

"Yeah."

"You love me, too."

"I do." She smiles brightly.

"Words, baby."

Sighing heavily like it's a burden. "I love you."

"I know."

She bursts out laughing. "So cocky."

I press deeply into her, her back and neck arches as she turns her head to the side and groans my name. The best sound in the world.

"Did you say cocky?"

"Mmm."

I plunge my tongue into her mouth, caressing, tasting. The kiss isn't gentle. It's heavy breaths and pounding hearts and bruising lips. She grips the back of my neck, keeping me close to her. It goes on for minutes. Hours. I don't know, and I don't care because I have her beneath me again, and holy hell I missed it more than I even realized. Allowing my anger over what happened to cloud my love for her. I realize how lucky I am that she's giving me another chance, and no way in hell will I do anything to screw it up again.

I skim her throat, running my thumb down the center. She arches beneath me, giving me room to reach around her and unclasp her bra. I toss it to the side, allowing her full breasts to tumble free in the process. Her body is changing so much, and this is one of my favorites. She always had beautiful boobs, but now? They're heavy and sensitive, and I can't get enough playing with them. So, I don't waste any more time. I travel south, kissing as I go. I slide my hands up both sides of her, pressing them together and taking both tight nubs into my mouth at the same time. She cries out, scratching the sheets, my back, my scalp as I continue to lick and suck. Giving both attention at the same time. I lift my head and bury my face between them before giving each side individual attention.

Because I'm a giver.

The sound of her moans is making me harder than I've ever been, and it's straining against my boxers, begging to join the party.

"You gonna let me give it to you, baby?"

"Mmm hmm."

"Open up for me."

I kiss my way down her belly, delving my tongue into her belly button. She giggles and moans at the same time, twisting her body this way and that. My fingers wrap around her panties and slowly drag them down her body.

She spreads her legs, her knees hitting the mattress. I look up at her and wink and she rolls her eyes.

"Annnndyy..."

"Did you want something?"

I lightly blow on her center before tasting.

"That," she groans. "Oh, hell yes. That."

I take my time, enjoying the sweetness and her sounds. Sounds that I'm the cause of her making. The way she says my name when I'm making her come. Her moans that sound like they're coming from deep in her toes. She continues to twist and turn, and I place my hands on her lower stomach to hold her steady.

I suck on her center and relish in the way her body begins to tremble. I slide two fingers into her, twisting and curling, and within seconds, she's thrashing beneath me, screaming my name so loudly I wouldn't be surprised if her voice is hoarse tomorrow.

When she's coming down, I crawl back up her body, shedding my boxers along the way, kissing her again because I can. Because she's still mine. Because I didn't lose her. And I let her taste herself. Because she loves it.

Without waiting, I press into her, the feeling so overwhelming I have to give myself a few moments before I move. I swear since she got pregnant, she feels tighter, swollen maybe? Or maybe it's just the fact that I know she's carrying *my* child. That she and I created something together.

"Honey," she whispers, her touch on my back so light that it makes me shudder. I bury my face in her neck and suck. "I need you to keep moving." She emphasizes her statement by rolling her hips, causing the friction between us to build.

"I don't want to forget this moment."

"It'll be pretty forgettable if you don't move."

I lightly spank the side of her butt. "Brat."

"So, do something about it."

I lean up and smirk. She raises an eyebrow in challenge.

I rise up on my knees, pulling her legs up, bent at the knee. I push her left leg back, keeping her leg bent and place her right leg over my shoulder. Exactly like we did our first time together. She reaches behind her, grasping at the pillows on the bed. We might need to invest in a headboard with slats when she moves in to my place. Which she will.

"So deep," she moans.

"Yeah," I grunt.

The sounds of the ecstasy we're sharing, the scent of her arousal, the sight of her spread out below me, sweat glistening her skin, stomach slightly rounded with my baby, has me ready to come before I want to.

When she screams, "I can't hold back any longer!"

"Yes. Come. Come now," I growl as I obey my own command.

I'm pretty sure I see stars as I collapse on top of her, careful to keep some of my weight to the side.

"Holy shit," she pants.

"Yeah," I croak, words not being something I care to focus on.

"I love you."

"Christine. I love the shit out of you."

W hen Aidan called me today to let me know he was in trouble and he needed me to come to the school, I didn't even blink. I was in the middle of making a batch of scones, and I left everything. I told Emma to take over and hightailed it out of there. Four hours ago, I was still holding strong to my anger.

Two hours ago, I was about to burst into tears from Andy's apologies.

And right now, I'm confused.

Confused because Andy's tearing through my house. Naked. Throwing every box he can find from my basement up the stairs.

"Honey? Care to tell me why you're redecorating while your whacker is still hanging out?"

He stops mid-throw and bursts out laughing.

"Whacker?"

"Well, what do you call it? Nope. Never mind. Just explain to me what's happening here." My hand doing an up and down motion as I speak.

"Explain what?" he asks, turning his head to the side and giving me that grin that could make a preacher's wife swoon.

"Andy, you're still naked. Not that I mind. At all. But what's with the boxes?"

"You're moving."

"Pardon?"

"To my house," he clarifies

"Really? When did we decide this?"

He prowls up the steps, naked as the day he was born, and arrests my lips in a soul-crushing kiss.

"Move in with us?" He doesn't even try to mask it as a question, but that does nothing to change the fact that my stomach flutters from the declaration.

"Like... now?"

"Yes. I spent two weeks without you because I was an idiot, Christine. I'm not spending more time away from you two." He places a hand on my stomach as he says it, but his eyes never leave mine. "And before you get all pregnancy-hormonal on me, I want you with me. Not just because you're carrying my baby. I want there to be no question."

"I wasn't..." But I can't finish the sentence, knowing it would be a lie. I can't deny the fact that I was a little worried about that. I don't question his love for me, but it did cross my mind that he could want me back simply because I'm carrying his baby.

"I know that's where your head was going. And I know it's my fault that the thought even crossed your mind. I'll never make you question that again. That's my promise to you."

"It's a good promise," I murmur quietly.

"It is. I love you, Christine."

It's not the first time he's said it; it's not even the first time he's said it in the last thirty minutes. He's definitely open with his I love yous. But it doesn't matter. Every time I hear it, my heart flops. "I love you, too."

"So, you will? Move in with me and the boys? If I come home without you in tow I think they'll throw my ass out of my own house."

"Don't you think we should discuss this?"

He rears back like he's surprised. "What's to discuss?"

"Well, the fact that we just got back together a couple hours ago for one thing."

"But you said you forgave me."

"And I did." He raises his eyebrows, so I correct myself. "I do. I'm not mad anymore, but I don't think jumping into moving in together is the answer."

"That's not why I'm doing this," he tries to explain.

"I know, but don't you think we still have a lot to figure out?"

He pulls at the hair on his head.

And he's still naked.

Standing right in front of me.

All I would have to do is reach out my hand a mere few inches and I'd be able to grip him.

This entire conversation is feeling more than a little awkward for that reason alone.

"Can you put on some clothes, maybe?"

"Am I making you uncomfortable?"

He takes a step closer.

"Andy," I groan, looking down with my head in my hands.

Bad idea.

Now I'm just staring right down at *him*.

"Christine," he mock groans.

"I'm serious. We can't go from fighting to having sex to moving in together! Not without talking to the boys first."

He studies me for a few beats. "You're right." He marches

off, walking into the front room where some of our clothes were discarded in our haste to get our hands on each other once again.

He reaches into the front pocket of his jeans, pulling out his phone.

He taps a few times then brings the phone up to his ear.

"Aidan. Get Reece on speaker."

A few moments pass, and I nibble on my thumbnail, shifting from one foot to the other.

"You both there? Good. Hang tight."

He pulls the phone away, taps again then walks over to me.

"You want Christine to move in with us, boys?"

"You fixed it? You got her back?" Reece says loudly, excitedly.

"I did, but she seems to be on the fence about where she's supposed to be living."

I gape at him, hardly believing my ears.

"With us, Dad. Make sure you tell her she's supposed to be living with us," Aidan says.

He gives me a look, and I do my best to glare in return. He plays dirty.

"I'll make sure to let her know," he says, grinning from ear to ear.

"You are such a brat!" I whisper.

"Is that her?"

Dammit. How did they hear that?

"Do you boys have bat hearing or something?"

"Christine, please," Aidan begs. "We want you to live with us. We need a woman's touch!"

"Aidan Simpson you did *not* just say that!"

"What? You know it's true."

Andy chuckles. "Thank you, boys, you did your job."

"So, you'll move in?" Reece asks, so much hope in his voice I have a hard time not just saying yes to him and giving in.

"Your dad and I need to discuss it, but..."

"Make it happen, Dad!"

"How about your dad and I figure everything out, and we'll be over with supper in a little bit?"

"With your stuff," Aidan says with authority.

"Let's just take things one day at a time, shall we?"

"Fine. But, Christine, we want you to know... we're more stubborn than you are. And, we're willing to play dirty." So much like their father. I'm screwed.

"Reece!" I cry out his name, appalled. I tsk. "I swear. It's always the quiet ones you have to watch out for."

"Yeah, you've told me that a time or two. It would be easier to watch out for me if you lived with us, you know."

I gasp. Totally walked into that one.

"You do play dirty," I say, narrowing my eyes at their father. Who is... still naked. And completely unashamed about it, too. In fact, I'm pretty sure he's... yep. He's hard. As in, standing at attention, pointing in my direction hard.

Oh my.

My eyes seem to have lost their focus. Or gained it, depending on which way you look at it. I can't tear them away from him.

"See you soon, guys! We'll clear some space in Dad's closet!" Aidan hollers before they hang up.

"Clearly, your sons get their tactics from you. That was low, Andy. How am I supposed to say no to them?"

He shrugs, uncaring. "Kind of the point."

"Why aren't you putting clothes on?"

"Why? So that when I convince you to move in with me, I have to undress again before we have sex right here on the living room floor? Think about it. Once you live with us, you won't be able to be as loud as you want."

"I thought you were trying to sell me on this whole idea?"

"I am. See, funny thing. I've learned a little about you. And, aside from me behaving like a complete moron in recent weeks, I get you. I also know that you care more about those boys — and hopefully me — than screaming like a banshee during sex."

"You're so annoying."

He nods his head seriously. "I know. It would bother me to be around someone who's right all the time, too."

I growl. I can't help it. He's such a smart ass. So cocky and full of himself. But he somehow makes it loveable.

He steps closer, dropping his phone to the couch, and wraps his hands around my biceps.

"Christine. Is it so awful that we want you living with us? Is there really anything wrong with that? You knew it would happen eventually. Now that I pulled my head out of my ass, I'm ready to keep moving forward."

"But you literally *just* pulled it out of your ass."

"Not exactly," he murmurs, and I narrow my eyes, about to ask him what that means, but he continues on before I get the chance. "Just because my head was up there doesn't mean that I didn't miss the hell out of you. Or think about you constantly."

"I thought about you, too," I admit.

"Of course, you did." He smiles, spreading his arms out to his side then points to his... yeah. He's pointing to what's pointing at me.

I roll my eyes in return.

"You might want to get that checked out, that whole eye rolling thing. You do it a lot to me." He jumps out of the way when I reach for him, ready to smack him on the chest. He backs away until he's in the kitchen, out of my reach.

"You're so annoying!" I repeat.

I hear him open the fridge.

"What are you doing?"

"I'm hungry!"

"Now?"

"Why not now? I worked up an appetite earlier. Didn't you?"

Food?

Oh yeah.

"I could eat."

And then my tongue gets stuck in my throat, and I have to cross my legs where I stand to stop from peeing myself because there stands Andy, in a whipped cream bikini.

He's smiling, completely unashamed, as he runs an index finger through the white foam covering his right nipple, bringing it up to his mouth so he can suck it clean.

He moans, closing his eyes and dropping his head back.

It should be weird.

It's mesmerizing and erotic and has me peeling my clothes away in my living room like a wanton slut. I don't know if it's his goofiness or simply him that I love so much.

His nostrils flare as I get closer.

He grabs me roughly, bringing us chest to chest, whipped cream smearing between us.

"Now we match," he says in a low voice.

"Hmm. Whatever are we gonna do about it?"

The wicked gleam in his eyes proves to me that he knows exactly what he intends to do about it, and his plans match nicely with mine.

We don't make it back to his house for a few hours. My stuff is far from packed, but I know there's time for that. When I walk up to Andy's house, a big handmade Welcome Home sign hangs on the entrance door greeting me.

Beneath the sign, stand the boys and a crib.

I look at Andy and scrunch my eyebrows.

He scrubs a hand along the back of his neck and shrugs.

"So, uh, a few nights ago I went for a drive. Needed to clear my head. I ended up at your place."

"What? But you didn't come in?"

"No. I realized that you deserved more than me showing up in the middle of the night. So, I called Barrett, told him I was heading into the shop to go through lumber. He asked why, and I told him he'd find out soon enough." He smirks because he knows that Barrett was probably dying to find out the reason. "I brought it home and..." he gestures to the crib.

"Wait, you *made* this?"

"I did."

"In... a day?" I exclaim because it's... well, it's beautiful. And perfect.

It's stained a dark walnut finish and has detail carved into the head and foot of the crib. I walk closer and notice the detail isn't just some random scrolling. It's an S. For Simpson.

"But, how did you..." My voice trails off, and my tears don't even have time to threaten spilling over. They just make a fast trail down my cheeks.

"I had a little help," he says with a shrug.

I look at the boys who are both beaming with pride.

"You did this?" I ask, my voice barely above a whisper.

"We all did. They stained and varnished it. It was a team effort."

I don't even know what to say.

A few days ago, I felt alone. And now? Now I have more family than I could have ever dreamed of.

"Thank you," I tell the three men in my life, and it doesn't feel like enough, but by the looks on their faces, it is.

Andy pulls me back outside and kisses me softly on the lips, his fingers skimming through my hair.

"I love you," he says against my lips, and I whisper the words back to him that I know we'll tell each other for the rest of our lives.

And when Andy picks me up to walk me over the threshold, I know that with him it would always feel like home.

THIRTY-SIX

ANDY

"I seriously have no idea what you're talking about," I lie. I glance at Barrett and notice he's sporting a shit-eating grin, so I quickly look away.

"Oh really? You have no idea, huh?"

"Nope!"

"Uh huh. So, you have no input on why Christine is glowing these days? Even after you were a raging idiot and basically broke up with her."

I roll my eyes but ignore the second part of his question. "Not a clue."

"You're so full of shit."

"And you're so damn nosy."

"I don't deny that. See how that works? I don't deny truth... you don't deny truth..."

"You're such a pain in my ass."

"Yet you still love me! Funny. I'm just that much of a likable guy."

"What are we talking about in here?" Josh, says as he walks into his and Barrett's joint office.

I groan, knowing that between the two of them, they won't

let up until I start divulging some information they think they're privy to.

"Ah, just in time. Andy was just going to fill us in on why Christine is so happy and glowing these days. I mean, aside from the fact you pulled your head out of your ass and realized you were being a jackass."

He just can't let it go. "Thanks. I appreciate your kind words. And, no, I wasn't about to say anything."

"Oh you were? Oh goody. I mean, we have our theories, but we would definitely prefer if you just told us the truth. It's really an inconvenience, us always having to talk about it behind your back and all."

They're both leaning back in their office chairs that face each other in their office, only separated by their desks. Barrett chuckles, and I roll my eyes. The thing is, though, I really need to talk to someone about what's happening. Because if I don't, I'm likely to lose my shit, and that's kind of the purpose of our meeting. I was the one who requested it, after all. But that doesn't mean I want to give in so quickly. Watching these two squirm is more fun.

"You are hopeless."

"Full. Hope-*full*. There's a difference. We're hopeful that you finally just tell us that Christine's pre..."

"Josh! Shut up, man! Let him tell us!"

I stand up from the chair I was sitting in and swipe my Dreamin' Beans coffee cup off the table, making my way toward the door like I'm going to leave. Before I can make it three steps, they both spring out of their chairs and dart in my direction. Barrett puts his arm in front of the doorway like he's going to block my exit. Josh moves to stand next to him.

"No. Please. Don't leave!" Josh's voice is frighteningly close to whining.

"Yeah — come on, Andy! We'll be good. And we're vaults. We promise. Anything you tell us we keep a secret."

I raise an eyebrow at his blatant lie. They're the worst secret keepers in the world. "Why do you think there's anything to even tell you?"

They squint their eyes at me and I sigh, knowing I can't just leave.

"Okay, fine!" I stomp over and sit down again.

They tap their fists against each other's in triumph without taking their eyes off me and close the door before they settle back in their chairs, moving them away from their desks and in front of me, leaning over with their elbows on their knees.

Idiots.

"Christine... she might be..."

"Yeah? Yeah?" Josh says, leaning over farther.

"Well, for a couple months now she hasn't really been feeling the best," I admit.

"Is she going to be okay? How long do you suppose this strange illness will last?" Barrett asks, thinking he's sneaky. He even winks at Josh.

"I don't know. I guess it's different for everyone. Some people are sick for longer, some only a short period of time."

"What could have possibly caused this bizarre illness?" This from Josh; he lifts a hand to Barrett as if to say, 'I got this'.

"Is she still upset about your moronic behavior? Or was it something else you did?"

I almost roll my eyes at their ridiculousness. Instead, I shrug my shoulders and fain indifference. "Could be anything, really. But my best guess would be that it's because she's..." I stop and look around the room.

"Yeah?"

"She's..."

Josh falls out of his chair, the wheels on the bottom spinning around. He quickly recovers, setting it back up and taking a seat as if nothing happened.

"Out with it, dammit!" Barrett hollers then presses his lips together tightly like he didn't just have an outburst.

"She's pregnant, all right?"

The two idiots high five each other without taking their eyes off me. I chuckle, shake my head, and lean up to high-five their now outstretched hands in my direction. Soon they're pulling me out of my seat and wrapping me up in a Barrett and Josh sandwich. It should be awkward — with any other two people it probably would be. But with them, it's just what you expect.

Barrett reaches into his desk and pulls out a bottle of whiskey and three shot glasses. Seems odd to me he had those at the ready, but whatever.

"Shots! To the new daddy!"

"Opa!" Josh shouts. I think he secretly wants to be European. He's always trying out different accents and words, whether they're British, Italian, or today's choice, Greek. None of them really work, his British, Irish, and even Australian accents pretty much crossover, but he tries, nonetheless.

Barrett knocks back his shot without even flinching at Josh's word. I chuckle but do the same. I feel the burn all the way down. How people can do shots without making faces is beyond me.

"You just happened to have that here? Did I miss the memo about drinking on the job?"

He shrugs. "I may have brought it in when we started suspecting. And when you asked for the meeting, I had to fight back bringing in cigars, too."

"Did I miss it?" The door to their office swings open so hard it hits the wall, and James's voice booms from the doorway. He notices our empty shot glasses and narrows his eyes at Barrett. "Dammit! I did, didn't I? I told you to hold him off!"

"It's okay, brother, better luck next time." Barrett reaches into his drawer and pulls out a fourth shot glass, fills it to the brim, and slides it over to his brother-in-law. James tips it back then lifts his glass in my direction.

"So, is it true?"

"What's that?" I ask him.

"Don't play dumb with me, man. Is it true? Are we expecting a little bun in Christine's oven?"

"We?"

All three men look at me like I'm dumb. "Of course, we!" Josh shouts like he's offended, and the other two nod their heads in agreement.

"How is this a joint effort with you three assholes?"

"Umm, because we're going to be the little squirt's uncles. Duh," Barrett says as though it's obvious.

"I'm a little disappointed and hurt that you even had to ask," James says, shaking his head.

I pinch the bridge of my nose, praying this whole ordeal is going easier for Christine than it is for me.

"So, what's the plan?" Barrett asks, pulling me out of my thoughts. What I thought would have been the worst day of my life, turned out to be the best.

"Plan?"

"Of course, plan. What's next?"

"What's next is we're having a baby. She's still a little freaked out, too. It's not like she's that young, you know?"

"She looks amazing though. And she's already got that beautiful glow to her," Josh says and I growl, causing him to howl in laughter.

"Whoa, man. Calm yourself. I'm a perfectly happy married man. Just stating a fact."

"Fact or not, keep your eyes to yourself."

James raises his eyebrows at me and smiles knowingly. His

wife is gorgeous, too. Obviously, he knows it, but he isn't so keen on anyone else thinking it.

"What did the boys say? Bri?"

"Bri can't wait. She's a little nervous, too because she understands the risks that come with Christine's age and pregnancy. But in the end, she just wants her mom happy. The boys? They're almost as I am. They love Christine, want her to stick around. The boys looked a little more than shocked when we told them. It was a humbling experience, for sure. Obviously, we've talked about things, but them being aware that their dad had sex with someone he wasn't married to... yet... was not a fun conversation to have. Add to that we weren't careful and she got pregnant. I think next week I'll smash my fingers with a hammer and see if it's as much fun."

The guys all grin, and Barrett offers up an, "I'll bet."

"As for our plans? We're together. Now that I have her back, I need to convince her to put my ring on her finger, take my last name, and life will be good." I lean back in my chair, hands folded together on the back of my head.

"You're planning to marry her?" Josh asks.

"That was always the plan. I think I knew it when we first started hanging out after Heather. It was never awkward. It has always felt right between us."

"Wow," Barrett says, picking up his phone, which I yank away quickly.

"Stop it, you news-spreading girl!"

He raises his hands. "I wasn't doing anything!" He tries to defend himself but we all know he wouldn't have kept that one a secret.

James shakes his head laughing. "And he wonders why I had to just drop to one knee when he didn't expect it."

"I'm hoping to do it in a more romantic setting than immediately after seeing someone get arrested." James proposed about two minutes after they watched Carly's ex-husband, Vince, get arrested for assault against James, among other things.

"And I missed it, too. Still not something I'm over," Barrett grumbles as he shoots daggers in James's direction.

"Why would you need to be there?"

"Tate and Will both saw it! Pardon me if I think it's bullshit that your gym owner got to see it and not me. Plus, Will got to be there for your first date!"

"He owns the shooting range we went to. It's not like he was *there* for the date. And they were there because we were together when we got the call that Vince was at the house," James reminds him.

"Whatever. Still bullshit. Could have called me," Barrett grumbles.

"Hello! I did. You just weren't quick enough."

Barrett simply narrows his eyes.

"You're so nosy," Josh says.

"Hi pot, I'm kettle. Look at that! We're both black."

"So..." James says, probably trying to get these two nutjobs back on track. "You're planning to ask her to marry you? Things are okay between you two again? You squared that away? What do the boys think of that?"

"Any other questions, man?" I tease, but continue. "We're good. I apologized for being an idiot. She showed me what it means to be an adult. The boys? Well, let's just say they're definitely on board the marriage train."

THIRTY-SEVEN

CHRISTINE

"Are you gonna tell us or not?" Lauren asks, settling herself in on my couch, both legs tucked under her body.

"Tell you what?"

She throws her hands in the air, exasperated.

"You two are so annoying! We deserve to know what's up, you know? Now that he got over whatever was up his butt for a little while there and you two are back together, you have some explaining to do. Besides, you're the one who called this little informational meeting. So, fess up. Now, dammit!"

"Geesh, Carly. Marriage has made you rather demanding, you know?"

"I know!" she says proudly. "Seriously. Are you two okay now? Everything is settled?"

"Yeah. He... freaked out, I guess. Putting it mildly. But, when Aidan got in trouble at school, I think it opened his eyes. We're moving on."

"Christine, you know we're here for you, right?" Tess says and I nod, reaching over to hold my hand, always the mother hen. Unless margaritas are involved — then it's every woman for herself. "And I'm glad to hear that. I hear Mrs. Lyons pulled him by the ear. She's hysterical."

"She did. I bet she loved that."

"So... I mean, tell us when you're ready, but I really think you should be ready now," Lauren laughs. "Want wine? Sometimes it helps, takes the edge off a bit, you know." She gives me knowing grin.

"I'm good."

"Oh? Why is that? I thought you normally enjoyed a glass or two of wine." Lauren. What a stinkin' brat.

"Okay, fine! I'm prego, okay?" I see Carly hand Tess some money and grumble that Barrett was right. No one is saying anything, so I continue on. "You know, I'm in a family way. Bun in the oven. With child. Knocked up. Bat in the cave."

"You have a booger in your nose, too?"

I cover my nose and jerk my head back. "What? Do I have a booger?" Carly looks and shakes her head.

"I'm confused."

"Bat in the cave. It means you have something in your nose."

"No! Bat in the cave. It means I'm pregnant."

"No, that's not what it means at all."

"I disagree."

"Let's look it up."

"Lauren! Stop! Who gives a crap! Christine just told us she's pregnant! With Andy's baby! Wait." She turns wide eyes toward me and gasps. "It is Andy's, right?"

I look at Tess like she's insane. "Of course, it's Andy's! Who else's would it be?"

"I don't know! I didn't want to assume!"

"Tess."

Who does she think I am?

"I realize that you and Andy are together but hey, I'm not here to judge you. It's the twentieth century."

"Actually, it's the twenty-first." Carly just can't turn off teacher mode.

"No shit? How does that make sense?"

"Nuh uh. Tess is right."

"No, she's not. Sorry you two, but there are instances in the world where you're wrong."

"I disagree with that also. I don't believe it. That doesn't even make any sense."

"Believe it... because the first years, like zero to one hundred, were in the first century. So, one hundred one..."

"Carly! Stop *teachering* right now! We get it, okay? You're smarter than we are!"

I'm watching the three of them with amusement. If they're talking about this, maybe they'll leave me alone for a bit.

"I didn't say I was smarter. I would never say that out loud. But in this case, I am. Also, teachering isn't a word. It doesn't even sound good."

"You know. You used to be nice. Before James. BJ — ha! See what I did there?" Tess laughs to herself. "BJ you were nice. AJ, which doesn't have quite the same ring to it, you're just all smart-assy and mean. My brother has really corrupted you."

Carly grins, obviously proud of the impact James has made on her.

I stand slowly from my place on the couch, hoping to get by with just my announcement and not needing to reveal much else. I don't make it two steps.

"Stop right there, chica." I slowly spin around and look at the ladies who have become my best friends over the years. I sit down and sigh. It's not that I'm not willing to give them more information. It's just that everything feels so new, and I kind of liked having it in our protective bubble. Once it's out there, it's out there. I'm not exactly young to be having a child, so the risks we know are involved are more real. It's terrifying. This little bundle growing inside me might not have been something we planned or expected, but we make up for it in how much we want him or her. Her, if you ask Andy.

"We need more details than that. When are you due? How are you feeling? Is Andy excited? A boy? A girl? Twins?" Tess gasps.

"Uhhh..."

"Oh, my gosh. What if you have another set of twins, like his boys?"

"Well we only heard one heartbeat so..."

"You heard the heartbeat already?" Carly shouts, standing up and throwing her arms in the air.

"Yes, you goofball, we've been to the doctor several times. Given the fact that I'm forty-one years old, they're keeping a closer eye on things."

I don't tell her that all three kids went with us to an early ultrasound also.

"Pssh, you may be forty-one in actual years, but you're so healthy it's more like dog years."

"So, I'm six?"

"What? No! You know what I mean. Stop being so literal!" Lauren laughs. "But seriously. You're in excellent shape, and holy crap your kids are going to be gorgeous. Andy's hot. And don't give me that look. I love my husband, but *damn*, girl. Andy's got it goin' on."

"What would Josh say if he heard you say that?"

"Oh, please. Like he doesn't know. I don't lie to my husband."

How can I not laugh at that? Sitting in this room, though, are three of the most faithful and loving wives ever. And their husbands are the same.

"Well, yeah, I would have to agree with you on that. Andy is definitely hot. And…" I gulp and look away before whispering, "young."

"Oh stop. He's not *that* young," Carly insists.

I raise an eyebrow at her. "He's six years younger than me."

"So? You think that bothers him?"

I grab the box of Wheat Thins off the coffee table, one of the things I crave and can't stop eating. Andy and I have boxes of them scattered everywhere. I eat a couple of crackers before I continue. "No, I know it doesn't bother him. He's made that perfectly clear. But, it's hard to explain. We get looks."

"If y'all get looks, it's only because you two are a smokin' hot couple and everyone is wondering if you two are celebrities." Tess nods her head at the other ladies for their agreement.

"You're such a suck ass."

"I am not! I don't lie! Right, ladies?"

"Oh damn," Lauren says, looking around the room excitedly, bouncing in her seat on the couch.

"What?"

She stands up and clutches her phone to her chest then looks down at it again and sighs. When she meets my eyes, she smirks. "Remember those pictures of that guy with his baby in the sling against his chest wearing that insanely sexy leather jacket and aviators?" Her smile is so broad, and her eyes are sparkling.

"What? What picture?" Tess and Carly both ask.

I smile, knowing exactly where she's going with this. Because that picture made women's ovaries explode all over the place. And yeah, I've thought about it. Just a few hundred times. He's already a hot dad to his boys. But they're teenagers. Picturing Andy with a baby? I basically have to chase my ovaries to England, where they exploded to.

"It was going all over Facebook! How did you not see it?"

"So, you can be all judgy of Facebook when people are

posting status updates, but not when someone is posting a picture of a hot guy?"

"Of course."

"Oh *hot* damn," Tess says. "Have mercy." She's looking down at her phone and looks up with wide eyes and fans her face. "I'm thinking maybe you should ban him from doing... that." She points to her phone.

I've thought the same thing, too.

I see how some of the women in our town look at him.

I'm not blind.

"Holy crap, that picture is panty melting." Carly's eyes are a bit unfocused as she stares at it then clears her throat. "So, back to you guys. Is he excited?"

"Umm, yeah. He is. At first? I think he kind of freaked out. He made me pee on a dozen sticks. He went to Walgreens and bought every kind he could then stood in the bathroom with me while he made me chug down bottles of vitamin water to get me to pee."

"Quite the bonding experience." Lauren giggles.

"Right? Nothing says love like using the facilities in front of each other."

Lauren, who sat back down on the couch, sits up straight and stares at me. "Wait. Did he do it, too?"

"Do what?" I ask dumbly. I can't believe I slipped up like that. No, that's a lie. I can totally believe it. I would never be able to keep the baby's sex a secret when we find out. I'm about as bad as Josh and Barrett.

"Pee?"

"Why would he pee?"

"To make you feel better!"

I gasp. "How did you know?"

She points at me. "Ha! I knew it. He totally peed on a stick, didn't he?"

I burst out laughing, wishing I could deny it.

"He had to brace his arm on the wall to make sure it aimed in the right place!" I shout through my laughter.

We all fall over, tears coming out of my eyes when I think about that night. I was so worried, and he made it a game. He calmed me down and eased my worries.

"Oh, bless his heart," Tess says, her hand covering her chest. "He's such a sweet guy. I can just picture his grin."

When I finally stop laughing, I sit back up on the couch and tuck my feet under my butt. "It was sweet. He got down in front of me while I was trying to pee, holding up a bottle of water with a straw in it, encouraging me to keep going, telling me not to worry or be embarrassed. Then he said, 'We got this, yeah?' When I started crying, he kind of nudged my knee and said, 'My turn. Let me do it this time. I wanna see what it's like.' I laughed so hard, I peed. Right then. I was so horrified, so he said he would pee on the stick, too. The whole thing is so gross, but it's a good memory. By the time we had used all of the tests and only one came out negative, obviously being his, we didn't have much of a choice but to accept it. He smiled at me and repeated, 'We got this, yeah?' and I knew we did.

"He was a little concerned about his boys, and how they would take it. But they've been wonderful. And they're all pretty sure it's a girl, even though we really don't know, yet. And now Andy is just this super protective, caring, even more affectionate man. Especially after everything that went down."

"Oh man. You're blushing! The sex is hot, huh?"

"Carly!" I laugh. "Seriously, not even the same person." I can't help but smile at her, though. "Okay, you're my people. So, yeah. The sex is uber hot. Which isn't easy since he has the boys, but since Bri isn't home, we have a little more freedom at my house when he's over. The stamina that man has... it's both exhausting and invigorating."

"Are you going to move in together? Get married?"

"Yes, we're going to move in together, but I think we're going to have to add an addition on to his place to make room for me, the baby, and a room for Bri when she's home. Married? I don't know. I would love to be his officially. But we haven't talked about it, not in the marriage sense."

"What do you mean?"

"I mean, we've talked that we love each other in a forever way, but I've been too nervous to bring up marriage. Honestly? If he asked me right now, I'd haul his ass over to the court house and marry him on the spot."

"Ooh, Bri would be upset if she missed it."

This is true. Plus, Andy and Bri have gotten surprisingly close since we've been together. She had a great father figure in Barrett, but the bond she shares with Andy is different. It's been a beautiful thing to watch.

"I don't think I have anything to worry about there," I admit.

"What do you mean?" Tess reaches her hand over to me, squeezing it once when I don't respond. "Talk to us, Christine."

"I don't think Andy really wants to get married. Heather did a number on him, you know? She just... she was just so bad." I don't dive back into everything that happened with his terrible ex and definitely don't want to bring up anything that happened with Todd and her. So far, Bri hasn't heard any of the grumblings around town, and I want to keep it that way. Her memories of her father, even when he was sick, are wonderful ones. I want to keep it that way because no matter what junk was going through his head or how stupid he behaved, he was an incredible father.

"And the way she's just up and left those boys?" I shake my head and shrug, wiping away a stray tear that starts making its way down my cheek.

"Hey—" Carly comes over and sits on the other side of me

while Lauren makes her way over, sitting on the coffee table in front of me. Surrounded by my three best friends, I know I'm not in this alone. I might be having a baby at forty-one years old, but I have the love of my life by my side and the best friends a girl could ask for.

"Listen here, you beautiful, incredible, fabulous woman. Andy knows how lucky he is to have you. He loves you. I bet he's looking for rings right now. Do you know how much he talks about you? Have you seen how he lights up when you walk into the room? It doesn't matter if he hasn't seen you in hours or minutes, his response is always the same. And I can only imagine how much he wants you to take his last name."

"He looks at me a way?"

"Oh yeah," they all say in unison.

"I'm surprised your panties don't melt off from his looks alone," Tess giggles.

I'm not sure they haven't a time or two. I hate feeling this way, but I can't help it. I loved someone with all I had in me once, and he ended up leaning on someone else, rather than coming to me, when he was at his lowest. As much as I've tried to not let it get to me, it isn't easy. And the more I lean on Andy, the closer we get and the harder I fall for him, the more nervous I get.

Tess leans over and lifts my chin so I'm looking at her. "Listen to me, and *hear* what I'm telling you. Do not let your mind get in your way at this moment. *Feel.*" She presses her hand to my heart then moves it to my stomach. "How does he make you feel? How does he feel knowing you're growing someone you made together? By the look on your face, I would imagine that he loves it more than just a little bit, am I right?"

I nod my head, feeling overwhelmed by their words.

"Damn pregnancy hormones." I sniffle.

"Oh, they're the worst," Lauren says. "And I only had to

deal with it once. But I had a boy and girl in there at the same time. It was like my body was going through whiplash."

"Thanks, girls. I don't know what I'd do without you," I say as the waterworks increase and I start weeping. "We're having a baby!" I wail, half laughing.

"Don't cry! Then I'll start crying!" Carly wipes at her eyes that are already leaking.

"A baby!" Lauren shouts, throwing her arms in the air, trying to lighten the mood. "I can't wait to snuggle it and smell it and dress it up!" Lauren, I can only imagine the clothes she'll buy this little bundle.

"Me either!"

Soon we're all huddled together on the couch, each of us crying and laughing.

"I think it's safe to say she told them," James's voice carries over us.

I lift my head and nod, seeing Andy's smiling face. His eyes soften as soon as we make contact.

"Babe," he murmurs, making his way toward me on the couch. The ladies move aside as he crouches in front of me and leans up to kiss my stomach. "How're my girls feeling?"

I hear the ladies behind me aww, and the guys snort.

"I'm good."

"Yeah? Then what's with the tears?" He wipes at my cheeks with his thumbs then kisses me softly.

I shrug my shoulders, not wanting to admit how self-conscious I feel about... well, everything. He raises his eyebrows at me, not satisfied with my lack of answering.

"Talk to me," his voice quiet and so damn sexy.

I glance around the room and notice that six pair of eyes are on us.

"Don't mind us," Barrett says with a cheeky grin. "Just keep talking, pretend we're not here."

Tess rolls her eyes, softly hits Barrett in the stomach, and walks over to me.

"We'll let you two chat. Incredibly happy for y'all. You're gonna be amazing parents. That's one lucky kiddo you got growing in that belly of yours, mama." She leans down and kisses my cheek then squeezes Andy's hand, turns and grabs a grumbling Barrett, and shoves him toward the door.

Everyone else says their congratulations and good byes, and soon we're alone.

"Talk to me," he says again. "It's just me here." He's so reassuring and thoughtful.

"It's just... you're amazing."

He gives me a crooked grin and winks. "And this makes you cry?"

"No! I... you really want this? With me?"

He looks at me with furrowed brows. Just last night I was blissfully happy for us. I couldn't wait to tell everyone that I was carrying his child, and less than twelve hours later I'm a nervous wreck. No doubt he's experiencing some whiplash of his own. "Christine, where is this coming from?"

"I don't know."

"Bullshit."

I scoff and roll my eyes, scrunching my nose up at him. "You're so annoying. Why do you know everything?"

"I love it when you do that, scrunch your cute little nose. I wonder if she'll do that," he says, glancing down at my stomach. "And, I don't know everything. I just know *you*. And I know you're getting inside your head right now. Are you having second thoughts about me? I thought..."

"What? No! Why would you think that?"

"Well, gee, I don't know. I walk in after we've told our friends about the baby, and you're not exactly shouting your happiness from the rooftops."

"It's not that, I promise."

"So, we're still good? You and me?"

"Yeah," I say, but I can hear the doubt in my own voice.

"Christine," his voice less soft than it was.

"I don't know how to say this out loud."

"Try me."

"Ugh! These stupid damn hormones! One minute I'm perfectly sane then... this!" I gesture to myself and he says nothing, simply gives me a look of understanding. I take a deep breath and rip off the proverbial band aid. "I wanna get married!" I shout then cover my face with my hands.

"Now?"

I remove my hands and look at him. His chocolate brown eyes shine, his smile wide.

"What do you mean?" I ask him in a whisper, fearful that I'm misreading his response.

His eyes soften, and he turns his head slightly. He leans in close, resting his forehead against my own. I inhale deeply, taking in his warm comforting scent that's all him. "Christine, you've gotta know. I'd marry you yesterday."

"Why didn't you say anything? I thought marriage was off the table after Heather."

He scowls at me. "Don't say her name and ruin our proposal day."

"Pro..." I clear my throat. "Proposal day?" I squeak out.

"Well, it wasn't necessarily planned this way, but I'm taking my lead from James, I guess. I've had this, well, for a while now." He reaches into the front pocket of his jeans and pulls out a little black velvet pouch. "I had to take it out of the box. That thing was annoying the shit out of me in my pocket. But I never wanted to be away from the ring, kind of like you. The boys helped me pick it out. And Bri. I asked her first."

I suck in a breath and move my eyes from the object in his

hands to his mouth. His tongue sneaks out and licks his lips, his teeth grazing his bottom lip. I take in a shaky breath, resisting the urge to bite his lip. It seems that I've hit the horny stage of this pregnancy, and even though I couldn't keep my hands off him before, it's only gotten worse. Or better, depending on how you look at it. I look up in his eyes and can see that he knows exactly what I'm thinking.

"You... what?"

"I took the kids out for pizza," he explains, and the fact that he says kids and he's including all three as if they're one does something to me. "And I asked them what they thought. They're excited. All three of them. So excited, in fact, that they dragged me to a jewelry store as soon as we were done eating. They're probably going to be pretty pissed that I did this without them, actually."

I couldn't stop the wetness on my cheeks if I tried.

"Christine," he raises up on one knee, kneeling in front of me. He takes the ring out of the pouch and slides it over the tip of his forefinger while I wipe the tears from my face and sniffle. "You told me once that I needed to be happy. I listened. You. You're my happy. You're Reece and Aidan's happy. You're Bri's happy. And soon, you'll be our little girl's happy."

I giggle and snort and try to remain looking cute but it's just not possible with the ugly crying that's happening right now. "You're just so sure it's a girl, huh?"

"Hazel's gonna even out our brood, you know?"

I nod my head, not being able to speak, but I know my smile is watery. He's so sure of us, of her, he's named her. And it's the perfect name. My green eyes. His brown.

"Neither of our lives have been easy, but that's okay with me, because I think that going through the crap? That's what brought me to you. But I do wish more than anything that I was your first love, and that you were mine always. I wish we could have shared all those moments together from the start. I wish no one had come before me to have your heart, and I pray I'm the last one to have it. I wish that person who had you first hadn't hurt you. I wish he wouldn't have taken advantage of the best thing you have to offer. But most of all, my wish is that you'll know I'll never forsake your heart, I'll never take it for granted, never forget that it's the most precious gift that you could ever give me. And, if you'll let me, I'll care for you, for the both of you." He leans up and kisses my stomach again. My hands go into his hair and he looks up at me, tears shining in his eyes.

He reaches for my left hand and blows out a shaky breath. "You're the love of my life, Christine. I don't want to wait a second longer. For the rest of our lives I want to wake up to you next to me in our bed. I want to have the privilege of loving you forever and knowing you're always mine. I want to travel the world with you by my side, I want to cook breakfast next to each other, clean up baby puke, watch our boys play sports, see Bri graduate from college and help her start her life, maybe adopt a puppy, choose paint colors, potty-train this little nugget, argue over who last emptied the dishwasher and what movie to watch and where to vacation next, curl up on the couch together and binge watch shows on Netflix. I want my last name to be yours. I want to show our kids what a real marriage is like for the rest of our lives. Will you marry me?"

There's no other answer I could give him. Even before the proposal he just gave me. I nod my head quickly and sob. "Yes! Of course!"

I throw my arms around him, knocking him down and back into the coffee table.

"Oomph."

"Sorry, got a little excited." He just smiles and twists so we're lying on the floor between the couch and coffee table, him hovering over me.

"I have one more question, and I want you to think about this, and we'll have to talk to them, but... if you want..." He hesitates, suddenly looking nervous and shy.

"Hey, what is it?" I graze the stubble on his face with my fingers, and he closes his eyes, leaning into the touch.

"The boys. They love you so much. I know it's early, and I don't expect this to be decided now. But I want to know if you're open to discussing adoption with them?"

My heart does a double tap against my chest, tears springing to my eyes immediately.

"Yes." I don't hesitate.

His answering smile comes quickly and widens across his face. "That's two yeses. Damn, I'm a lucky man. Can I put this on you, now?" He shows me the beautiful cushion cut diamond ring. It could turn my finger green or be a Ring Pop for all I care.

"What are you waiting for?" I stick my hand up and wiggle my finger, anxious to have the sign of his everlasting love on my finger, and he effortlessly slides it on. We both watch, and as soon as it's in place he lifts his eyes to mine.

"How'd you know my size?"

"One day when you were taking a nap I sized your finger with a string," he admits with a slight tinge of blush to his cheeks.

I choke back a laugh and can just picture him trying to be stealthy. Though I'm a little concerned by how out of it I am while napping. "You did?"

"Once I got that ring on your finger, and a yes out of your mouth, I only want to see it on, never off, so I wanted to make sure it fit."

"I love you so much, Mr. Simpson."

He grins his wide grin, the one that reaches his eyes and makes them sparkle. His tongue snakes out and he licks his bottom lip, and it makes me want to devour him. "I love you so much, almost-Mrs. Simpson."

Grasshoppers jump in my stomach like it's the first sign of summer. "I like the sound of that."

"It'll sound a whole lot better without the almost included." His voice is husky and deep.

"I agree."

"Tomorrow?"

"Tomorrow what?"

"Want to get married tomorrow?"

A laugh bubbles up out of me. I don't care about a big wedding. We've both been there and done that, and we've learned that a wedding doesn't make a marriage. I meant it when I said I would marry him in the court house.

"Well soon, yes. But not tomorrow. I doubt Bri can be home, and I won't do this without her."

"I don't like the word soon, remember?" He looks so vulnerable, and hearing him remind me of it makes me hate his ex-wife even more. Every time he asked when she would give him the divorce her answer was "soon."

"Right. Well, how about... two weeks? I'm sure we can convince Bri to be home then, and it will give the girls a chance to find something to wear because you know Lauren will expect to be a bridesmaid. That better?"

"Better." And he kisses me soundly to seal the deal. "In two weeks. I'm gonna marry the shit out of you," he mumbles against my lips.

"Mmm." I can't form any coherent words because at the moment his hands have me distracted, running up and down my sides, sliding under my shirt and up to cup my breasts, squeezing just lightly. They're still tender, and he knows this.

Mercy, he's so sexy. My body melts beneath his. I wrap my arms around his neck, keeping him close. Our tongues tangle, our breaths intermingle, and our bodies crash together. He lowers his center, grinding himself against mine, and the sensation sends bottle rockets through my body, causing me to moan deeply. He lifts his head and moves his mouth, kissing me on the cheek, my jaw, my neck.

I pull at his shirt and he lifts slightly, yanking his shirt off in one swift movement. He tosses it to the floor, and once again his mouth is on me. Our tongues tangle with each other, his lips soft and punishing at the same time. I can taste the cinnamon of his gum that he's always chewing. My hands graze the smooth contours of his chest, down to the ridges of his abs and up his back. I grip his shoulders, digging my nails into his skin. He moans and shifts, pressing his hardness against my center when I wrap my legs around his waist, locking my ankles together.

He lifts up and looks down at me, breathing heavily.

"I love you. You said yes, right?"

"Why would you question that? Andy, I think I've loved you since you took me to the cabin."

He smiles and leans down, lifts my shirt and kisses my belly, moving higher with each graze of his lips. Just as he's about to remove my shirt, we hear a pounding on the door.

"Let us in! The girls want to see the ring then you can get back to having all the sex!" Barrett's voice booms loudly through the closed door.

"Shit," Andy mumbles. "Why is he such a pain in the ass?" His voice raises through the last words.

"Heard that!"

"Good!"

"Don't let Andy put his shirt back on!" Lauren shouts. "What? Dang, Josh, you don't have to growl at me!"

"Stop staring at him!"

"I can't help it!"

"Are they watching?" I whisper shout, horrified at what our friends could have seen. I thought they had left!

Andy looks over his shoulder, I lean up on my elbows and sure enough, through the windows off my front porch stand six of our best friends staring in, completely unashamed at their Peeping Tom tactics.

Carly waves like a maniac, smiling widely, James's arm around her, who leans down and kisses her on top of the head. Tess and Lauren have their faces and palms planted against the window like one of those old stuffed Garfield cats. Josh and Barrett both have their phones up and aimed at us.

"Were you recording us?" I screech.

"Not the sexy time. Just the proposal part. But we can do that, too, if you want!" Barrett shouts. "Come on! Let us in!"

"You guys left through the same door you're standing on the other side of, it's not locked, you dumbasses!" Andy shouts.

He barely gets the words out and the door flies open, Josh and Barrett tripping over each other through the doorway, Josh landing on the floor first.

"Dammit! That's the second time I've fallen today!" Josh grumbles. He pops up with a jump, smiling as though nothing happened. "Congratulations! Ha!" He points to Barrett then around the room. "I said it first, suckers!"

Andy pinches the bridge of his nose and moves to get off me. He stands, giving me his hand to help me up before he reaches down to swipe his black t-shirt off the floor.

"Please. By all means. Come in. We weren't in the middle of anything." He wraps an arm around my waist and kisses my temple.

"Oh please, y'all can get back to it. We just wanted to make sure you guys were good, and we're glad we did, otherwise we would have missed the proposal!" Carly claps her hands.

"Ever occur to you that it was a private moment?"

"No." Barrett looks at us and raises his phone to take a quick picture.

"I'll take a copy of that," Lauren teases.

"Would you stop! I'm right here!"

Lauren looks over at Josh and shrugs before mumbling an apology.

"For real, y'all. We're so dang excited for you guys!" Tess bounces over and hugs us both.

"Woman! Hands off shirtless Andy! Andy, my man, do us a favor and cover that up? You're making us look bad."

"Speak for yourself, brother. I didn't get the nickname Captain for nothing."

"Oh, shut it."

"Just sayin'." James shrugs his shoulders.

"He's not lyin', either," Carly agrees quickly, but blushes and bites her lip.

"Mine! How many times do I have to tell you that?" James says oddly as he reaches over and removes her lip with his thumb. Those two are so weird. I feel like we're in some weird dimension right now where kids are adults and adults are kids. But I wouldn't have it any other way. Our friends might have their moments of immaturity, but it's all in good fun.

Andy grins at everyone and slides his shirt on, and I sigh. Lauren's right. It really is a shame to cover up his abs. He's incredibly good looking with a shirt on but without? They could put him on a billboard and it would stop traffic.

"All honesty, now that we don't have the distraction of Andy's bare chest..."

"And abs," Tess adds in helpfully, making Barrett sigh and shake his head, rolling his eyes.

"Yes, that. Congratulations again, you two. We couldn't be happier for you. Between the baby and the engagement, you two deserve all the happiness in the world, and we are all so excited for you."

"Thank you. It means a lot to us to have you guys by our side."

I look over at Andy and he looks back at me; the love I feel radiating off him is overwhelming at times. He fixed a part of me I didn't know was broken. When Todd turned to someone else rather than me when he was at his lowest, I didn't realize how deeply it affected me. I had always brushed it off that it was just something he did because he was going through a hard time. Looking back, I realize that yeah, that was the reason. But it doesn't excuse it or make it right.

And I know, without a doubt in my mind, that Andy will never do the same to me. That he'll fight for us, no matter what we're going through. I was meant to be his forever, and I feel ready to accept that gift.

EPILOGUE

CHRISTINE

"This was a horrible idea. A stupid, ridiculous, horrible idea that you got us into. Why did I listen to you?"

"Me? How is this my fault?"

I look pointedly down at his crotch, and he guffaws.

"Oh, yes. Blame him. Makes sense."

"I thought so. If it wasn't for him, we wouldn't be he... aggghhh!"

"Breathe, baby, breathe. You got this." Andy is by my side in a flash, crooning words of encouragement into my ear.

"She's trying to kill me, Andy. I know it. There's no other explanation. Bri was never this mean," I scream/grunt/groan through another contraction as I squeeze Andy's hand.

"So, now you think it's a girl?" he teases, trying to lighten the mood.

"Oh, please," I grumble, annoyed.

"You're the strongest woman I know, sweetheart. And I'm so proud of you. You're doing so amazing."

"Whatever. Tomorrow we're going to force a watermelon out of your pee hole and see how it works out for you."

"Gee, I think I'll pass, but thank you for the sweet offer."

I relax between contractions, wishing like hell I had come in earlier and not tried to be tough and labor at home for so long.

"Andy. I think I need a do over on today. And don't you dare say I told you so, but I think you may be right — I should have come to the hospital earlier. This no drugs thing is bullshit."

"There's literally nothing in the world you could threaten me with that would get me to admit I was right."

"Why did you let me stay home for so long?"

"I'm not answering that either."

"Aghhhh! Andy!" I pull him close as another contraction hits.

I may have underestimated how quickly I would move through labor. I mean, it was nineteen years ago the last time I went through this. *Nineteen!* I figured my body wouldn't be jumping back on the labor bandwagon. Not to mention that I'm old as the hills.

I stayed at home, minding my own business, fighting through the pain of each contraction, not really paying attention to how quickly they were coming. My water hadn't even broken yet. Meanwhile, Andy, the caged animal that he was, paced around the house until he finally stepped in, demanding I let him bring me to the hospital.

Once we were settled in the pickup, I called to let them know I was coming, and they asked me how far apart the contractions were, to which I moaned, considering a contraction hit at just that moment.

"Okay, is there any chance your husband can maybe get you here a little... quicker?" the kind nurse asked.

"Uhhhh," I groaned, looking over at Andy. He was sweating, breathing heavily, and leaning over the steering wheel cursing like a mad man at anyone who got in his way.

"I don't think that will be a problem," I assured the nurse, who then told me they'd have someone waiting for me by the ER to escort me back to OB.

"Oh, that's not necess... aggghhhh!"

"Let's just pretend that you need him to make him feel useful, shall we?"

"Yeah, okay. Maybe that's good."

"Let's also maybe have your husband step on it? Unless he's in the mood to deliver your baby in the car?"

She was clearly not the most reassuring person to have on the other end of the line while I was freaking out and trying to keep Andy calm.

We came sliding into the ER parking lot, Andy slamming the pickup into park before it fully came to a stop, causing it to rock back and forth. He ran around to my side, opened the door, and helped me out.

When we got to the ER entrance, there was an orderly waiting for us with a wheel chair.

"Mrs. Simpson?"

"That's me. I got this, though. No need for the wheel chair."

And then I peed on the floor. Well, not pee. My water broke, gushing all over the floor beneath me.

The orderly looked down at the pool of fluids, up to me, back down, and up again.

"Humor me?" He tried for a smile. Didn't work.

"Fine. But I can totally walk on my own."

"We know you can, baby, but let the man do his job. I'm sure he lives for this. Pushing cranky pregnant ladies through the halls."

"Dude. Did you just..." the orderly said just as I finished his thought.

"Did you just call me cranky?"

"Nope."

"I'm gonna kick Carly's ass. Like she better watch her back," I growl.

"She knows boxing moves." Andy raises his eyebrows at me, looking thoroughly amused by my current state of miserable and dying.

I wave him off. "It doesn't matter. She's not gonna know what hit her when I get to her. Do yoga, she said. It will help with the labor, she said. It will help you move things along, she said. She's such a bitch."

Andy laughs loudly. Carly is the furthest thing from a bitch, but right now I kind of hate her for getting me healthy during my pregnancy, thus causing this baby to come so quickly that I got to the hospital at nine centimeters dilated, thus *no drugs*! No happy juice. No blissfully pushing a baby out my vagina and not feeling a thing.

"Knock, knock," a sweet voice calls out.

"Well, speak of the devil!" I yell.

Carly's face appears in the doorway, her wide smile dies the instant she sees me.

"Oh, shit. What happened to you?"

"Seriously?" I screech, pointing to my stomach.

"But..."

"We got here and she was at a nine," Andy answers her unasked question.

"Already?" Oh, now it's her turn to screech.

"Wow, yoga actually works," she mumbles.

"Helpful!"

"Sorry! But... wow. I didn't realize it would actually help THAT much!"

"Come here, Carly. I wanna tell you something." I crook my finger at her, but she's shaking her head, stepping behind Andy.

"I'll just..." She starts making her way out the door, pointing behind her.

"No! Don't!" Andy shouts, obviously not wanting to be left alone with me and my grouchiness.

Another contraction hits, and I fold over. "Aghhhh! Holy hell! I think my insides just split into a million pieces. Check, Andy. Make sure that nothing just fell out."

"No way."

"Okay, yeah. I think I'll just... get Bri. Or... someone, anyone else. Good luck!" Carly babbles.

"Traitor!" Andy hollers at her, as she bolts out the door like the hounds of hell are chasing her. And I'm pretty sure the luck she was wishing was to Andy rather than me.

"Make it stop. There's so much pressure. So. Much."

"I'll call the nurse. Maybe it's time?" he asks, rushing toward the door.

He opens the door, peeks his head out, and in a moment of his own panic yells, "Someone get your ass in here! Now! I think she's ready!"

He walks back in, calm as ever, like he didn't just scream into the hallway.

"Someone will be right in, baby." He leans down and kisses my forehead. "We're almost to the end, I'm sure of it."

"Mm hmm. You know this because..."

"Because I can't take anymore, and if she's not gonna come out on her own now I'm going in after her."

"Let's take a look, shall we?" Dr. Matthews's voice cuts in as he walks into the room.

"Yeah! Let's do that!" My voice is sunshine and rainbows.

"Oh, you're nice to him?"

I shoot Andy a dirty look.

His eyebrows kiss his hairline.

"Feeling a bit uncomfortable, are we?"

"A bit, yes."

"I was asking your wife, Andy."

"Oh," he says sheepishly.

"I'm great! Just ready to get this show on the road!" I say in my most pleasant voice, not wanting to anger the guy who will be staring at my most private area for the next however long. I'm thinking ten minutes, tops. I've been doing this labor thing for long enough now.

Dr. Matthews chuckles. "Right." He pulls on a pair of gloves and takes a seat while the nurse who walked in with him comes to my side, directing Andy to hold the leg she's not holding. She looks like she's about my age, in fact, I think it's one of Grady's friends' moms. Blake maybe? I can't be sure.

"You're doing amazing, Christine. Seriously."

"I don't feel like I am."

"I promise." She smiles.

"Blake's mom, right?"

"Yup! Lisa."

"Right. I knew you looked fam... aghhh! Holy mother! This can't be... nor... gahhh!"

"Breathe, honey. Breathe. You're doing great." Lisa pats a damp washcloth on my forehead while Andy leans in close, allowing me to grip his hand with hulk-like strength.

"Good, Christine. Nice breathing. I'm going to check you now, see how we're coming along."

He presses one hand to my inner thigh and the other, well, he just gets all close and personal. "Little bit of pressure here," he says in warning.

"Mm hmm." I grit my teeth as Andy brushes the hair from my forehead, kissing me on the temple.

"Christine? Andy? You ready? You're at ten centimeters."

"Thank God. Get her out," Andy growls, his forehead resting against the place he just kissed.

Beside me, Lisa giggles, and I roll my eyes.

"It's been a little while since you've done this, Christine, but nothing has changed. Remember to breathe through the contractions like you've been doing, bear down, curl your body into a C. Lisa and Andy will help hold your legs, and things will go smoothly."

"Smooth. Right."

"We got this. She's coming, and you're amazing and beautiful and I love you more than I ever thought possible and I don't think I've ever seen you look sexier than you are in this moment, your eyes are blazing and skin flushed, you're determined and sweaty and..."

"Now's not the time, Andy!"

"Right. Okay, yeah. Doc? Just... don't... I mean... please don't hurt her. Either of them."

"I'll do my best, Andy. I promise." Dr. Matthews throws me a wink, but I don't have time to even smile my thanks for his calming words because another contraction hits, and this one is stronger than any of the others.

"Aghhhhhhhhh! Andy!" I squeeze his hand.

"Okay, Christine. You need to push."

"No shit?"

I curl my body like I learned in my Lamaze classes. It had been so long since either of us went through this that we decided to go to the classes again. And I'm glad I did. I had blissfully forgotten so many things about childbirth.

Lisa starts counting to ten, and I suck in a breath before pushing for what feels like a hundred counts, blowing out a deep breath when I'm finished, collapsing back onto the bed.

"Good. Good. You're doing really well, Christine."

Lisa is right there with a damp washcloth, dabbing my forehead. Andy lifts our hands to his lips and kisses the back of mine softly, his eyes never straying from me.

"You made some progress. You're doing great," Dr. Matthews says, shifting on his seat by my feet.

I barely have time to relax before another contraction hits, and soon I'm pushing with everything I have in me.

I curse.

I push.

I scream.

I push.

I curse.

A lot of cursing.

I push.

A lot of pushing.

A lot of screaming.

An hour. An entire freaking hour goes by before the doctor looks up at me with worry in his eyes. "Okay, the baby isn't shifting. The shoulder keeps getting stuck against your pelvic bone. Right now, baby is doing fine, but we need to get things moving along. I need you to bear down with everything you have on your next contraction or I'm going to have to go in."

"Go in?"

"Yes. We can't have either of you going into distress."

"No."

"No?" he asks me.

"No," I answer with conviction. I try to sit up a little taller, even though it doesn't really work with my feet in the stirrups and their hands wrapped around my legs, which only causes me to almost take out my poor doctor by nearly whacking him in the side of the head with my foot. "No. I can do this."

"Christine..." Andy looks like he's about ready to throw up.

"I said, no. If she starts going into distress, I won't fight you, but I promise you, I can do this. And I will."

"Two more pushes," he says, his brown eyes lighter than normal, looking up at me from his position on the stool. "Then I'm going to have to go in."

I nod my head as another contraction threatens to rip me in two.

Lisa grips my hand and pulls my leg up, Andy following her.

"Christine, you can do this. Push, girl. Push. I know it hurts. I know you feel like your body is going to break, but you're the strongest woman I know," Lisa's reassuring words cheer me on.

I look at Andy, and he nods, encouragingly. "We got this." It's been his motto since he suspected we were pregnant and he's said it countless times since then.

"Yeah. Okay," I grunt out as the contraction peaks.

I close my eyes tightly and push, resisting the urge to use any of my energy in making the noises I really want.

When I don't think I can take another second, Andy's left arm wraps around my back, lifting me up farther off the bed, his right arm still holding up my leg.

"Keep going, Christine. You got this! You're so strong. So incredible. Come on, baby."

He's chanting every encouraging thing he can think of. Tears are streaming down my face as the last of the contraction hits, and Dr. Matthews announces that her head is out.

"Lots of dark hair. Peek around, Daddy," Lisa says after getting a look.

Andy stares at me for a moment before shifting to the end of the bed.

"Oh, my gosh. She's here, baby. One more push. Come on. You can do it."

He's back by my side just as another swell hits, causing me to rise up and push with everything in me.

"Last one, Christine. This is it. Just one more big push and you're done," Dr. Matthews says, his voice calm.

And then...

The most beautiful sound in the world.

The tiniest of cries fills the small hospital room.

And then...

"Congratulations, you two. You have a daughter. Do you want to do the honors, Daddy?"

I collapse onto the bed and watch as Andy reaches around, taking the scissors from Dr. Matthews's outstretched hands before cutting the cord that tied our daughter to me for nine months. I watch in awe as Dr. Matthews places our baby on my chest after quickly wiping her off. I place my hand on her back and Andy bends down to kiss her head. Tears spring to my eyes when Andy looks at me with glassy eyes of his own.

"She's the most gorgeous thing I've ever seen," he says, a sound of complete wonderment in his voice.

Andy lifts Hazel from my arms so the nurse can finish everything she needs to. She takes measurements and pictures, bundling her in a blanket after cleaning her up a bit more, all while Andy hovers, watching closely. I wince as Dr. Matthews finishes everything up, pushing on my stomach and stitching me up.

Once Lisa is finished, she hands the baby to Andy, the sight of him holding her close making my heart swell.

My smile is watery as I hold my arms up for him to bring her to me. He bends down, kisses her on the forehead, then walks over to me, kissing me on the cheek and laying her against my chest at the same time.

"Thank you for this gift. I love you. More than I ever thought possible."

"I love you, too, Andy."

My eyes drift down to our baby girl, her dewy wrinkly skin, mess of dark hair, eyes unfocused as they gaze up at me. Her soft mewling sounds and jerky movements tugging at my heart.

"Do we have a name?" Lisa asks.

"Hazel Brielle Simpson," Andy tells the nurse, not looking

away from either me or our daughter, the palm of his hand covering the back of Hazel's head.

We had discussed middle names, but Brielle wasn't one of them. Andy chose both the first and middle name for our baby girl. Most women would be upset. Me? I'm ecstatic. I wouldn't have picked a better name.

"Beautiful name for a beautiful girl." She smiles at us.

And before I know it, it's the three of us. Andy has taken approximately twelve hundred pictures on his phone. Kissed both of us at least as many times, and we've shed countless tears.

"I'm going to get the kids, okay? Are you ready for them?"

I nod my head, another wave of emotion hitting me, and he kisses me once more before walking out the door.

When he returns, the boys and Bri are following him.

Bri already has tears streaming down her face, and the boys' eyes haven't left their new little sister.

"Oh, my gosh, she's beautiful," Bri says, rushing to my side.

"Kids, I'd like you to meet Hazel Brielle."

Bri gasps then hiccups through a cry, picking up her baby sister from where she was resting on my chest, cradling her close.

"She's... Mom..." Bri tries to speak but becomes too emotional, cuddling her baby sister close, kissing her cheeks, smelling her hair, tears streaming down her cheeks.

Reece and Aidan are standing near, leaning over to get a closer look.

Aidan sniffles, and Bri leans her head against his. "She's so tiny," he muses, lifting the back of his finger to her cheek. "I can't believe how..." He chokes on his words, causing Bri and me to both let out a sob. He turns to me, carefully leaning over and hugging me.

"Thank you. I didn't know I wanted a baby sister so bad."

I wrap my arms around him and kiss the top of his head. "I love you, kiddo."

"Love you too, Mama."

He and Reece both started calling me Mama shortly after we got married. It slipped out from Aidan first, his face flamed red, and tears immediately sprang to my eyes. I asked him why he was blushing, and he shyly asked if it was okay that they call me Mama. I told them they could call me whatever they were comfortable with, and I love that they chose the name Mama. It's something unique for just me.

"Can I hold her?" Reece asks.

"No," Bri teases, making us both laugh as she cuddles Hazel closer before handing her over.

For the next thirty minutes, our new family of six coos and awws and gushes over the perfection that is Hazel before she begins getting fussy. The nurse interrupts, letting us know that we need to try to feed her, so Bri offers to take the boys for supper.

"I don't know if I can hold them back much longer, so as soon as you're done with the first feed, are you open to visitors?"

I don't even have to ask who she's trying to hold back.

Andy chuckles. "Yeah, you can send them in when she's done here."

"Do you remember how to do this, Christine?" Lisa asks.

"I think so, but..." I position Hazel, and after a few failed attempts, she latches on. She sighs contently while Andy watches in admiration. Lisa leaves the room, letting us know that she'll leave us alone and be back to check on our progress.

As soon as the door clicks shut, Andy lifts his eyes to me, a sparkle twinkling. "I know this is not the most appropriate time, but I don't think I've ever been more turned on in my life. Seeing you with our daughter... holy shit, Christine. It does things for me. It's going to be a really long six weeks, you know that?"

I wince as a laugh bubbles up, trying to stay still so Hazel doesn't lose her hold on me.

He kisses me on the lips then on the forehead. With Bri spending time with the boys, Hazel in my arms and Andy next to me, I finally feel like home.

Andy

I ALREADY KNEW my wife was strong. I already knew she was beautiful and incredible and amazing and determined and just... so much more than I ever could have hoped for.

I finally admitted what I've been thinking ever since she went into labor, and what do I get in return? Christine's laughter.

"Oh, my gosh. Only you, Andy."

"What? I can't help it! You should see you right now!"

"If watching another woman nurse her baby turns me on then I think we have a problem."

I give her a sly grin, knowing that she'll get hers soon enough. "Oh, just wait, baby. Just wait."

"Whatever. You think I don't already know you're gonna be the hottest Daddy ever?"

I grin, not being able to help it.

The fact that Christine still thinks I'm *hot,* in her words, makes me feel like I could conquer the world.

She finishes nursing and presses the button to call the nurse, who comes in just a few moments later.

"Everything go okay?" Lisa asks, smiling as she walks in, placing her hand under the hand sanitizer contraption by the door and rubbing her hands together.

"It did. Took a bit and I had some cramping as she was nursing, but we'll get it figured out. She drank herself to sleep."

I snicker, the words *Like mother like daughter* on the tip of my tongue, remembering Margarita Madness, and she shoots daggers in my direction.

Too bad a smirk followed so closely behind, along with an eye roll.

"Seriously, guys. She's one of the most beautiful babies I've ever seen. And I'm not just saying that."

No way am I denying that. Hazel is gorgeous. And I'm afraid I'll never have ownership of my balls for the rest of my life, knowing that she and her mom now securely hold them in the palm of their hands.

"Are you ready? They're getting incredibly restless out there." She makes an eek expression with her mouth, and we both laughed lowly.

"Five more minutes," I tell Lisa, and she nods her head before quietly leaving.

"I love you." I kiss Christine on the forehead then lean over to Hazel. "And I love you, baby girl." I lift her from Christine's arms and cuddle her tightly to my chest.

I walk to the window, giving Hazel her first view of the world.

"My promise to you, Hazel. I'm going to do my best to slay your dragons, to watch you soar, and pick you up when you fall. I'll be by your side helping you to achieve your dreams and will hold you when you need held. I'll never leave you, sweet girl."

I breathe in her sweet scent and brace myself when I hear the door open, knowing our private moment is about to be shattered.

"About time that warden let us in. Holding me back from my niece," James says. I turn to see him rubbing his hands together much the same way Lisa did when she entered.

He holds his hands out to me, somehow stiff arming all three girls in the process, and lifts Hazel out of my arms.

His hand cradles the back of her head, and he brings his face down to hers. "Hi, Hazel. I'm your uncle James. The cool one. Don't let any of these clowns tell you different."

"You're so full of it," Barrett mumbles, and Tess giggles.

I watch as our friends pass Hazel around, each of them falling in love with her as quickly as I did. And as Bri and the boys tumble back into the room, all I can think is, I've never felt so at home as I do in this moment.

EXTENDED EPILOGUE

Extended Epilogue
Bri

"I can't tell her, Andy." I can hear through the door that my mom is crying, and it makes my stomach hurt.

I've only been home from college a few days, and most of that time has been spent cuddling and playing with Hazel.

I can already see that the boys basically treat her like the little princess she is.

"We've been over this. She has a right to know."

"No. She doesn't. Drop it. I'm telling you, now, don't go there."

"Christine, I love you. You know I do. I couldn't be more in love with you. But this? She needs to know. You realize now that Heather has it in her head after Preston left her, she's gonna spread that shit far and wide. I know she is. And if she doesn't? That asshole little brother of his will. Especially after all the shit that went down with him and Grady. You need to make sure she hears it from you, rather than the damn Liberty rumor mill."

What?

What does Grady and Dawson have to do with what's upsetting Mom? I hear a sniffle and then Mom ask for a tissue.

"I don't want her to think differently of him."

"If she hears it from you, she won't. You explain it to her how you explained it to me. Make her see it the way it happened, not the ugly everyone else is going to turn it into."

I hear more sniffling and take a step backward, not wanting to hear what I know is something that will change my life forever. Unfortunately, when I move back, the heel of my foot lands on one of the damn dog's toys, and it squeaks.

"Boys?"

I blow out a breath, knowing I can't just sit here in hiding like I want to.

"No, it's me." I walk around the corner into Mom and Andy's bedroom. They're sitting on the bed, Mom's head is on Andy's shoulder, always her pillar of strength. The baby is asleep in the bassinette next to the bed on Andy's side; he never allows her to be too far away from him, so it's no surprise that's where he set it. Mom tried moving it to her side, so it would be easier when the baby would wake up in the middle of the night to feed her, but Andy kept moving it back to his side. Eventually Mom just gave up and let him have his way.

When Andy and Mom got married, Dad had been gone for so long. And seeing them together? It feels like it was always supposed to be them. I loved my father, but I don't remember seeing my mom in love the way she is with Andy.

"Bri?" Mom lifts her head from Andy's shoulder and she wipes under her nose. Andy rubs my mom's shoulder, and she looks at him like she's begging him for something. He nods a couple times then stands up and leans back down to kiss her on the cheek.

He walks over to me and places both hands on my shoulders and looks into my eyes.

"What is it?" I ask, my voice is quiet and unsure.

"Just listen to her, okay?"

"You're kind of scaring me," I admit, a quiver in my voice.

"Don't be scared. Your mom and I love you, that's all you need to remember. But promise me you'll listen to her."

I look back and forth between his dark brown eyes, the exact color of his twin boys', and Hazel's. "I promise," I whisper and look at Mom, who's wiping tears from under her eyes.

"What's wrong?" I ask, after I hear the door click closed behind me.

"Nothing's wrong, sweetie. It's just something I should have told you a long time ago. And you need to hear it."

"Okay?"

"First of all, you know Andy's ex-wife Heather was with Preston, right?"

I nod but *don't* really know. "Yeah. But I don't understand why he's a factor," I admit.

"Well, I didn't at first, either. In fact, I didn't know it until just recently. As in, yesterday."

"Mom. Please just tell me what's happening. You're making me super nervous."

"I'm just going to explain it as best I can and with all the details. Just listen to me and don't interrupt. You can ask questions later."

"Mom."

"Yeah. Okay. So. Andy caught Heather having sex with Preston."

I nod because, of course, I know that much.

"Right. So, what I just found out is that Preston is Dawson's older brother."

"What?" I ask, my voice barely above a whisper.

"I know. Little punk following his older douchebag brother. Man, I hate that family," she says angrily.

"So, what does that have to do with us, though? I mean, aside from the crazy coincidence. Wait..."

"What?"

"It's just... that night that, you know." I gesture up and down my body, and she closes her eyes. We haven't talked very much about the night Dawson wouldn't take *no* for an answer.

Grady and I had gone to the field party together, just like every other week. But that night I was pissed at Grady for not realizing that I wanted more. I've been in love with Grady since I was eleven years old.

Dawson had been asking me out on a date for a few years, and I always turned him down. It wasn't only Dawson who I wasn't interested in. It was every other guy who didn't go by the name of Grady Ryan. He was my only and forever.

That night, Dawson cornered me. Luckily, he didn't get far — though he definitely got far enough. He gripped my arms and wouldn't let go then jammed his disgusting tongue down my throat. I tried to move my head away from him, and that's when he got really pissed.

"You're such a fucking tease, Bri. No wonder your mom couldn't hold on to her husband. I bet you learned everything from her, huh?"

"What?" I ask, continuing to try to push him away.

"That's right. My older brother told me all about it."

"Told you what?" I ask again, genuinely confused.

He smiles a smarmy smile then grabs me again; he yanks my body against his so quickly I lose my footing, slamming into him.

"I knew you'd come around eventually."

"No. Stop," I plead, tears already streaming down my face.

I push and squirm, trying to get away, but he is too strong.

He reaches around, grabbing my butt in his hands and squeezes hard.

"It's gonna be so much fun breaking you in. I bet Grady hasn't done it yet, has he?"

I use the heel of my hand to hit him in the nose, and the next thing I know he has me on the ground. When I continue to fight, he slaps me across the cheek.

"Stop fighting, and it'll be so much more fun. I promise." He grinds his pelvis against my center, and I whimper, begging him to listen to me. To stop. "Oh, come on, Bri. I'll show you what you've been missing, hanging around Grady like a lost little puppy."

"Stop. No. Dawson, please. You don't want to do this."

"What the hell?" Someone shouts, and suddenly Dawson's body is lifted off mine.

"Answer me, you piece of shit!"

"We're cool, right Bri?" Dawson says, glaring at me.

"GRADY!" Blake shouts. "Get your ass over here, now!"

"Preston really was right."

I still don't understand what he means by that but it doesn't matter.

Grady shut him up and came to my rescue.

Just like he always did.

"What about that night, honey?" my mom asks, bringing me back to the present.

"Um. Well, I guess I remember Dawson kept saying these weird things about how his brother was right, but it all kind of blurred."

"Preston wasn't the first guy she'd had an affair with. Heather was with another man, well — several — but one in particular."

"What are you saying, Mom?"

"The day we found out your dad had cancer, I also walked in on him with..."

"Heather."

She nods and looks away, swipes a stray tear and clears her throat.

"Dad cheated on you?" I whisper the words like they're unbelievable. Because — they are. Unbelievable. Dad loved mom like she was his lifeline. At least, that's what I always knew. Now I don't know what to believe.

"You need to know that it was his only time."

Scoff.

"It's true, honey. He was in a bad way. You know that. He was feeling fantastic one day, and the next day he wasn't. We had gone to the doctor and knew the possibilities. He was supposed to wait until I was with him to find out the results. He decided to go alone. You know what he found out. She was..."

"What? Mom. Just *tell* me."

"Obviously, I wasn't there, but he got home and had a few drinks. Well — a lot. He was upset. Rightfully so. And she saw his car in the driveway. She'd been kind of coming around wherever he was for a while. Trying to get his attention. You need to understand what a horrible place he was in. And drunk. Not that it makes it okay, but..."

She pauses, and I watch as her eyes close. As if trying to block out the memories.

"I walked in on her on top of him in the living room."

I gasp. I can't help it. If I walked in on Grady that way...

"But. I just don't get it. Dad was crazy over you."

Her eyes soften, and she reaches over and clasps my hand between hers.

In the corner of the room, I hear Hazel squeak, but she quiets down right away.

"He was."

"So, he just, what, decided his love didn't matter? Your love didn't matter?"

"No. See? This is why I didn't want you to know. He *did*

love me. It wasn't about that. His head space was messed up, and he just... made a mistake."

"Oh, so it's okay to cheat on the person you devote your life to if they're drunk and in a bad way? Mom. Do you know how messed up *that* logic is?"

She doesn't respond.

"This is just great. I can't believe you hid this from me all these years! I can't believe... dammit, Mom! How am I supposed to have faith in..."

"You stop right there. I know where your head is going, honey, and you need to stop. Love? Your love with Grady? It's real. It's been real since you were eleven years old. Before you even understood what it was to love someone on a soul-deep level, the way you two do. Your dad and I never had that. We loved each other, yes. I would never deny that."

"I need some space. Or something. I can't... I can't deal with this right now."

Mom stands up when I do. "Please, understand, Bri. Your dad had a momentary case of douchery." I choke out a laugh/cry and swipe with the back of my hand under my nose. "He had also just found out he had cancer. And here was this younger woman acting desperate for him. In the short moments after finding out that he wasn't going to live much longer, he clung to something that made him feel young again. If only for a moment."

"Doesn't make it right," I mumble.

She shakes her head, understanding in her eyes. "No. No it doesn't. But it makes it... I don't know. Understandable?"

"I'll never understand that, Mom. I love you, and I understand why you didn't want me to know. I do. It still hurts that you kept it from me."

"I know. I never quite knew how to tell you."

Suddenly memories assault me.

"Wait. When you and Andy broke up for a few days, is this..."

Her eyes dart to the other side of the room before returning to me.

She nods sadly. "Yes. Heather was making sure everyone knew about it. Claimed that I was only with him to get back at her." She rolls her eyes. "He was hurt. By her. And it messed with his head a bit."

I take it all in, feeling like my mind is mush.

"I think I need to be alone for a little bit."

She sniffles. "Okay. Yeah. I understand. But, don't go far, yeah?"

I lean over and hug Mom, which she returns with every ounce of might she has in her, and I make my way out to my car.

I turn my phone off.

Start up the engine.

And drive.

And don't look back.

You can one-click Waiting For Her, Grady and Bri's story now!
https://jennifervanwykauthor.com/waiting-for-her/

ACKNOWLEDGMENTS

My Heavenly Father. The one who blessed me with my life. With the ability (and desire) to sit down at a computer and tell stories and touch people's hearts. I'm humbled. I am so grateful that He's my leader and I pray I always follow His leading.

Republishing From the Ground Up, A Better Place, and Feels Like Home wasn't an easy decision for me. When Blue Tulip Publishing accepted my first manuscript, I cried so many tears of joy. To put it lightly, I was honored and humbled. Nervous. Excited. All the things. You gave me the courage to step out and do this self-publishing thing and I'll be forever grateful for your hand in it.

My family is such an encouragement and I'm so proud of being able to call them mine. My husband and children are by far my biggest supporters, even if they aren't exactly sure what happens in the publishing process. LOL And my parents, especially. They read everything I write and while some of the scenes might be a little awkward for them, they never hesitate to pick up my next release.

Rach. My MafiaQn. Thanks for teaching me the importance of passing the baton. For calming me down and being real with me. I love you so very much.

Kate. My little southern pumpkin. I didn't expect our friendship but dang if I'm not grateful it appeared in my life.

To the real teacher in the story. You really do rock. You know who you are.

My friends who are with me in the Walk. I didn't know I was missing something in my life until that magical day when you came along. You've changed me. And I thank you. Big whopper of a thank you to Michelle L for having the courage to start us walking together. It's a pleasure and honor to be with you ladies.

Jill. You keep me in check and remind me of how to not be a total and complete wreck. I'm honored to have you have my back and am in awe daily of how you do what you do.

Jennifer's Java Girls. Wow – I had no idea what a pleasure it would be to have you in my life. You all make me smile. Thanks for that and so much more.

Bloggers, thanks to so many of you who chose to read a previously published book or already read it. You all have such an important role in our book world. Thank you!

Readers, again, you're rock stars. We love falling into stories. It's the best, isn't it? Man, I really love reading. LOL So yeah – you're my peeps. Thanks for picking up my stories.

ABOUT THE AUTHOR

From the Ground Up was Jennifer's first published novel and now that she was bitten by the writing bug, has no intention of ever stopping. Jennifer makes her home in small town Iowa with her high school sweetheart, three beautiful, hilarious and amazing kids, one crazy Jack Russell terrier. This is where her love for all things reading, baking, and cooking happen. Jennifer's family enjoys camping, boating, and spending time outside as much as possible. You'll be her best friend if you can make her laugh and follow up with asking her what to read next. When she's not writing, you can find her cheering the loudest at her kids' sporting events (read as: embarrassing them), sipping coffee or iced tea out of a mason jar with her Kindle in her lap or binging on Netflix.

You can follow her on Amazon here: http://amzn.to/2vZV2Ic

Make sure you stay up to date by following her newsletter: http://eepurl.com/dcTJKf

Join her reader group to be first in the know on all things JVW books: https://www.facebook.com/groups/JennifersJavaGirls/

OTHER BOOKS BY JENNIFER VAN WYK:

From the Ground Up (Barrett & Tess Ryan):
https://jennifervanwykauthor.com/from-the-ground-up/

A Better Place (James & Carly):
https://jennifervanwykauthor.com/a-better-place/

Feels Like Home (Andy & Christine):
https://jennifervanwykauthor.com/feels-like-home/

Waiting For Her (Grady & Bri):
https://jennifervanwykauthor.com/waiting-for-her/

All I Need (Walker & Ellie):
https://jennifervanwykauthor.com/all-i-need/

Gone For You (Ethan & Olivia):
https://jennifervanwykauthor.com/gone-for-you/

Falling For You (Rex & Chloe):
https://jennifervanwykauthor.com/falling-for-you/

Staying For You (Owen and Cami):
https://jennifervanwykauthor.com/staying-for-you/

Made in the USA
Monee, IL
22 September 2020

42613676R00206